Mistletoe

and

Murder

A Midcoast Maine Mystery

Also by Lawrence Rotch

Gravely Dead: A Midcoast Maine Mystery
Bulletproof: A Midcoast Maine Mystery
Standing Dead: A Midcoast Maine Mystery

Mistletoe

and

Murder

A Midcoast Maine Mystery

Lawrence Rotch

SₘP

Shoal Waters Press

Printed in the United States of America

ISBN: 978-0-9839079-1-6

First Edition: October, 2013

Published by
Shoal Waters Press
Liberty, Maine
Shoalwaterspress.com

10 9 8 7 6 5 4

"Revenge is a dish best served cold."
Pierre Choderlos de Laclos,
Les Liaisons Dangereuses

Chapter 1

Late afternoon, December 24, 2004

The reservoir for Arlington, Massachusetts, affectionately referred to as the "Res," was conveniently located in the center of town. Being a suburb of Boston, Arlington boasted a sizeable population, many of whom took advantage of the recreational opportunities which the Res offered.

Annette Penrose was one of those people. Every Friday afternoon, regular as clockwork, she ran laps around the jogging and bike trail which circled the Res. She didn't have much company today, because it happened to be the afternoon before Christmas Eve, and most people were too busy getting ready for the Big Day to spare time for anything else.

There was a small bathing beach on one side of the Res, and a toddler, bundled up in a lime green snowsuit, stood on the sand and jabbed at the skim ice with a stick, while a woman in her twenties clung to the child's arm. The ground was bare of snow, but a cold, raw wind was blowing in from Boston harbor, and the mother was shivering as she clung to her charge. Annette Penrose glanced at the scene as she jogged by. She turned away abruptly, irritated by the emotions welling up in her mind. Suddenly, the Christmas lights seemed less festive.

Annette and Harry Penrose were ambitious people who had intentionally chosen to forgo the burdens of child rearing in order to pursue their separate careers. Still, at times like this, with the red and green blinking lights, Christmas music, people jamming the stores, and toddlers in lime green snowsuits, she felt strangely sad to think that she would never have children of her own.

The problem wasn't so much the relentless ticking of nature's clock that made children unlikely—Annette was only in her early forties, after all. No, the strains in her marriage centered around money. After two terms as governor of Massachusetts, Harry Penrose had made a disastrous run for the U.S. Senate, losing both the election and a large part of his fortune in the process.

Worse, he had not forgiven his wife for refusing to mortgage her own successful business to help fund his campaign.

Annette had gotten her second wind by the time she was half way around the loop. Her stride was smooth and effortless, her breathing easy, her mood brightening as she lost herself in the moment.

She nodded to a woman coming the other way with a Golden Retriever in tow. This was the first person she'd seen in a while, which just went to show how absorbed people were with the frenzy of last minute shopping, wrapping presents, and dealing with hyped-up kids.

Annette's mind drifted back the Harry. Like many out-of-office politicians, her husband had begun to take on the role of lobbyist, using his connections to smooth the regulatory and legislative pathway for those with the money to pay him. And money had recently come in.

A lot of it.

So much, in fact, that he was having an expensive yacht custom built in Maine. This discovery bothered her, largely because of his refusal to explain where the money was coming from. Who was paying Harry so much, and why?

Her feet clattered over a planked foot-bridge which spanned the pond's spillway. A little way ahead, the trail ran through a stand of brush and small trees. A bank of clouds had swept in, hiding the late afternoon sun and leaving the woods in gloom.

Annette instinctively picked up her pace.

A man stepped onto the path, blocking her way. "Hey, lady, what's your rush?"

This was ridiculous. The Res was one of the safest places in town. He was about twenty feet away, and Annette's legs flailed for a second as she broke stride, and turned around to head back the other way.

There was a second man blocking the way. Two quick steps and he punched her in the stomach. She doubled over and he punched her again.

Her first reaction was amazement. These things never happened here. In a vague, detached way she saw the knife, realized that she had been stabbed, not punched.

She turned, but the first man was there. She clawed at his eyes, her fingernails drawing blood, but his fist battered her injured midriff and drove the wind from her lungs.

———————

Not far from where Annette Penrose was being stabbed and beaten, Sean O'Malley was also jogging. In his increasingly grim battle with middle-age spread, Sean had taken to exercising three times a week when he was off-duty, Christmas Eve or not.

He was jogging along, a bit more slowly than Annette had been, his face red with exertion, his sweatshirt stained despite the cold, when he heard the unmistakable sounds of a struggle ahead. He surged forward and saw the outline of two men attacking what looked, in the shadows, like a woman.

"Stop, Police!" he bellowed. Sean carried his backup gun, a snub-nosed .38cal Smith and Wessen revolver, in a pancake holster at the small of his back, and he reached for it with one hand as he ran. Unlike a TV cop, who managed to shoot somebody between every commercial, Sean was a real cop, and like many real cops he'd never fired a shot in anger in all of his twenty-one years on the force.

And now when he needed it, the damn gun was tangled in the tail of his sweatshirt.

"Police!" he bellowed again. Sean began to worry that he'd arrive on the scene with his right arm caught behind his back.

One of the muggers paused, apparently unsure if the man bearing down on them with one hand behind his back was really a threat.

With a mighty heave, Sean freed the weapon and held it at the ready.

That was enough for the attackers, who ran off. Sean caught a final glimpse of them crossing the parking area behind a low apartment complex.

He kneeled over the woman, whose alabaster skin contrasted with her straight black hair. "You're safe now, lady. I'm a police officer, and we'll get you to the hospital in no time. Just take it easy, and you'll be fine."

She didn't say anything, and he wasn't at all sure that she would be fine.

He pulled out his cell and called it in, then unzipped her anorak. A wound in her chest bubbled as she breathed, and three more wounds in her abdomen were oozing blood. He took off his sweatshirt and used it to slow the bleeding as best he could, glancing behind him to make sure the muggers were really gone.

There was an odd hitch to her breathing now, as though she was having trouble getting air into her lungs.

He imagined a faint noise behind him and turned again to look. When he turned back, the woman had stopped breathing.

"Shit," Sean muttered, but she started breathing on her own as quickly as she'd stopped. "Hang in there, lady, the ambulance will be here any second. Just concentrate on breathing."

The bus would home in on his cell, and Sean figured they'd pull into the parking area behind the apartment block where the muggers had fled. From there it was only fifty-feet or so to where the woman lay. A piece of cake.

If she didn't die first.

Blinking and hooting, the ambulance parked right were he'd expected, the red and white flashing lights reminding him of a Christmas display on steroids. He waved and hollered as the EMT's unloaded a stretcher.

Sean moved back to make room as the EMT's went to work. With nothing but a sweat-soaked Tee shirt covering his upper body, he began to shiver uncontrollably.

"Has she said anything? Give you her name?" one of the EMT's said

"Unconscious," Sean managed through chattering teeth.

The EMT looked up, seeing Sean for the first time. "Jesus Christ, didn't you mother teach you how to dress in the winter?" He grabbed a blanket and handed it over before returning to the woman. "Middle-aged male, hypothermic," he murmured into his shoulder mike.

"She's got a fanny pack, probably has ID in there," the second EMT said. "They'll get her name at the hospital."

"She going to make it?" Sean said.

"I know one thing; she'd be dead now if you hadn't come along."

Sean walked alongside as the EMT's carried the stretcher over to the ambulance.

Suddenly, he realized the place was swarming with cops. "I should report in," he said.

"Later. Right now, you're coming with us before we end up carrying *you* off on a stretcher."

"But I can help—"

"Get in the goddam bus," the EMT growled, taking Sean's arm

to steady him. His voice softened. "Look, I don't know how aware she is of what's going on, but I do know that you're her Very Best Friend right now, and having you next to her could make a difference."

Sean O'Malley got in and put his beefy hand on hers. To his surprise, she clutched his fingers.

Chapter 2

Thursday afternoon, December 13, a decade later

Charlie's Tavern on Boston's Dorchester Avenue was not one of the city's premier establishments. It did have the advantage, however, of being one of those dimly-lit places in whose murky booths one could have a private conversation without being noticed, which was what Harry Penrose had in mind.

"You understand what I want," Harry said to his companion. "Start with the Medical Examiner, then Breener's sister and then Breener himself."

Harry paused and looked up furtively as the tavern door opened, admitting two men, a blast of icy air, and a gust of snow. Heavy snow was predicted for later in the afternoon, and Harry was anxious to get home before the roads became too bogged down.

"Yeah, I got all that," Vince Martell replied.

"Breener has to die on Christmas Eve, and he has to know it's coming and why. That's vital."

Vince stared at Harry and said nothing.

Harry Penrose was in his mid-fifties, handsome, successful, and distinguished, with a full head of iron-gray hair. He was also a man who did not take no for an answer. Like many powerful men, Harry expected to be obeyed by his underlings, which made his companion's behavior all the more irritating. "Is there a problem?" he said, suppressing his impatience. "I've gone over it all twice already. Is there something you don't understand? Should I be talking to somebody else?" Harry took a swallow of his martini, the third, so far.

Vince Martell, ten years younger than his companion, had been nursing a mug of draft for the past half-hour, and he took a tiny sip, eyeing Harry impassively over the rim for a moment before answering. "Three things," he said. "Ten days isn't a lot of time to do everything you want. All that stuff will take time and planning to get right. Second, what you want isn't going to come cheap."

"I have the first payment—"

"Third, and most important, *your* instructions are *my* guidelines. I'm the professional here, so push comes to shove, I'll handle the details my way without you or anybody else looking over my shoulder."

Harry thought this over for a moment. "Fine. You know what I want. He is to suffer, and then die. At the right time. That's all I require of you."

"And you'll get it."

Harry nodded and slid an envelope across the table. "Here's the retainer to get you started."

Vince opened the envelope, looked inside, and put it in his pocket. "I know Breener is in Maine, but where's his sister?"

"Hopkinton. She's got some kind of organic farm out there. It's not too far away, but if you play your cards right, it shouldn't be hard to lure her up to Maine."

Vince nodded. "And the ME?"

"I called him yesterday, anonymously of course, and he's heading up to Maine now. He has a cabin on a little pond near Breener's shack, owns a snowmobile and likes to ride it around. I'll give you his address up there."

"Snowmobiles can be dangerous," Vince said thoughtfully.

———————

By dawn, some fourteen hours after Harry Penrose's meeting at Charlie's Tavern, the snow had crept up from Massachusetts into Midcoast Maine and began to sift down from a gray, windless sky. It was snowing hard and starting to blow by mid-morning, and by noon the local TV channels were talking breathlessly about gale-force winds, white-out conditions, and two-feet or more of accumulation. By mid-afternoon, with gusts approaching hurricane force, the plows surrendered the back roads, where four-foot drifts took over within minutes of being cleared.

The power went out at four o'clock in the afternoon, and forecasters were predicting three feet of snow.

Hardened Mainers resigned themselves to an old-fashioned Nor'easter.

———————

Sarah Cassidy was not a hardened Mainer. In fact, this was her first winter in the state, having grown up in Massachusetts. She huddled and shivered under a pile of blankets and quilts. Her head throbbed, her throat was sore, her chest was congested, and every joint ached.

She had slept fitfully until the wee-small hours of the morning, when a sudden thud shook the building and woke her with a start. She listened for a while, but heard nothing beyond the howling gale and decided it was probably a tree limb hitting the cabin. In any case, there wasn't much to be done before daylight, which was hours away. She glanced at the bedside clock, but the power was still out and the numerals were dark.

She buried her head under the covers as a blast of wind swept across the pond and pounded her cabin, shaking it to the foundation.

———————

The wind was still howling at dawn. Sarah reluctantly clambered out of her warm bed, put on her heavy dressing gown and lined slippers, and made her way to the cabin's "Great Room," as Brian Curtis, Burnt Cove's Realtor, had grandiosely described the twelve-by-twenty-foot space when she took the rental. The Great Room ran the length of the water-facing side of the three-room cabin and contained the kitchen, eating, and sitting areas. It was also icy.

With the power out, there was no furnace or running water, not to mention lights or a variety of other creature comforts she hadn't thought of yet.

There was, however, a sizeable woodstove in the center of the room. Sarah descended on it eagerly. A couple of twists of newspaper, some scraps of cedar kindling from Oliver Wendell's boatshop, a few logs, and a match started a satisfying blaze.

She poured a glass of orange juice, all her stomach could handle, and sipped it while she stood beside the stove, coughing and shivering.

Sarah Cassidy was in her early-ish fifties. Though the dreaded double-nickel was approaching, she had held onto her figure reasonably well and prided herself in being able to pass for someone ten years younger—in spite of a few tell-tale grey strands in her dark, shoulder-length hair.

After a few minutes, she felt warm enough to make her way over to the sliding door and pull back the insulated drapes far enough to let in some light. Having been built in the 1940's when building restrictions were more lax, the cabin's front porch was only ten feet from the water's edge.

It could have been ten miles from the water for all Sarah could tell. A wall of swirling white pressed against the glass, and the wind had found a tiny crack between the sliders, bringing with it a small but growing snow drift, which crept across the floor. Sarah shuddered, closed the drapes, and crammed more wood in the stove.

After refilling her glass of juice, she retreated to her bed.

———————

Sarah was up, and loading more wood in the stove when her cell phone chimed an hour later.

It was Oliver Wendell, with whom she had become involved over the last summer.

"How are things going down there?" he asked. "Your voice sounds awful."

"My sinuses are killing me, my throat is sore, I'm coughing and wheezing, and the power is out," she replied. "And don't peck at me about not getting a flu shot. I forgot, all right?"

There was a hurt silence and Sarah tried to reign in her temper, but the unfairness of it all made that difficult. Oliver had a back-up generator in a shed behind his boatshop, so he had power for water, heat, and light, while she shivered in the dark. To make things worse, his wood-fired furnace produced scads of hot water as well as hot air.

"Do you have enough water?" Oliver said, as though reading her mind. He had cajoled her into buying a case of bottled water last fall. She had resented his insistence at the time.

"So far," she replied, thinking that Oliver had probably taken a hot shower this morning. The image of his long back, glistening with hot water and soap, rose unbidden in her mind.

"Have you been plowed out?" Oliver said.

"I haven't heard a plow since yesterday evening." She would scream if it turned out that he had.

"Neither have I. They've probably got their hands full just trying to keep the main roads open."

It wasn't as though she had to be here, alone in this primitive and drafty cabin. Oliver had asked her to move in with him any number of times. She could have accepted his offer and been taking a hot shower herself this morning, steaming her bronchi, perhaps washing Oliver's back, and visa-versa—

She broke into a spasm of coughing.

"Shouldn't you see a doctor?"

"And how would I do that in this weather? Besides, I used to be a nurse, remember? I know when to see a doctor," she wheezed.

There was a muttered word that sounded a little like "stubborn," to her congested ears, but could have been something else beginning with an "s."

A drop of ice water landed on Sarah's head, followed by a sizzling noise from the woodstove beside her.

The cabin's ceilings were wooden tongue-and-groove planks, painted white, a nice rustic touch. Except that water had begun dripping through the seams. A lot of water.

"I've got to go," she said. "It's raining in here."

"It's what—"

Sarah broke the connection and looked up. Water was coming down from half-a-dozen places.

What was going on? Had some sadistically malignant force zoned in on her lust for a hot shower? What unspeakable evil had she committed to warrant this punishment?

Grabbing every container she could find, Sarah set them out to catch the rapidly spreading collection of drips. She had never thought about the attic in the nearly three months she'd been here, but of course there must be one. And there must be some way to get into it.

A hallway ran from the Great Room to the back door. There were two small bedrooms, one on each side of the hall, with a bath and a utility closet flanking the back door.

The utility closet held a small furnace and a tank for the water pump. The walls were lined with shelves which held an assortment of ancient paint cans, a pile of scruffy paint brushes, a tool box, and a half-century's worth assorted bits and pieces. There was also a removable panel in the ceiling.

Retrieving a paint-stained step ladder from behind the door,

Sarah pushed the ceiling panel out of the way and stuck her head into the attic.

The space was low, barely high enough for a person to walk doubled over. Tiny windows, one at each gable end, provided the only light. The window sash at her end of the cabin appeared to be held in place with nothing more than a pair of nails driven into the casing.

The window at the far end was missing and a growing mountain of snow had blown through the opening. There was no insulation up here, and Sarah figured that the woodstove must be providing enough heat to melt the snow, thereby creating a perverse form of morning shower.

She descended the ladder with a groan.

A while later, dressed in her winter clothes, parka, mittens and boots, and carrying a sturdy metal dustpan—along with a hammer and nails for good measure—Sarah clambered into the attic.

A narrow catwalk of flooring ran the length of the cabin. She moved a box of chipped plates, a dusty assortment of framed prints, and the inevitable crate of moldy *National Geographic* magazines to make a path.

Sarah made her way, hunched over like Quasimodo, to the snowy end of the attic and set to work with the dustpan.

Shoveling snow out a window into the teeth of a gale, while armed with only a dustpan, proved to be hard work.

"That which doesn't kill you, makes you stronger," her mother used to say, and Sarah repeated this mantra as she toiled away, wondering all the while which was the most likely outcome of her labors, death or strength.

At last the job was done, and Sarah was relieved to find the window sash lying unbroken beneath the snow. She nailed it back in place and sat, panting and wheezing, in the sudden stillness.

Somebody had left a shoe box and a paper shopping bag beside the window and Sarah picked them up. Both their bottoms were soggy from the melted snow. Thinking vaguely about drying them out downstairs, she took them, along with the hammer and dustpan back to the storage room.

Back in the Great Room, Sarah refilled the stove and stood in front of it while she tried warm up and catch her breath. As she feared, shoveling snow out of the attic had not proved to be therapeutic.

Tea, she thought. Toast an English muffin over the woodstove, drink a mug of tea, and curl up on the sofa in here where it was warm. With the quilt and a couple of blankets. Or more. She filled the kettle from one of the gallon water bottles Oliver had forced her to buy, and put it on the stove.

There was a pounding on the door.

"Now what?" Sarah growled as she stamped up the hall.

Chapter 3

Friday morning, December 14

Ziggy Breener, Burnt Cove's can man, spent much of the year pedaling his bicycle around town in search of cans in order to collect the deposit. A man of mystery, he usually went away for the winter. "Cans are like flowers; they bloom in the summer," he was fond of saying. This year had been an exception.

It was rumored that Ziggy's parents had met at the first Woodstock Music Festival in 1969, and had discovered nine months later with the arrival of a son, that free love wasn't quite free after all. Zigfield Follies Breener, the result of this discovery, stood on the doorstep, his navy-blue knitted watch cap pulled low, and his scruffy beard caked with snow. He wore what had once been an expensive charcoal-gray tweed overcoat, while on his feet were a pair of knee-length rubber fisherman's boots. The toe of the right boot was heavily wrapped with duct tape.

"Good morning, Ditch Lady Sarah," he said. Sarah had been climbing out of a roadside ditch, after nearly being killed by a hit-and-run driver, when Ziggy first encountered her last spring. He never let her forget.

"How did you get here?"

"On my new Yukon Jim snowshoes, on sale at Reny's," he said proudly, nodding to where the objects in question were sticking out of a snow bank.

"But it's two miles from your place." Ziggy lived in a one-room shack amidst a collection of livestock and junk, known locally as "Ziggy's Zoo," on Meadow Road.

"Only if one is limited to following roads. I prefer to think of myself as a crow, free of burdensome highways and able to travel straight and true. It's only a mile for a crow." He paused for thought. "Not that I am a crow, but there's a snowmobile trail at the top of your pond."

The snow was up to Ziggy's knees, and some of it was spilling through the open doorway. Behind him, more of the pesky white-stuff filled the air. Having already spent far too much time shoveling out the cabin, she let Ziggy in and escorted him over to the Great Room table, where he removed his cap with a flourish and shook the snow onto the floor.

He seemed oblivious to the occasional plops of water, which were still falling into various containers. Perhaps, Sarah thought, leaky roofs were the norm at the Breener homestead.

Sarah sat down across the table. "Why are you here?" she asked, trying not to sound too ungracious.

"I've come to spread Christmas cheer."

"No, I mean why haven't you gone south for the winter, like usual?"

Ziggy peered up at the ceiling as he pondered the question. "As a new member of the landed gentry, I have responsibilities that keep me here."

Having recently inherited several acres of prime waterfront land in Burnt Cove after the death of the reclusive Myra Huggard, Ziggy would become a relatively wealthy man once the estate was settled. Perhaps, Sarah thought, he did feel certain new obligations.

She was convulsed by a coughing fit, and Ziggy gazed at her owlishly while she subsided into strangled wheezing.

"Standing in breezes makes coughs and sneezes," he informed her.

"It's just the flu."

"I had a little bird, its name was Enza. I opened up the window, in flew Enza," he replied in a sing-song voice.

"Enough with the home-spun clap-trap, Breener."

It was said that Ziggy had once been an Emergency Room doctor before starting a new career in the can-collection business. Some believed that a nervous breakdown had brought him to Burnt Cove, while others thought that he'd fried his brain on some illicit drug.

She broke into another bout of strangled coughing. Sitting seemed to make it worse.

"Tea," Ziggy announced.

"I'd just put the kettle on when you arrived."

"And I happen to have brought some medicinal tea," Ziggy murmured, extracting a plastic baggie from his overcoat.

"Medicinal tea?" Sarah eyed the baggie suspiciously.

"It's my own special blend, cunningly made from selected herbs, grasses and blossoms," he said proudly.

"That's very generous of you, Ziggy. Maybe I'll have some later."

"It's not the cough that carries you off, It's the coffin they carry you off in."

Sarah figured if the man's tea didn't kill her, his endless sayings would.

"Later may be too later," he added gloomily.

"Later will *not* be too later," she retorted.

Ziggy responded by extracting a much folded piece of paper and handing it to her.

It was a degree in medicine from Duke University. So the rumors were true. "Do you always carry your diploma around with you?"

"Only when I make house calls. It comforts me." He leaned

forward earnestly. "I must swear you to secrecy, Ditch Lady Sarah; Don't tell anybody about this."

He pointed to the diploma. "That comes from a different astral plane that must not cross into our present universe."

The trouble with Ziggy, Sarah reminded herself, was that there were two of them in there, like bats in a closet, and you never knew which one would pop out when the door was opened: the shrewd canny Ziggy, whose eyes seemed to see all, or the dizzy Ziggy, whose ramblings meant nothing—or everything.

He got to his feet and headed for the tea pot, announcing, "Carpe Diem!"

"A glass of orange juice would be fine," she said hopefully, but Ziggy was fishing around under his overcoat from which, after a certain amount of searching and muttering, he extracted a tea ball, filled it from the baggie, and put it in the teapot.

Ziggy sat down again while the kettle was heating. The box and bag which Sarah had rescued from the attic were sitting on the table and Ziggy started to move them out of the way.

"Careful, the bottom of the bag is—" she began, too late.

The soggy paper gave way and a human skull rattled onto the table top.

The jaw had been wired on loosely and it wobbled in an alarming way as Ziggy lifted the skull. He sat, staring at it for a long time, his face a mask. "Alas, poor Yorick—" he began in a low, tentative, voice.

Sarah groaned, which led to another coughing fit.

A flashlight was sitting on the table. Ziggy picked it up and shone it into the skull's base while he stared nose-to-nose into the eye sockets.

"Think of it," he said, "an entire life was lived in there—all the joy, sadness, love, hate, deceit, passion, boredom—all hidden away in this little container. Yes, and memories of evil and death, too."

As she watched, a reddish glow seemed to emanate from the skull's eyes and light Ziggy's face.

"For God's sake put it down, you're creeping me out."

"It's a dangerous thing to let a skull wander away from its owner," he said.

"What were you doing, and why was it glowing red?"

"You, oh Ditch Lady Sarah, who seek out the evils living in the ditches of life, should appreciate the malevolence which can live in a—"

She snatched the skull away from Ziggy, and peered into an eye socket. "It's filled with red cellophane." She noticed that the top had been cut off and glued back on. An autopsy? That would have made it easy to unglue the pate and put in the cellophane.

The kettle began to boil and Ziggy rose to fill the teapot.

"Shouldn't we call the police?" Sarah said.

"There are more than seven billion skulls walking around even as we speak, all of them filled with life. Why bother the police with an empty one when they have so many full ones to worry about?"

He poured the tea into their cups. "Seven billion skulls. Just think how many second-hand ones must be rattling around in the world."

The aroma of mint and grasses greeted Sarah's nose. "But why hide it away under the attic floor?"

"I've mentioned before that it's not wise to spend too much time exploring the gutters of life." He glanced at the ceiling. "Or the attics. Do as I do and soar like the wise and crafty crow over sordidness."

Sarah sighed.

"You can buy skulls on the internet," Ziggy commented, sipping his tea. "'Skulls-R-Us,' or some such firm. Empty skulls, of course."

Sarah sniffed the brew cautiously. "Purple monsters aren't going to pop out of the wall and attack me if I drink this, are they?"

"Are there purple monsters in your wall?"

Sarah wondered if Ziggy carried his diploma around often. How many people had he shown it to? Somehow that raggedy piece of paper did reassure her.

Sarah took a tiny sip of the herbal concoction. The taste of mint covered a subtle collection of other flavors, making it impossible to guess what was in it.

"Do you think the red cellophane was just for effect, like a Halloween thing?" she said.

Ziggy stared up at the ceiling again, where a drop of water was forming as it prepared to fall into the stew pot Sarah had placed on the useless electric stove. From this angle she could see that his shaggy, white-streaked beard looked as though it had been roughly trimmed recently with dull scissors.

"You should put the skull back at once," he said. "I see evil in it, seeking to get out."

"Gimme a break."

The droplet fell into the pot with a faint splash. She took another sip of tea.

Ziggy looked at her, a troubled expression on his face. "This house is cursed, Ditch Lady Sarah. I see evil reaching out to the unwary."

"A skull in the attic does not mean the house is cursed." She took a defiant gulp of tea. Now that she was used to it, the stuff tasted pretty good.

Chapter 4

Friday morning, December 14

The town of Burnt Cove embraced all fifteen miles of the Squirrel Point peninsula from Route One down to the seaward tip of Squirrel Point itself. Including the coastal road, which circled the peninsula, plus various cross roads, there was a generous amount of highway mileage in town, and Ziggy pedaled most of those miles in his job as chief can collector for Burnt Cove. As a result he was in excellent physical shape.

Unfortunately, bicycle riding develops very different muscles than snowshoeing, which Ziggy had not done much of. As a result, his legs began to tire as he plodded the mile of deep snow back to Meadow Road. The snowmobile trail made for easier going, but nobody had come this way for an hour or more, snow was falling heavily, and drifts were already filling in the trail.

He was relieved, therefore, to hear the whine of a snowmobile approaching from behind him. A freshly packed track would make his life much easier.

He worked his way off the trail to allow plenty of room, since the blowing snow made visibility difficult and he could hear that the machine was moving fast.

Too fast.

The blow caught him in the lower leg, tossed him into the air and into the woods.

The snowmobile didn't stop, and after a short while snow began to cover Ziggy Breener in a layer of white.

———————

The skull sat on the table and watched, eyeless, as Sarah put more wood in the stove. It gazed silently as she emptied the last of the teapot into her cup. It observed without comment as she carried the blankets, pillows, and comforter from her meat locker of a bedroom, and arranged them on the sofa where it was warm.

With some cheese, crackers, yogurt, and tea—all her stomach felt up to—on the coffee table beside her, Sarah nested under the covers.

For the first time in two days, she was beginning to feel almost human. Her mind seemed clearer, her senses sharper, her cough dissipating, her chest less congested. Could Ziggy's tea be working already?

Yorick peered at her out of the corner of his left eye socket with a grin on his boney face, as though he was agreeing with her about the tea.

It was just the angle she was looking at him, of course, but still—

"Stop staring at me like that," she growled, "Make your own tea if you want some, but don't expect me to do it for you."

Sarah wondered if Yorick was a he or a she. Could one tell the gender of a skull?

"Where did you come from?" she said. "And stop drooling over my brunch," she added peevishly.

Yorick continued to grin at her in silence, and Sarah glared back while she finished her yogurt. After a few minutes, she dozed off while the skull, which had been sleeping in the attic for a long time, stood guard.

———————

Sarah was awakened an hour later by her cell.

"How are you feeling?" Oliver inquired.

"Did you make poor Ziggy come all the way over here in this weather?" she said.

"Nobody can make Ziggy do anything he doesn't want to. Did he give you some of his tea?"

"Yes."

"What color was it?"

"Tea color, what else?"

"I mean the slip of paper in the baggie."

"Slip of paper? Oh, that. It was red, I think. Why?"

"Don't drink too much of it at one time," Oliver said. "His red-tag tea is strong stuff."

"Red-tag tea? What do you mean 'strong stuff?' What's in it?"

"God knows. All I can say is that it works like a charm. Did he show you his diploma?"

"I thought it was supposed to be a secret."

"It is, but if he shows it to you, that's Ziggy-speak for you should be in a hospital."

"Don't start in on me, Wendell—"

Sarah glanced at Yorick, who seemed to be laughing at her.

"Hang on a second." Sarah grabbed a Hannaford Supermarket shopping bag, put Yorick in it and stuffed the bag under the kitchen sink.

"Just tidying up a little," she said on returning to the phone. "I found a skull in the attic."

"A skull in the attic? Does this have something to do with it raining inside?"

Sarah reluctantly recounted her morning adventures.

"So you spent the morning shoveling snow out of the attic,

while you're suffering from pneumonia? Are you nuts?"

"What else could I do?" she demanded. She could hear the whine of a snowmobile in the distance, but the blowing snow was too thick to see anything.

"Calling for help would be an option," Oliver commented.

"I'd have been up to my knees in ice water by the time anybody got here." The snowmobile was on the pond and getting nearer.

Oliver muttered something unintelligible that concluded with, "Thank God Ziggy was willing to make a house call."

Sarah could see the glow of an approaching light through the falling snow. "I'll have to call you back. A snowmobile is coming."

———————

"Wicked cold out there," Jeff Rice said as he removed his helmet and stamped his feet on the hall floor, adding more snow to Ziggy's still-melting collection.

"Too soon to start shoveling out, isn't it?" Sarah replied. She had hired Jeff, a sturdy High School senior, to clear snow for her. The easy winter hadn't required much shoveling, until now.

Jeff held up a large key ring for her inspection. "There's fifteen cottages on the pond, and twelve of them are empty in the winter, so I take care of most of the summer cottages over here. I made a run over to see how much drifting there was and make sure the places were okay after the storm." Jeff lived with his mother and older sister in a double-wide on Meadow Road, just across from Ziggy's Zoo.

"Come in and warm up," Sarah said.

Jeff stood close to the stove and looked at the half-empty wood box. "That all the wood you got?"

"There's a big pile of it beside the back porch, under a tarp."

"Is it all biscuit wood like this?" he said.

"Biscuit wood?"

"My Grammy used to cook on a wood stove," Jeff said.

"Whenever she wanted a hot oven, she'd send me out to get an armload of wizeny little sticks like those, 'cause they'd burn hot and fast. Biscuit wood. Trouble is, they burn fast, but don't last."

"There might be some bigger logs outside," Sarah said, "but I'm not sure." The fact was that she hadn't used the woodstove much, relying on the furnace to keep her warm.

"I'll check your wood on my way out," Jeff said, his voice reflecting a hint of the long-suffering patience which native Mainers sometimes use when explaining the obvious to an ignorant flat-lander. "I'm dressed for it."

Sarah suspected that Oliver was also behind Jeff's visit, and his examination of her wood pile. She wasn't sure whether to be pleased with his concern or irritated.

"You came across the pond. I didn't think it was frozen hard enough for snowmobiles."

"Solid enough here, but it's open water a little further up," Jeff replied.

"Sounds risky, from all the warnings I hear on TV."

"It's no problem so long as you keep moving. I wouldn't do it," he added piously, "but some people will run right over a patch of open water. They say you can skip over a pretty good stretch, if you go fast enough."

———————

Perhaps because of Sarah's concern about the ice, Jeff decided to take the trail around the head of the pond on his way home. Besides, it was shorter, and Jeff was getting hungry for lunch.

Another machine had been through this morning, so Jeff was able to make good time.

If it hadn't been for a boot standing at the edge of the trail, Jeff would have gone right by. As it was, he almost took it for a stump half-buried in the snow.

Jeff's heart gave a lurch when he pulled the boot from the snow.

He looked around, started to paw frantically at a mound of drifted snow nearby.

The face was gray and cold as ice.

"Zig! Zig! Jesus, Ziggy, say something!" Jeff cried.

The side of Ziggy's head was caked with blood, his watch cap lost in the snow.

Jeff continued to sweep away the snow. Ziggy's left foot, the one without its boot, was bent at an odd angle.

He cradled Ziggy's face in his bare hands for warmth while his mind churned for traction. God, the guy was cold.

"I flew like a crow." The words flowed thickly from Ziggy's frozen lips.

Jeff nearly collapsed with relief. "You flew head first into a tree, from the looks of it."

"I flew...through the air..."

"That's nice, Zig." Jeff pulled out his cell. "Ma?" he said in a shaky voice, "Ziggy's had an accident."

"Like a crow..." Ziggy added.

"Where are you at?" she demanded. "Have you been out on the pond again?"

Ma! Ziggy's hurt bad. He hit his head, and he's talking funny."

"He always talks funny, Jeffery."

"I flew..." Ziggy insisted.

"He thinks he's a crow, Ma! And his head is bleeding real bad—"

"Heads always do that."

"—and his foot is broke."

That brought her up short. "Are you sure?"

"It's bent all out of shape, is all I can say. I'd tie him on the back if it weren't for his foot flopping around."

"Through the air!" Ziggy bellowed.

"Jesus Christ, will you shut up for a minute? And stop flapping around like that."

"Okay," she said with a sigh, "Deke's got a sled for his skidoo.

I'll have him go over. Where you at again?"
    "On the trail right at the head of the pond."
    "May take a few minutes. Keep him warm."
    "Like a crow!"

Chapter 5

Friday midday, December 14

Sasha Borofsky was in her mid-forties, with ash blond hair, a pale complexion, and a body that was slender almost to the point of emaciation. Clad in the briefest of bikinis, she lay in a lounge chair beside the pool with her huge blue eyes hidden by a pair of oversized sun glasses.

Anton Borofsky lay beside her, a study in opposites. He looked older and was built like a bull, with dark hair showing a touch of grey at the temples. A furry pelt covered his chest, which glistened with sweat, while his bathing suit had long since given up trying to cover the ample stomach. His round face was deeply creased with the smile lines of one who enjoys the good things in life that great wealth can provide.

Their guest, seated in a chair beside his hosts, sweltered in a sports jacket.

"We have a lot of spare bathing suits, Vince," Sasha said. "I'm sure we can find one that will fit you."

"The water is really very warm," Anton added, his voice betraying an accent.

"I never learned to swim," Vince said.

"Really?" Sasha said, taking off her sunglasses to stare at him.

"You must learn during your visit with us."

"Sasha is right," Anton said. "The ability to swim is a survival skill. You never know when it might be needed."

"Maybe later," Vince muttered, feeling trapped. The intensity of the woman's eyes gave him a twinge of nervousness.

"We'll start you off at the shallow end after lunch," Sasha announced with finality. She put her sunglasses on again and lay back in the lounge chair, a smile flitting across her thin lips.

Vince wished he'd thought to bring his sunglasses. He pushed out of his chair and went to the pool's edge. Stooping, he put a tentative hand in the water. "That's almost hot."

"Sasha doesn't have any insulation to speak of," Anton explained, "so she needs the water hot."

"I do like it hot," Sasha murmured.

"I think we can help each other," Anton said briskly. "After all, we do have a common goal."

"No, we don't," Vince replied, his hand roiling the water.

There was an awkward silence while Vince straightened up and returned to his chair.

"But we can work together, even so," Anton persisted.

"I've never seen a house that had a swimming pool on the third floor," Vince said as his gaze moved from the Olympic-sized pool up to the high, peaked ceiling with its big skylights and dazzling recessed lighting. "Can you actually get a burn from those lights?"

"Of course," Sasha said.

"It's incredible what you've done."

"It wasn't easy," Anton said. "First, there were the high-priced architects and building engineers, and then the problem of finding decent contractors to do the work—"

"It was a nightmare," Sasha added. "I didn't think they'd ever finish."

"We're completely independent here," Anton said. "We even have our own power plant. We have to, what with the power going out half the time. There's no real infrastructure around here. Don't get me wrong; we love Maine, but it is primitive in places."

"And some of the people—" Sasha gave a shudder. "Well, you've heard about that."

"Still snowing," Vince commented, as he gazed up at the skylights.

"Is it?" Sasha said disinterestedly.

"The United States is a great country," Anton said, waxing eloquent. "Truly a land of opportunity. Anyone who is smart and willing to work hard can do well here."

"It looks like you have done well," Vince commented dryly.

"And I will protect what I've got."

Vince looked at his hosts for a moment. "Maybe we can help each other after all," he said. "But I have to do things my way. I don't want you to hurt the man."

Anton's lounge chair creaked as he shifted his weight.

"I'm grateful that Harry Penrose contacted you and that you were willing to let me stay here for a few days," Vince said, "but I won't put up with any interference." His voice was as cold as the snow that whistled outside.

Anton sat up and glared at Vince, his face red. "Have you seen the hovel that man lives in? Can you imagine him moving all that trash right next door?"

"It's not just us," Sasha said. "It will destroy property values in the whole area. Everybody is up in arms about it."

"And those fancy lawyers you hired can't stop him?" Vince asked.

"That old witch left the property to him in her Will, and we couldn't get it overturned," Sasha said in disgust.

"To make matters worse, there are no zoning laws in this town," Anton said. "That man is planning to bring in all his animals and a bunch of rowdy teenagers, and turn them loose practically in our back yard. I won't let that happen. If you don't stop him, I will."

"Mind your blood pressure, dear," Sasha said.

"But how could he afford a decent lawyer to defend the Will?"

Vince said.

Anton took a deep breath. "He's got this friend, Sarah Cassidy—"

"Who nearly burned down our house," Sasha interjected.

"—who has an ex-husband who happens to be a lawyer, and he found a pair of high-powered Boston attorneys to defend the bum and the Will."

"And now it looks like he's won," Sasha said. "Can you believe it?"

"You can see why we have to put a stop to the man, one way or another," Anton said.

"This Cassidy woman," Vince said. "I'll want to look into her. She may be useful."

"Fine. Have it your way, for now," Anton grumbled. "But this had better be resolved by Christmas."

"It will," Vince said. His tone seemed to chill the air, in spite of the radiant heat and artificial sunlight pouring down from the overhead lamps.

After a while, Vince asked, "Out of curiosity, how did Harry Penrose come to know about you and Breener?"

"I helped fund his run for congress back in 2004," Anton said, "so Harry called me last month when he read about the man living right here in town. Apparently, Harry thought he'd died years ago until the newspapers mentioned his name earlier this month in conjunction with the lawsuit."

"It's too bad he didn't die years ago," Sasha murmured.

"Better late than never," Anton said.

"That's true," Sasha said, brightening, "and this way, we have the pleasure of Vince's company."

Vince looked at his hosts in silence, a slight frown on his face.

———————

Eldon Tupper was in his mid-twenties, stood six-foot-six-inches tall, and tipped the scales at a muscular 300 pounds. The Tupper clan had lived in the Midcoast area for generations, and he had grown up on Burnt Cove's Meadow Road before moving to an apartment in nearby Rockland after college. He was also dating Sally Rice, Jeff's older sister. As a result, Eldon was tuned in to the Meadow Road grapevine and he'd heard in graphic detail about Ziggy's injury, his rescue by snowmobile out to Route One, the closest plowed road, and his trip from there to the Pen Bay Medical Center, where he was listed in fair condition.

As befit his size, Eldon drove a large, if somewhat battered, GMC pickup. This vehicle had little trouble making its way through the blowing and drifting snow to the hospital.

Ziggy appeared to be asleep when Eldon arrived, and the young man stood in the doorway for a moment, gazing at the motionless form buried under the covers. Ziggy's face, what little was visible around his unkempt beard, looked white and pasty compared to his usual ruddy, weathered complexion. The ratty watch cap that was his almost constant companion had been replaced with a turban of gauze bandage, which left a bald spot exposed at the top of his head. The overall effect was one of disquieting vulnerability.

Ziggy's eyes popped open and swivelled wildly about the room before settling on Eldon.

"I flew through the air," he said hoarsely, "like a crow."

"You're one hell of a lucky crow," Eldon replied, approaching the bedside. Ziggy seemed to have aged twenty years in less than a day. "How are you feeling?"

"I must leave at once." Ziggy made a feeble effort to rise.

From close up, Eldon could see fear in Ziggy's eyes. It was strange how doctors, even former doctors, seemed to be terrified of ending up as a patient. Assuming, of course, that he really had been a doctor and wasn't just a crazy loon with a fake diploma.

"Jesus, man, you've got a broken ankle, a concussion, and you nearly died of exposure," Eldon said reasonably. "Take it easy for a day or so until you get some strength back."

"The crow must fly."

"Cut the crow crap for chrissake, and lie back down."

"My clothes are around here somewhere."

"It's still snowing like crazy out there, so you couldn't get back home anyhow."

A cunning look slithered across Ziggy's face, making Eldon nervous.

"The crow could roost with you," he suggested hopefully, "until the weather got better."

"I ain't going to sneak you out of here, no way," Eldon replied.

"I should have migrated, like a sensible bird. Blizzards don't suit crows."

Eldon had no idea about the migratory habits of crows, and he suspected that his companion was baiting him out of simple peevishness.

Eldon changed the subject. "What happened, anyway?"

"I was struck from behind by a hawk."

Eldon bit his tongue. He should have known better than to complain about the crow business. Now, it would be wall-to-wall bird talk for the rest of his visit. "Did you see who did it?"

"I was too busy flying through the air—"

"Like a crow," Eldon finished.

Ziggy eyed his guest suspiciously.

"You didn't get a glimpse of the hawk as it flew away? No registration numbers? What about the color of its feathers?"

"They were the color of death." Ziggy replied. He ostentatiously closed his eyes and turned away from his visitor.

———

Maine is a state that knows how to deal with snow. By afternoon the army of snowplow operators, who had been tag-teaming the blizzard for twenty-four hours straight, began to sense that the storm was beginning to wind down and another half-day or so would bring victory within reach.

While the snow was being battled outside, a quieter struggle was being waged inside the Pen Bay Medical Center. Ziggy, in his own lunatic way, was wise in the ways of hospitals, and he managed to wangle a wheelchair, in which he cruised the hallways, muttering about crows. His actions didn't hint at the bird's crafty intelligence.

By mid-afternoon, the nursing staff had become so accustomed to Ziggy's harmless, antic rambles that he became virtually invisible.

It was nightfall before anybody realized that Zigfield Follies Breener, the vociferous bird-man of Pen Bay, had flown the coop.

Chapter 6

Saturday morning, December 15

Sarah had cocooned herself under her quilt and blankets, and spent the night on the sofa near the woodstove. She pleasantly surprised herself by sleeping soundly until sometime around one o'clock on Saturday morning, when the whine of snowmobiles, their sound torn and shredded by the still-blowing wind, lifted her to a place somewhere between wakefulness and sleep. Lying in that dreamlike state, she heard what could have been a series of gunshots, or perhaps tree branches breaking, and then nothing more.

She slept like the dead after that until well past dawn, when the rumbling of a snowplow clearing the street woke her up. For the first time in days, her head felt clear, her fever was gone, the congestion in her chest was reduced to an occasional cough. Once again, she wondered about Ziggy's tea. There was just enough left to make another cup, or possibly two, and Sarah resolved to question her eccentric friend about his concoction.

She got up and dressed hurriedly in the frosty room, the woodstove having long-since gone out. Laying a fire, she noticed that the supply of kindling, which she had brought home from

Oliver's scrap wood pile, was getting low. Why hadn't he called? It was certainly late enough in the day.

He was probably out shoveling snow, she concluded. She would call him after breakfast. For the first time in days, she was hungry—ravenously hungry. The power was still out, but Sarah had followed Jeff's advice and placed the contents of the fridge in a sealed bucket in the storage room, a place which was, she figured, at least as cold as any refrigerator. The contents of the freezer sat in a cooler on the back porch. Jeff, ever practical, had even showed her how to flush the toilet using a bucket of melted snow.

Sarah got bacon, eggs, and juice from the storage room and made a sizeable meal, feeling pleased with herself, secure in the knowledge that she could hold out for days without electricity, if necessary. At least until the food ran out. Or the kindling.

With the stove warming the room, she pulled back the drapes over the slider and looked across the pond. It had stopped snowing, as near as Sarah could tell. The wind had swung into the northwest, a fair-weather direction in Maine, and was whipping wind-devils of snow across the pond, obscuring the far shore. She could see a hint of brightness where the sun was trying break through the clouds.

———————

Sarah was just finishing the last of Ziggy's tea when the roar of an oversized snowblower greeted her ears. She watched from the back door, feeling as though she was being rescued from a North Pole jail as Jeff Rice maneuvered the machine down her precipitous driveway, a great rooster tail of snow streaming off to the side.

A few minutes later, her driveway cleared, Jeff was sitting at the table with a steaming mug of coffee in his hands.

On a whim, Sarah brought the skull out of its spot beneath the sink.

Jeff laughed. "So you found Old Nick."

"Old Nick?"

Jeff picked up the skull and rapped on its pate. "Doc Carnell got it from someplace, and he used to shine a flashlight into it to light up the inside. There's cellophane in there to make the eyes shine all red, and he'd wave it around when us kids came over trick-or-treating on Halloween. Used to scare the sh—, bejesus out of us."

"I thought that was it," Sarah replied glibly, scolding herself. Why had the skull seemed so ominous yesterday? Of course she'd been running a fever then. Probably just the flu making her jumpy. "Ziggy saw the skull yesterday. It seemed to make him nervous."

"Don't know why. He must have seen it before. Ziggy and Doc Carnell hang out sometimes when they're both here in the summer."

"Did Ziggy have any other friends from away?"

Jeff thought for a moment. "There is somebody else, and older guy, Doc Tierny. He has a cabin on the pond and comes up sometimes in the winter to go snowmobiling.

Suddenly, the refrigerator rumbled to life. Sarah gave a startled yelp.

"Looks like your power's back," Jeff said as he rolled Old Nick between his hands. "Doc Carnell never let us kids touch Old Nick—kept it hidden away, except for Halloween. He used to say there were evil spirits would get us if we played with it. Pretty scary for us kids." He put the skull down. "I haven seen that fool thing for a while."

"Well Old Nick is going back into the attic, later. He gives me the creeps, even under the sink."

Jeff shrugged, no longer interested in skulls. "The town will have to keep plowing 'til the wind dies down, and they'll probably wing out tonight, so I'd stay here 'til they're done, or else you'll have to shovel your parking spot out when you get back."

"I'm not going anywhere."

"That's good," he replied. "The wind is some cold, but I imagine you found that out already."

"I haven't been out yet."

Jeff gave her a surprised look. "Somebody has, 'cause there's footprints around the side of the cabin. I figured you were out looking for leaks in the sashes."

"Footprints?" Sarah tried to imagine a peeping Tom tramping around in the middle of a blizzard. "Are you sure?"

"They were pretty much all drifted in, just dents in the snow in places, but it sure looked like somebody was out there last night checking the windows."

"Where were the tracks, exactly?"

"I didn't look all that close, but it seemed like they went around the end of the cabin," he said. "Like I say, I figured you went out to check on things."

"Well, it wasn't me, and I can't imagine anybody wandering around the cabin in this weather. I did hear snowmobiles out on the pond last night, though," Sarah said. She didn't mention the gunshots, which were probably just the wind, after all.

"Last night? Jeez, you'd have to be crazy to go out on the pond at night with all the open water, unless you stayed close to shore."

Sarah wondered if some would-be burglars on snowmobiles had stopped by in the middle of the night to case the cabin, before discovering it was occupied. The storm would have provided good cover for a break-in.

"Might want to keep your doors locked," Jeff said, apparently thinking the same thing. "Just to be on the safe side. Kids will break in to these cabins once in a while over the winter. Just looking around."

Sarah's closest neighbors were the Orrs, who lived four cabins down, but that was a long way off in a storm like the one they'd just had. "I'll do that," she said.

Jeff looked at Sarah thoughtfully. "You don't look half as punk as yesterday, but I wouldn't spend too much time out there even so. That wind could blow the hide off a polar bear."

"I do feel a lot better." She looked wistfully at her empty teacup. "I wonder if Ziggy has any more of his tea."

"He ain't around right now." Jeff shifted in his chair. "He takes off in the winter, mostly."

Sarah had raised a teenage son, and she was familiar enough with the species to smell a rat. "Are you telling me that he went off in the middle of the blizzard, without saying anything?"

"Hey, the guy does his thing. He'll go off sometimes, just like that, nobody knows where."

"And he doesn't tell anybody? What about all his livestock?"

Jeff fiddled with the coffee mug. "We keep an eye out, where he lives right across the street, and feed his animals if he don't seem to be around."

Sarah gave Jeff a long, skeptical stare. "Is Ziggy all right? And don't try to con me."

Jeff pushed the mug away. "He had a little accident after he left your place yesterday. Got hit by a snowmobile on his way home. Got banged up and broke his ankle."

"Is he all right?"

"I imagine," Jeff replied vaguely as he stared at the snow swirling across the pond. "We had a helluva time getting him out to where the road was plowed. They took him to Pen Bay."

"God," Sarah said. "I feel awful. If he hadn't come over to give me that tea, this wouldn't have happened."

Jeff returned to the examination of his mug. "Can't say about that, one way or the other."

She could tell that Jeff still wasn't telling her the whole truth. "I'll call him at Pen Bay. It's the least I can do."

Jeff sighed. "He ain't there. Checked himself out last night."

Sarah gaped in disbelief. "He checked himself out? In the middle of the storm? With a broken ankle? Where did he go?" She leaned into Jeff's space. "What the hell is going on?"

Jeff returned her gaze, distress and worry etched on his face. "Jesum Crow, I wish I knew."

Sarah bundled up and followed Jeff outside for a look at the mysterious footprints. Thanks to the wind, which was still whipping around the end of the cabin, there wasn't much to see beyond indentations in the snow.

"I didn't follow them all the way around, 'cause the snow was drifted in so deep." Jeff said.

In fact, the snow was drifted up to Sarah's waist, light, fluffy, and cold. "Somebody went to a lot of trouble to peek in my windows," she said as they made their way to the first window.

"Good thing you had 'em locked." Jeff commented as they pushed through the snow.

"I just did that to try and cut down the draft."

"Could have been the snowmobiles you heard last night."

Sarah shivered, and not just from the cold.

"I'm not so sure this was kids looking to break in, though," Jeff said. "Most people around here know which places are empty and which aren't, anyhow. Of course, it could have been somebody who was too drunk or stoned to care."

"In that case, why not just kick in the door?"

Jeff shrugged, looking uneasy.

"What?" Sarah said.

"It probably don't mean anything," he said reluctantly, "but I plowed the Borofsky's driveway early this morning, right after the town went through—he's real fussy about staying plowed out—and I could see snowmobile tracks running up his driveway, looked like they were made yesterday."

"I can't imagine why Anton Borofsky would sneak over to prowl around my cabin. On the other hand, if the Borofskys have a snowmobile, they could have run Ziggy down yesterday. They have a grudge against him over his inheriting Myra's land, so there's motive to do it. It would have been easy to follow the snowshoe tracks from his shack."

"You don't think Borofsky would try to kill poor Ziggy over a piece of land, do you?" Jeff said.

People have been killed for a lot less, she thought to herself.

———————

Sarah put more wood in the stove and gazed out the sliding door after Jeff had left.

The last day or two had seemed strangely unreal, almost like a dream. She had put it down to the flu with its fever. The eerie feeling she'd gotten from the skull was probably just the flu as well, or maybe Ziggy's tea. But she wasn't imagining the footprints or what happened to Ziggy.

The sound of the snowmobiles and gunshots she'd heard could have been a dream, too, or possibly burglars casing the cabin—it had been hard to tell how close the machines were with the wind blowing so hard.

She looked out over the pond where the swirling snow still hid the far shore, and wondered what was going on.

Chapter 7

With the snow cleared from her driveway—at least until the wind blew it back—and the power back on, life was looking a lot better. Sarah decided to call Oliver and share her news.

Oliver wasn't interested in her adventures.

"Can I call you back later?" he said as soon as she spoke.

Sarah clearly heard a woman's voice in the background saying, "Would you like some tea, dear?"

"You have company?" Sarah asked, wondering who would be visiting with so many of the roads still un-plowed.

"Things are too crazy around here to talk right now."

"Are you all right?"

"Call you later," he said, breaking the connection.

Sarah stood, confused. It wasn't like Oliver to hang up on her like that—at least not in the eight months she'd known him. And who was that woman in the background? *Would you like some tea, dear?* What was that about? Calling a casual acquaintance "dear" was common Maine practice, though it was usually pronounced "deah," with a long "e" and two syllables. In any case, whoever was talking didn't have a Maine accent.

Sarah watched the snow blowing across Pimm's Pond, and scolded herself for overreacting. Just because her ex-husband was a philandering sleazbag didn't mean that Oliver was from the same mold. Besides, sleeping with a man didn't give her a claim on him, not in this day and age.

She got out the vacuum cleaner and slammed around the cabin, tidying up.

Later that morning, the maid brought lunch up to the pool for the Borofskys and their guest: clam chowder, fresh salad, biscotti, and wine.

Despite their protestations, Vince Martell left right after the meal.

"I like Vince," Sasha said.

"I don't trust him," Anton muttered.

"What do you mean, you don't trust him? He'll be staying here while we're away. Are you afraid he's going to make off with the silverware?"

She looked at him playfully. "Are you jealous?"

Anton gave her a dark look. "That's not what I mean, and you know it."

Sasha stretched sinuously in her lounge chair. "Because you're my only Teddy Bear."

"The man is a loose cannon," Anton said. "Besides, he doesn't work for us. We have no control over what he does, and that makes me nervous."

"Who cares, so long as he gets the job done? He seems very competent."

"I'm not worried about *whether* he can do the job; I'm worried about *how* he does it."

Sasha lay back in her lounge chair with a sigh. "You're being too controlling again. What does it matter how Vince gets rid of that awful man, so long as he does it? He's just a bum riding around on a junky bicycle, after all. Who's going to notice or care what happens to him?"

"Collateral damage," Anton replied tersely. "It's the collateral damage that I worry about. Martell doesn't care about that, but we have to live here."

"Live here? Come on, Anton."

"Well, we do, at least part of the year. This is a small town and some of those people have long memories when they feel crossed."

"Maybe we could hire him ourselves, for our other problem," Sasha mused.

"I'll deal with that myself. I've got my own contacts. People who'll do what I tell them."

Sasha was quiet for a while. "I wonder where Vince went off to?" she said at last.

"Doing whatever it is he does."

"Do you suppose we'll be able to fly out this evening? It's such a dinky little airport. I wonder if they can plow it out in time, after all this snow."

Meadow Road was a narrow byway which ran down the middle of the Squirrel Point peninsula. Unlike nearby Squirrel Point road, which followed the shore and was home to a collection of pretentious homes, the most garish example being the Borofsky's mega-mansion, Meadow Road was lined with battered cottages and run-down double-wides. Included in this collection was Ziggy Breener's shack with its assortment of what Mainers call "cultch." A derelict car, with its seats removed and one door missing, sat in the front yard where it served as a hen house in the summer, while a rickety structure consisting of a few boards nailed to a pair of saplings provided shelter for Ziggy's goat, Annabelle Lee. A pig named Oswald, who spent the summer rooting in the backyard, had gone to his reward—and Ziggy's freezer.

Nearly three feet of snow had been kind to the overall appearance of the Breener estate, mercifully covering all the smaller random junk.

In all fairness, Ziggy's Zoo wasn't all that much messier than some of his neighbors, whose collections of discarded appliances, broken lobster pots, wrecked bicycles, outgrown toys, and other obsolete artifacts were also buried and out of sight. The overall effect was to give the neighborhood a deceptively pristine, almost bucolic look.

Cindy Rice took a long drag on her cigarette as she stared sourly out the kitchen window of her double-wide. The town of Burnt Cove had just plowed Meadow Road, a skimpy and hurried job, but then this was a skimpy neighborhood compared to the mansions on Squirrel Point. In fact, her son Jeff was out plowing the driveways of several of those mansions. Money was money, wherever it came from.

Ziggy's Zoo being right across the road, Cindy had a good view of the place, and she watched, stubbing out her cigarette, as a car with out-of-state plates pulled up in front of his dooryard. Ziggy had shoveled narrow paths—mostly drifted in by now—to his shack, wood pile, and goat pen, and the stranger limped through the snow to the door.

The man didn't knock, just slipped an envelope under the door before returning to his car, where he stood for a moment and looked around. Cindy could see his gaze following Jeff's footprints from Ziggy's goat pen, across the road, and up to her porch.

Like Cindy's family, most of the residents on Meadow Road had lived here for generations in a tight-knit community that did not welcome strangers easily.

Ziggy Breener was an exception. The inhabitants of Meadow Road tend to admire, or at least tolerate, those who are eccentric and self-reliant, those who mind their own business and, above all, aren't pushy. These were all character traits with which Ziggy was well endowed. Though he'd moved in less than ten years ago amid great suspicion, the Can Man was now accepted as part of the Meadow Road community.

So it was that Cindy's protective instinct caused her to don her worn parka and go out to confront the stranger.

"He ain't home," she said from across the street.

The man squinted up at her, sunlight off the snow partially blinding him. "You keep an eye on the place?"

"My son tends the animals when he's away."

The man nodded. "I left an envelope under his door. It's important that he get it as soon as possible."

Cindy wondered what that was all about as she studied the stranger. Word of Ziggy's new-found wealth, thanks to Myra Huggard's Will, had gotten around, and she suspected that this stranger was hoping to scam her neighbor out of all he could get.

"You'll have to take your chances, 'cause I don't know when he'll be back. Could be away 'til spring." She didn't think the stranger looked like a lawyer, but he sure looked like trouble of some kind.

The man crossed the street. "Do you have any idea how I could reach him?"

Cindy hadn't bothered to put on her boots and her feet were going numb in her slippers. "No," she said curtly.

The stranger looked bigger and more ominous from close-up. "But you must have some way of getting a hold of him in an emergency."

Cindy took comfort in the thought that a dozen eyes were probably watching, but the man was spooky, even so. She wished Jeff was here. "Ain't you heard a word I've said? People around here mind their own business, so if you want to find *Mister* Breener you'll have to do it yourself."

The stranger gave her a look of controlled rage. "It looks like I'll have to do just that," he said in a tone that dripped of threat.

Cindy noted the car's plate number as the stranger pulled away, but she figured it was a rental.

———

P. Melvin Delroy worked most Saturdays, as befit a workaholic billionaire, so he was at his desk when his secretary rang through to him. "Mr. Harry Penrose is on line three," she said. "Shall I put him through?"

P. Melvin muttered an oath.

"I can tell him you're unavailable," she suggested.

"No, I'd better take the call." P. Melvin was a distinguished-looking man in his late fifties, with well coiffed iron-grey hair, and a slightly chubby face. He adjusted the cuffs of his custom tailored silk shirt before picking up the phone. "Good morning, Harry. Been a while, hasn't it?" he said, thinking that it hadn't been long enough. "To what do I owe the pleasure of this call?" he added with barely suppressed sarcasm.

"It's about Doctor Breener, P. Melvin."

Of course, the tycoon thought. He wondered what had taken Penrose so long. "Doctor Ziggy Breener? The man who treated your wife?"

"The man responsible for her death."

"Yes, of course."

"Have you read the papers?"

P. Melvin rolled his eyes. "I seem to remember something about a Ziggy Breener in the *Boston Globe* a few weeks ago. Didn't he inherit a piece of land from some old woman up in Maine? Didn't the heirs contend that Breener coerced the old woman to leave him the property? What was the old lady's name?"

"Myra Huggard."

"A nasty business, taking advantage of a senile old woman like that." There was a creak of leather as P. Melvin sat back in the chair. "Surely you don't think this is the same Breener who treated your wife? The *Globe* didn't mention this Breener being a doctor."

"I've been working with Anton Borofsky on it, and I'm convinced it's the same man," Penrose said stubbornly.

"Who is Anton Borofsky?"

"I'm sure you've met him—born in Russia, emigrated here, and developed a process for treating fish to keep them smelling fresh. Modest means, worth around fifteen million."

P. Melvin was worth closer to fifteen billion, with a "b," money he had earned the hard way, starting out as a trader during the Savings and Loan debacle. Using a shrewd combination of insider information and timely short-selling, he'd walked away with his first ten million. The Dot Com bust tripled his net worth, but it was the bank deregulation movement that really feathered his nest. It had been hard work, a lot harder than some Russian chemist coming up with a way to peddle rotten fish.

"Yes, I remember him now," P. Melvin replied. "I met him and his wife at some get together or other a few years ago. She was quite well assembled as I recall."

"Her body is certainly well assembled," Harry replied, "but as for her head, not so much."

"Anton is very protective of her, as I remember."

"And she provides a steady series of men for him to protect her from."

"An odd relationship, but who are we to second-guess someone else's marriage?" P. Melvin thought about his own marriage, and his wife's inexplicable urging that he retire. Surely, she kept saying, they could live comfortably on fifteen billion if they budgeted carefully. She didn't seem to understand how much he relished the thrill, the satisfaction of out-hustling the competition in the money chase. Even deeper in his psyche, though, P. Melvin was plagued by the miser's terror that somehow it wouldn't be enough, that an unforeseen disaster would snatch away his hard-earned nest egg. Rationally, he knew his wife was right, but the old fears still gnawed at him in the wee-small hours of the night, like a rat nipping at a slum lord's dozing baby.

"For God's sake, Annette died way back in 2004," P. Melvin said. "After all those years, you really need to let go. Think of your political career if word gets out that you're waging some kind of vendetta against a harmless bum living in the back woods of Maine."

"I *can't* just let it go."

P. Melvin prayed for God to save him from fanatics like Harry Penrose. "I'm trying to let bygones be bygones and advise you as a friend, Harry. No good will come from this."

Harry wasn't interested in advice. "It's just that I've had to hire somebody to work on the problem, and it's been more expensive than I thought—"

"How is your boat, Harry? Did you go out sailing much last summer?" P. Melvin didn't wait for an answer. "We had an agreement, and you were well paid. You got a free pass last time, but I warned you about pushing your luck. I will not be crossed again."

"This is chicken-feed, really, just a loan for a few months. I only need another thirty or forty—"

"The Ringling Group paid you seven million for Annette's firm when she died," P. Melvin said coldly.

"It's worth ten times that now."

"You were paid a fair price. I put out a lot of money and hired a lot of good people to turn her company into what it is now. Are you telling me the seven million is gone already?"

"No, no, it's just a temporary thing, what with starting up my new campaign for Congress, and contributions being a little slow to come in. And I'm having to be extra careful with all these watchdog groups, too."

"You should be worrying about your own reputation as much as watchdog groups, Harry. Your political effectiveness is based on the fact that people respect you. If everyone sees you going on some kind of witch hunt, you'll lose that respect." P. Melvin sighed into the phone. "And you want me to help fund this boondoggle?"

"I know we had a disagreement in the past," Harry said, "but I was hoping we could put all that behind us."

"A disagreement? Is that what you call it?"

"We can still help each other."

P. Melvin thought for a moment. Harry's fixation on revenge was probably little more than an irritation which seemed unlikely to make trouble for the firm, but one could never be too safe. He fiddled with his phone console to create a clicking sound.

"I have another call coming in that I have to take, Harry, so I've got to go, but I'll give you thirty, with the understanding that I may have some minor work for your man. My secretary will have the check this afternoon."

P. Melvin cut the connection. He supposed that Penrose might be right and this Breener was the real thing, unlikely as it seemed. He pondered the implications of that possibility and decided to have one of the firm's younger partners look into the situation, just in case. Giving Penrose the money could be useful if some extra-legal action was required. Better to keep his hands clean and let Harry's thug to do any dirty work.

After all, one could never be too careful.

Chapter 8

Saturday evening, December 15

It was after dark when Vince returned to the Borofsky mansion. He opened the massive door and stood in the entryway for a moment. The three-storey front hall, with its great sweeping stairway and second-storey balcony, reminded him of *Gone with the Wind*, only much larger. A vast crystal chandelier, the size and weight of a luxury SUV, hung from the lofty ceiling. Its lights were turned down to an orange glow, which danced over the cut-glass pendants.

It had been a long thirty-six hours for Vince Martell, much of the time spent freezing his ass on Anton Borofsky's snowmobile. He'd planned to just bump Breener a little, but he must have cut it too close, and the next thing he knew the guy was in the hospital. That would have been okay, except the nut-case had vanished before Vince could deliver his letter. Weren't hospitals supposed to keep track of their patients, especially the weirdos?

Where the hell was Breener, anyway? The last thing Vince needed was to have the guy disappear right before Christmas. He'd checked the Cassidy woman's cabin last night just in case Breener had gone there, but she was alone. There had been no luck at his shack when he dropped off the letter either, though it was likely that the woman who lived next door knew more than she was telling. The way she had studied his face and the rental car made him nervous. Most people didn't look twice at a stranger, but he figured she would know him for sure if he turned up again, in spite of the fake limp and phony glasses.

In any case, he would have to find some other way to flush Breener out.

Thanks to the uncertain lighting, it took a moment for him to spot Sasha as she stood in the doorway to the library with a drink in her hand.

"Is this place big enough for the two of you?" he said.

Sasha took his quip seriously. "We only stay here for short periods of time."

In the dim light and from across the vast hall, she seemed to be wearing what looked like a dressing gown.

"I thought you two would be on a plane by now."

"The flight was cancelled, so Anton is driving down to Portland to catch a flight into The City."

She was referring to New York, of course, since Boston was merely a village to those from the Big Apple's upper crust. Vince began to feel uneasy.

"He won't have an easy drive, with the snow drifting across the turnpike," he said.

"Anton is very committed to his work." Sasha shrugged. "Why don't you change into some dry clothes and come down for a drink? It will be hours until supper is ready and I have a proposition to discuss with you." She paused for a beat. "A business proposition."

———————

"Sure you don't want anything stronger?" Sasha said, handing Vince a glass of club soda when he returned later.

"This is fine," Vince replied. A small sofa faced the fireplace and he sat there, soaking up warmth from the hearth. The trouble with castles, even brand new ones, was that they were cold.

Sasha was mixing a drink for herself. It appeared to be something that contained a generous quantity of vodka. She sat beside him on the sofa, closer than was necessary in his mind.

"Here's to success in our new joint venture," she said, raising her glass.

Vince frowned. "I don't take on more than one job at a time."

"Do you really have to wait until Christmas to deal with that man?" she said.

"My employer has very specific instructions."

Sasha pouted and took another swallow of her vodka. "I suppose I can wait that long." Her dressing gown was tied loosely at the waist and as she turned toward him, her knee brushing against his, he could see the gown was covering a filmy negligee and little else.

"Mmm," she said sniffing the air. "Nika is starting supper. I wasn't sure when you'd be back, so I told her to serve at seven. That way, you'll have a good three hours to thaw out after being out in the wind all day."

"Nika cooks too?"

"She does everything, cooking, waiting table, cleaning. We've had her for years and take her everywhere. She's the only help we need on short trips like this." Sasha sipped her drink. "Best of all, Nika is discrete. So many domestics have loose lips when it comes to the family secrets." She gave a little laugh, her hand brushing Vince's cheek. "All families have secrets, Vince. But I imagine that you must know all about discretion in your line of work, too."

He looked at her, trying to keep his gaze off that negligee, and trying to gauge how drunk she was. Vince believed in being discrete alright, but he never counted on the discretion of others—that was dangerously naive. "So, what is this problem you want to talk about?"

A brief flash of triumph crossed her face, convincing him the Sasha was more sober, and more dangerous, than he'd originally thought. She leaned forward, her hand resting on his shoulder.

"What do you know about Anton's work?" she said.

"Not much, except that he came up with some kind of chemical to make old fish smell better."

"An oversimplification," she said dryly, removing her hand, "but the general idea is correct. Anton is a chemist in the food industry and he developed a way to treat fish in order to delay, and even partially reverse the decaying process—what you might call 'the bad fish smell.'"

As you can see," she added, gesturing around the room, "his discovery has made us quite wealthy."

Her hand found its way to the nape of his neck as she slid a little closer. "The trouble with breakthroughs like Anton's is that they attract copy-cats, ruthless people who prey on those of us who are truly creative." She looked into his eyes earnestly. "History is full of examples of people who have their inventions stolen and are left penniless. We do not intend to be one of those sad cases."

Her dressing gown seemed to be undressing itself, leaving less and less of Sasha to the imagination. "But you can't prevent competition," he said.

"Prevent competition? In the land of the free? God, no, I just want to slow it down long enough to solidify our business."

"How?"

Again, there was that quick triumphant flash in her eyes. "There's a certain individual, lets call him John Smith, who is in the process of trying to muscle in on Anton's invention. We can't let that happen, which is where you come in."

"And what, exactly, do you have in mind?"

"I leave that to your discretion, but a fatal automobile accident would seem appropriate to me." The drink glass had vanished, which enabled her to run her fingers along his thigh in addition to his neck.

Vince began to realize how complicated his life was becoming. "I don't work for free."

"You'll be well compensated," she purred, patting his leg. The dressing gown had fallen open to reveal an extraordinarily short and shear negligee. "I have a good deal of cash at my disposal."

"Cash is good," he managed.

"Would five-thousand be an adequate retainer to start with?"

"You have that much money lying around here?"

"I have a safe in my bedroom."

"Of course you do."

"We can go and get it now, if you like." She smiled at him. "To seal the deal."

She abruptly slid away. "There is one thing. Anton must never know about our arrangement."

"Of course not."

"He thinks of himself as a tough guy, who can take care of the problem by himself. It's a macho thing."

Vince nodded.

"But he's really just a cream-puff, and I'm worried that he'll get in over his head. I mean, he talks tough, but what does a chemist know about your line of work?"

In Vince's experience, cream-puffs did not usually become self-made millionaires in a competitive business. A measure of ruthlessness was required for that.

Sasha studied Vince for a moment. He was ten years younger than Anton, trim and fit.

"Let's go upstairs and get your retainer." She rose, tugging at his arm. She looked up. "Oh, look, there's a sprig of Mistletoe over the doorway. Nika must have put it there."

Vince Martell sensed that he was about to have a lively evening.

Chapter 9

Sunday morning, December 16

Morning dawned sunny and calm, as though the weather gods were apologizing for having plastered Burnt Cove with nearly three feet of snow over the weekend. Sarah had finished cleaning up the breakfast dishes, and was just putting on her boots when a pounding rattled the cabin. She knew of only one person who could knock on a door like that.

"Good morning, Eldon," she said, opening the door. "Would you like some coffee?"

"No time. You and I are supposed to drive to Oliver's place."

"Has he forgotten how to use a telephone?"

"Things are a little strange up there right now," Eldon replied enigmatically. "We'd better take my truck."

Sarah nodded, remembering the woman's voice offering tea when she'd called yesterday. "I can drive myself, if I decide to go."

"We'd better take my truck," Eldon repeated.

"You don't think I can drive in the snow?"

"You been up to the road?"

"I was just on my way."

The path that Jeff had cleared up to the road yesterday was pretty much drifted in, so they trudged through knee-deep snow for most of the way.

"Where is my car?" Sarah said when the reached the road.

"Under that snow drift, I imagine."

Between the snowplowing and the wind, the drifts were well over Sarah's head. "My poor car," she moaned, looking at the shapeless mound of snow, "I won't see it until spring."

"I expect Jeff will be over to dig you out sooner or later."

It didn't take long for Sarah to appreciate the ability of Eldon's oversized pickup to churn its way along the still-drifted back roads.

"You have no idea what this is all about?" she asked.

"Just that Oliver sounded hassled, and he wouldn't say what was going on." He gave Sarah a quick glance. "I can guess, though."

"Me too."

They made their way to Route One, which was well cleared, and crossed it to Hound Hill road, which was not so well cleared.

They had driven about five miles inland from Burnt Cove by now, and the snow was noticeably deeper here. Half way up the hill, they encountered a huge front-end loader, which was laboriously digging back the drifted snow. Its bucket looked big enough to swallow up a car.

"My car is going to be destroyed," Sarah groaned, "picked up and dumped in a ditch."

"I doubt it'll get all that stove in," Eldon said mildly, "so long as they remember it's there."

The wind had swept a lot of the snow off the field in front of Oliver's elderly colonial, and the driveway was well plowed.

Beside the barn-turned-boatshop, which adjoined the house, there was a mound of snow. "Poor *Owl*," Sarah said. Her classic Herreshoff sixteen-foot sailboat had vanished under an icy blanket. The warm summer days spent at *Owl's* helm seemed impossibly far away.

"You got a good cover, so she'll be fine under there," Eldon said.

A woman, who appeared to be in her early forties, met them at the kitchen door and ushered them inside. She had long brunette hair, which reached nearly to her waist. An overworked scrunchy struggled valiantly to control the billowing tresses. "We got visitors," she bellowed at the interior of the house.

Wes, Oliver's black-and-white Springer Spaniel, vaulted into the room to greet the arrivals, barking and wagging his tail with delight.

Sarah's suspicions were confirmed when Ziggy hobbled into the kitchen on crutches.

"Should you be walking around like that?" Sarah asked him.

"I fly like a crow," he replied.

"Could you lay off the crow business for one minute?" The woman heaved a great sigh. "I'm Annabelle," she said, "Ziggy's sister, God help me. You must be Sarah. I've heard a lot about you. And that giant behind you must be Eldon."

Oliver entered the kitchen, squeezing in behind Ziggy. Tall and slender, his blond hair tinged with grey, he surveyed the group crowded into his kitchen. "Guess you've all met," he said.

To Sarah, he looked tired and, as Eldon had said, "hassled."

Annabelle sidled over to Oliver and took his arm in what seemed like an overly possessive way to Sarah. "Oliver has been kind enough to put Ziggy and me up for a while, until we can decide what to do next."

Oliver noticed Sarah looking at him. He shot a glance at Ziggy and rolled his eyes. Sarah felt a sudden pang of sympathy for this man who treasured his privacy, who had only slowly come to accept her into his life, and whose house had been invaded by these two obviously squabbling siblings.

"How about some coffee?" Annabelle said. "It won't take me a minute to start another pot."

Just then, Eldon's cell chimed. "It's Cindy Rice," he said, checking the caller ID before answering. He listened for a moment.

"Do I know where Ziggy is?" he said meditatively, staring up at the ceiling. "Maybe."

He listened a moment longer before handing the phone to Ziggy, who listened, his face going pale. Eldon reached over to steady him.

"What's going on?" Oliver murmured.

"Annabelle's sick, real sick, and it doesn't look good," Eldon replied in a stage whisper.

"I must fly to the rescue!" Ziggy proclaimed as he returned Eldon's cell.

"What's all this about Annabelle?" Annabelle said.

"She's Ziggy's goat," Eldon explained.

"You named a *goat* after me!"

"Annabelle is a noble beast," Ziggy said, "full of fun and true goat-wisdom."

"I've half a mind to break your other ankle," Annabelle growled. "How's that for goat-wisdom?"

"I need the keys to your truck," Ziggy said to Eldon. "I must fly to her side."

"No way you're going to drive my truck with a broken ankle."

"Then you must drive me to the rescue."

"Shouldn't we call a vet?" Oliver said.

"A *vet?* For Annabelle?" Ziggy said, scandalized. "No! We must all fly like crows to the rescue."

In the end, Eldon, Ziggy, and Annabelle jammed themselves into Eldon's truck for the trip to Burnt Cove. Sarah and Oliver followed behind in Oliver's elderly Honda.

"How long has Ziggy been here?" Sarah asked as they churned down the snow-covered road.

"Fifty-nine long hours, and neither of them ever sleeps, as near as I can tell," Oliver replied glumly. "He appeared on the doorstep around eleven o'clock Friday night, and Annabelle arrived at dawn on Saturday morning. I figure Ziggy must have called as soon as he got here, and she headed up right away."

"How did he get here from the hospital? The roads weren't all that good."

"He flew like a crow, of course," sympathetically muttered. He caught himself. "Sorry. That pair aren't the easiest of house guests. I don't know for sure how he got to the house. The first thing I knew, he was pounding on the door, waving a crutch in the air, talking about fleeing, and crows, and pleading for sanctuary. How could I say no? My guess is that he wangled a ride on one of the plow trucks, or maybe several plow trucks. The guy can be persuasive."

"Why go to your house? Why not the Rices, or his shack?"

"Beats me. Ziggy won't say anything sensible about that. Come to think of it, he won't say anything sensible about anything."

Sarah nodded sympathetically. "And Annabelle? Where did she come from and how did she get here?"

They crossed Route One and turned down the Squirrel Point road. The traffic was light and Eldon was lead-footing the big GMC, probably due to Ziggy's urgings.

"God knows how she got here from Massachusetts, though she mentioned a bus. Maybe she got a cab, or hitchhiked part of the way."

"Maybe she'll take him home with her. He can't live alone in that shack with his leg in a cast," Sarah said. "Are there any other siblings?"

"Just the two of them, according to Annabelle," Oliver replied. "Annabelle Lee Breener and Zigfield Follies Breener. The A and the Z of it."

"And she's the oldest?"

"The youngest."

"Then why isn't it Abner and Zaza?" Sarah inquired.

"Only a Breener could answer that question. I learned that she's divorced and lives alone on an organic farm down in Hopkinton, Massachusetts. I've never heard of any women in Ziggy's life."

"Ziggy Breener, man of mystery," she commented.

"That's an understatement."

"Their parents must have been true flower children, considering the names." she said. "Does anybody know where he usually spends the winter? Do you suppose he stays with Annabelle?"

"No. And I can't imagine the two of them sharing a house for any length of time. She'd kill him inside of a week."

"The crow talk does seem to bother her," Sarah said.

"I wonder where the crow thing came from. There's quite a knot on his head from the snowmoble accident. Maybe that addled whatever was left of his mind."

"Maybe," she replied. "When Jeff found Ziggy after the accident, he said that Ziggy kept babbling about flying like a crow."

"And he's been doing it ever since."

"Come to think of it," she said slowly, "he did mention that the distance from his place to my cabin was a mile away as the crow flies, when he came to bring me some of his tea. But that was just a comment in passing."

"Maybe the accident happening right afterwards got crows stuck in his head."

"I'm not an expert on head injuries, but I suppose it's possible," she said. "The brain is a strange thing."

"Especially his." Oliver closed the gap between them and the GMC. "I wonder if the crows mean more than we think."

"How so?"

"You know Ziggy. He always talks in circles. Maybe the accident hasn't made him as batty as we think. Maybe the crows are more than just a conk on the head, and he's saying something real. Something we don't understand."

"So what does a crow mean to you? What does it stand for?" Sarah said.

"It's a bird, the master of both land and air. It's also a symbol of sorrow, darkness, and evil, like Edgar Allen Poe's raven. Crows are a connection to the underworld."

"Crows are clever, smart and devious."

"A flock of them is referred to as a 'murder of crows,'" Oliver said.

"Let's hope Ziggy doesn't mean it that way." Sarah thought about the mysterious snowmobiles, and the skull.

Oliver fought for control as the Honda skidded around the corner. "Eldon is going to get *us* murdered at this rate," he grumbled. "Crows steal things, like a farmer's seeds."

"Which is why farmers shoot them," she said. "Speaking of shooting, I heard snowmobiles and gunshots on the pond around one o'clock on Saturday morning."

"Snowmobiles and gunshots? Are you sure?"

"I'm not positive about the gunshots. It was still pretty windy."

"Probably just some kids joyriding in the storm."

"Possibly," Sarah said doubtfully.

Chapter 10

Sunday morning, December 16

Cindy hurried out to meet the caravan as it pulled up. She was clearly upset. "Annabelle was fine when I fed her this morning," she said to Ziggy, "but when I looked out the window later, she was kind of staggering around looking wobbly. That's when I called Eldon." Cindy rested her hand on Ziggy's arm with uncharacteristic tenderness. "She collapsed and died right after I hung up. I checked and she wasn't breathing, and I didn't hear a heartbeat."

"I must fly to her side," Ziggy said, hobbling towards the path beaten through the snow. Annabelle followed close behind, trying to keep Ziggy from falling, while avoiding his flailing crutches.

Cindy shook her head sadly. "He's going to miss that fool goat." There was a hitch in her voice.

They gathered around the spot where Annabelle Lee lay in the snow. Ziggy managed to kneel beside the body, and he gently brushed a dusting of drifted snow off her head and chest. The two-legged Annabelle rested her hand in his shoulder.

After a moment, Ziggy struggled to his feet. "We have to take her inside."

"Of course," Annabelle said gently. "We can't leave her lying in the snow like this."

"I can carry her into your cabin," Eldon suggested.

"Where it's warm," Ziggy said emphatically.

"We can light the stove," Cindy said. "It won't take long to warm the place up."

"I don't think she'll mind being cold, Ziggy," Annabelle said reasonably.

Ziggy turned to Cindy. "We must take her to your house."

"You want to take a dead goat into my house?"

"We must fly like crows with Annabelle!" Ziggy said, waving a crutch in his agitation.

"You know how he can get when he's upset," Eldon said. "Might be best to humor him for a bit."

"By putting a dead goat in my kitchen?" Cindy looked at Ziggy's expression and sighed. "Fine. Whatever."

Cindy reluctantly led the procession to her house. Annabelle wasn't much bigger than a large dog, and Eldon carried her easily in his arms.

The thought of getting his beloved goat's corpse into the warmth of Cindy's kitchen had a calming effect on Ziggy. "I must gather some things," he said, turning towards his shack.

"You sure could use a change of clothes," Annabelle said.

Oliver went with Ziggy to help carry. The inside of Ziggy's shack consisted of a single room with a bed at one end, a cooking and sitting area at the other. A large wood-fired cook stove sat in the middle of the back wall.

"Take these," Ziggy said briskly, pointing to his worn medical bag and a large black suitcase that was nearly the size of a steamer trunk.

Oliver staggered across the road with his burden, and wondered apprehensively what his oddball companion planned to do with the medical supplies.

They found Annabelle-the-goat lying on a sheet of plastic on the kitchen floor.

"Annabelle must be on the table," Ziggy said.

"What are you planning to do with your doctor's bag?" Cindy said.

"Annabelle must be on the table!" Ziggy exclaimed.

"Your goat will be nice and comfy on the floor," Annabelle-the-person said.

"You're not going to autopsy a dead goat on my kitchen table, are you?" Cindy said suspiciously.

"Autopsy Annabelle? Are you crazy?" Ziggy's scraggly beard bristled.

"We eat on that table," Cindy pointed out.

"She *must* be on the table!"

"Might be best to humor him a little longer," Eldon murmured.

Cindy glared at Eldon. "Fine," she snarled, "but some day, I'm going to leave a dead goat in your apartment. On your bed."

They maneuvered the animal's body onto the table, where her legs flopped precariously over the edge.

Ziggy rummaged in his medical supplies.

"What are you doing?" Oliver said.

Ziggy filled a large hypodermic needle.

Cindy shook her head in despair.

"What the hell are you doing?" Annabelle screeched. "The damn goat is dead! Look at her, she's cold as ice!"

"I don't think that's a good idea," Eldon added, eying the syringe.

"You're a trained EMT," Ziggy said to Eldon. "You must give Annabelle the breath of life."

"Forget it," Eldon rumbled. "I ain't breathing into a dead goat's mouth for anybody."

Ziggy plunged the needle into the goat's chest, and turned to Sarah. "You were a nurse, *you* give Annabelle the breath of life." He turned to prepare another syringe.

Sarah rested her hand on Ziggy's arm. "Your sister is right, Ziggy," she said gently. "The goat is dead. Let her go. Let Annabelle rest in—" She gave a grunt of pain as one of Annabelle's hooves punched her in the stomach.

"Jesus Christ," Cindy said in awe.

"Post-mortem spasm," Eldon said.

Annabelle-the-goat gave a snort and began to struggle in panic.

"She's alive!" Annabelle-the-person said in amazement.

"Perhaps," Ziggy said calmly. "We'll know if she's really alive in twenty-four hours."

"What just happened?" Cindy said, her eyes bulging. "Do you mean she wasn't really dead after all?"

"Who knows when a dead goat is dead?" Ziggy replied. "Goats are tricky that way," he added, as he comforted Annabelle. "She needs a blanket."

Cindy hurried off, mumbling.

"What the hell was in that shot you gave her?" Oliver said.

"A cunningly contrived compound," Ziggy replied.

Sarah remembered Ziggy describing his tea in much the same vague terms. Once again, she found herself wondering if the man's behavior was just a sham, an intentional act to deceive people. Was he crazy like a fox, or just crazy? Did he have some kind of multiple personality disorder, switching personas at random?

"Annabelle was poisoned, wasn't she," Sarah murmured to Ziggy. "A paralytic, maybe?"

Cindy returned with a worn blanket, and helped Ziggy wrap it around Annabelle.

"Perhaps Atropine," Ziggy replied. "She was alive, but dead. She may still be dead. We'll know in twenty-four hours."

Sarah knew exactly what he was saying. There was a variety of poisons that killed by paralyzing the muscles. She tried to imagine Annabelle's experience: the inability to stand or even move, slow suffocation as the ability to draw a breath was lost, and finally death as the heart became still. All this while the mind was still conscious. Who would do such a thing?

Perhaps everyone was thinking along the same lines because the room was quiet as they arranged a cushioned spot on the floor and placed Annabelle on it. The goat eyed them warily for a moment before laying her head down with a sigh.

"We must buy her some new grain," Ziggy said.

"Where do you keep it?" Oliver asked.

"In the trunk of the old junker where the hens live," Cindy said. "There's no lock anymore, so anybody could get in there." Cindy looked at Annabelle lying groggily on the floor, one eye half open. "What are we going to do with her? We can't leave her here alone, and I have the afternoon shift at Reny's. Sally won't be back from her job until four or so, and God knows when Jeff will be home."

"She must come with me," Ziggy replied.

Oliver sighed.

Suddenly Cindy gave a start and reached for an envelope lying on the kitchen counter. "I forgot about this in all the to-do. Somebody came by and slid it under your door yesterday. I brought it in here for safe keeping until you turned up."

Ziggy took the envelope, turned it over in his hands for a moment, as though reluctant to open it. At last he removed the contents, looked at them, and let them flutter to the floor as he lurched back against the counter.

───────────

"Do you think Ziggy is really just an oddball?" Sarah said. She and Oliver were in his Honda, with the back seat folded down to make room for Annabelle, who lay in luxuriously padded comfort.

"I'm not sure we're competent to answer that question," Oliver replied. "Especially when you consider that we're the ones with a goat in the back seat."

"A pet goat."

"A pet goat the size of small pony."

She's not that big. You should be thankful that Annabelle is a young goat. Just think how much bigger she would be, full grown."

Oliver muttered under his breath.

"Give her a break; she's just come back from the dead."

"So we have a pet zombie-goat almost the size of a small pony in the back seat. I'm glad you cleared that up."

"She's awfully quiet back there," Sarah said, turning around to look at Annabelle.

"Maybe that's the way it is with zombie-goats."

"That's what I mean about Ziggy. I checked Annabelle while the two of you were getting his medical bags, and for all intents and purposes, she was dead: body cold, no pulse, no breathing, pupils not reactive, nothing."

Oliver shrugged. "Okay, so she was dead. I thought modern medicine was able to bring people back from the dead all the time. Why should goats be any different?"

They arrived at the Route One intersection and turned left towards the Hound Hill road, while Eldon and the others turned right to pick up fresh feed for Annabelle.

"It's just that Ziggy made it look so easy," she said.

Oliver nodded. "A few shots and Annabelle came back from goat heaven."

"It was the same way with the tea he gave me. I was really sick, fever, probably pneumonia, the whole works—"

"You sounded like hospital bait for sure."

"I felt like it too, but a few cups of his tea and I was better in just a few hours. I could almost feel it working."

"Ziggy's red tag tea is powerful stuff."

"Ziggy himself is powerful stuff," she said.

"I hope you aren't suggesting some kind of occult, voodoo witch-doctor thing."

"No," she said slowly. "I just think he's a lot better doctor than we realize. Brilliant comes to mind. At the very least there's a lot more to him hidden behind the craziness than we know."

The turn onto the Hound Hill road was marked by huge gate-posts of snow.

"Speaking of hidden," Oliver said, "what was in Ziggy's envelope? I saw you pick up two pieces of paper and palm them."

"Just for safekeeping."

"So dig them out and let's take a look."

"That's unscrupulous," she said primly.

"He's the one who dropped them on the floor."

Sarah fished in the pocket of her parka. "There's a Christmas card and an old newspaper picture of a man. The caption on the photograph says, 'Doctor Harry Hastings.'"

"That's all, just the name?"

"That's it. The rest was cut off, but it must be old because the paper is yellowed. It's a nice Christmas card, with a sprig of Mistletoe on it. The picture was probably inside." Sarah opened the card. "It says, 'Remember Christmas Eve.' I wonder what that means." She turned the card over and said, "Oh," in a small voice.

"Oh?"

"The back side says, 'Run and your friends will die.' What has Ziggy gotten into?"

"More important, what has he gotten us into?" Oliver said.

Chapter 11

Sunday afternoon, December 16

Vince returned to the Borofsky's palace around mid-afternoon and let himself in one of the side doors, carefully disarming the elaborate burglar alarm system. The place was empty, since Sasha and Nika had left for New York during the morning.

He was glad to see the last of Nika. The mousy, grey-haired little woman gave him the creeps, with her way of scuttling noiselessly around the house. Sasha had assured him a number of times the Nika didn't understand English, but he had watched the woman while he and Sasha were talking over supper last night, and he suspected the maid understood a lot more English than her employers thought.

Sasha had also assured him that Nika was the soul of discretion. He hoped so. He could picture Nika listening in on their fling last night. She wouldn't have needed English to know what was going on. He was a fool to have let Sasha lure him into her bed, not that it wasn't a pleasurable experience. The woman's ferocious love-making had scared him—and he was not someone who scared easily. No, it had been incredibly foolish to get involved with these people, including Anton Borofsky, who was almost certainly more dangerous than he seemed.

The vast emptiness of the place was unnerving.

He had picked up a supply of beer, and that Maine delicacy, an Italian sandwich, on the way over. He made his way into the immense, restaurant-sized kitchen and sat at the table.

Vince had spent the morning knee-deep in snow and he was cold. To add insult to injury, Nika had turned the temperature down when she and Sasha left, and the house was frigid. Vince muttered about his tight-wad hosts while he searched for the thermostat and turned it up to a more comfortable level.

He sat at the kitchen table and unwrapped his foot-long Italian. It was overflowing with lettuce, tomato, onion, pepper, and assorted cold-cuts, liberally sprinkled with oil. He ate contentedly, pleased with the morning's events.

Everyone on Meadow Road might be dirt poor, but they all seemed to own a snowmobile, and as a result there was a maze of trails threading the brushy woods behind the houses. He'd made good use of those trails to observe Ziggy's arrival and the subsequent events.

Poisoning Ziggy's goat worked better than he'd expected. Anton Borofsky had briefed him on the names and descriptions of the various players he might encounter, and Vince watched as Ziggy, a woman he figured must be his sister, Sarah Cassidy, her boyfriend Oliver Wendell, and a huge kid who must be Eldon Tupper, all arrived right on cue.

Their arrival had provided much information. Most important, it was almost certain that Breener was staying with Wendell.

Vince had watched as the goat was carried inside the Rice's house, and later as the animal was placed, alive, into Wendell's car.

Vince was oddly touched by Ziggy's compassion for the goat, and he was glad the animal survived. He didn't think of himself as a vicious man, a cold-blooded killer. He liked to believe that he disposed of people who deserved it, and that he was improving the world by taking them out of it.

Vince liked animals better than he liked most people, and it had bothered him that the goat should die just to flush Ziggy Breener out of the woodwork. In any case, dead or alive, the goat had served its purpose.

Still, he wouldn't have needed to do the goat thing if he'd killed Breener outright with the Borofsky's snowmobile instead of just banging him up like his client wanted. Left to his own devices, Vince would have finished Breener off that day and made it look like a hit-and-run, some kid joy riding too fast on a stolen machine. Quick, neat and clean was his motto, and this psychological torment business didn't sit well.

Vince took a swallow of beer. That was the trouble when you let clients tell you how to do a contract, he thought irritably. They turned a simple, clean hit into a mess. Vince had charged an arm and a leg to do this job, but now he was thinking that maybe he hadn't charged enough, or more accurately, that he didn't want the contract at any price.

Vince scolded himself. After all, a job was a job and he needed to get it done with. Still, this whole business was getting to him.

He put the Italian down, wiped olive oil off his chin and took another swig of beer while he thought about the players and considered his next step.

First, there was Cindy Rice. He didn't like the woman. She was hostile and, more important, her eyes were too shrewd and saw too much. Years of experience had taught Vince that a minor change in his appearance was enough to fool most people. He sensed that Cindy Rice was an exception, and therefore dangerous.

According to Anton Borofsky, Sarah Cassidy had come up with the lawyers who successfully defended Ziggy's claim to the land on Squirrel Point. That meant she was a friend of Ziggy's, which made her a possible target for Vince's campaign of revenge.

Then there was Oliver Wendell, who was harboring Ziggy Breener. That would require Vince's attention.

Of course, there was Ziggy's sister, Annabelle. He would deal with her and Ziggy last.

It was going to be a busy week.

Breener must realize by now that he was the target of revenge. The Christmas card would tell him that, and why.

Vince finished his meal, washing it down with the last of the beer. He looked around the kitchen. Where the hell was the wastebasket? Scanning the oversized and immaculate space reminded him that there was still one loose end to deal with on Meadow Road. He would tackle that job tonight.

The house was starting to warm up and Vince decided to finish thawing out his feet by exploring the place. He'd seen the cavernous front hall, and the third-storey swimming pool. Not to mention the master bedroom.

The back of the house, over the kitchen, was more modest and contained the servants' quarters.

He poked around Nika's room. The space was small and spare, like the woman herself. A handful of paperback books on the bedside table drew his attention—an assortment of cheap romance novels. They were in English.

Snow weighed down the young fir and spruce trees, making them look like stooped ghosts burdened by spectral cares. Sarah and Oliver plodded through the woods, their snowshoes sinking deep into the snow.

Wes had greeted this first big snowfall of the season ecstatically, leaping like a gigantic flea ahead of his slow-moving people. Now and then he'd pounce and bury his head in a drift as he pursued some hapless creature, amid snorts and muffled woofs. After a while, the flea act became tiring, and Wes contented himself with trudging along in the snowshoe tracks.

"You've lived all these years in Maine, and never had a Christmas tree?" Sarah said incredulously.

"Never saw the need for one."

Sarah knew that his wife had died a couple of years before he moved to Maine, and he'd been living alone since then, but even so...

"Well, it's high time you had a tree, especially where you have house guests."

"Don't goats eat Christmas trees?"

"Ziggy promised that she'll only be in the house for a day or two, and he'll keep her in the living room," Sarah said. "It's only until she's strong enough to be outside, and we did take out the rug, lay down tarps, and put down straw for bedding."

Oliver grumbled.

"The poor goat can barely stand up. Where's your Christmas spirit?"

"How is Santa going to get down the chimney with a bale of hay in the fireplace?"

"Think of it as having a real-life nativity scene in your very own livingroom," she suggested brightly. "At least the stable part."

"Ziggy's sister does help around the house, which makes a big difference," Oliver conceded, "even if she is almost as loony as he is."

They came to a huge boulder, which loomed over Sarah's head. She stopped to look at it.

"They're called 'erratics,'" Oliver said. "The glaciers dropped them all around this part of Maine."

"It looks so out of place, just sitting here all by itself for tens-of-thousands of years. Out of place, like Ziggy, who is pretty erratic himself right now. If he doesn't spend the winter with his sister, then where does he go?"

"Not even the Rices know. I asked Annabelle, and she has no clue where he usually goes, either."

"What does he live on? He can't possibly make enough money collecting cans."

"According to Annabelle, they inherited some money when their parents died—not much, but enough to give Ziggy a little income to live on." He glanced at Sarah, a bit defensively, she thought. "She's kind of fun when you get her away from Ziggy."

"What about Annabelle? The goat, I mean?"

"She stays at Ziggy's Zoo over the winter. The Rices take care of her while he's away."

"That's very nice of them," she said, "considering how Cindy Rice feels about incomers."

"She has a soft spot for oddballs like Ziggy."

They came to a piece of woods that had been cut over some fifteen years ago and had grown up to a stand of eight-foot balsam firs. They began shaking snow off some likely prospects.

"I wonder why Ziggy chose to move to Burnt Cove, or Meadow Road, or even to this part of Maine," Sarah said.

"You've heard the rumor that he was an Emergency Room doctor who had a nervous breakdown and moved here to get away. Well, this is away compared to a lot of places."

"Escape from his demons?" she said. "But still, why here?"

"Why not here?" After all Oliver thought, that's what he'd done after his wife died. Perhaps he had more in common with Ziggy than he realized.

Sarah knew enough of Oliver's history to know that she'd inadvertently hit a nerve. "Sorry," she said.

"Ancient history."

They set about selecting and cutting down a tree in silence.

Having packed the trail on the way out made the return trip easier, even with the tree slung between them. They were half way back to the house before Sarah returned to Ziggy. "Do you suppose he's been hiding from someone all these years and now he's been found? He got a lot of coverage in the papers a couple of weeks ago when he won his lawsuit over Myra's will."

"Blew his cover," Oliver said. "If your theory is true, then it begs the question of what's next for Ziggy."

Chapter 12

Sunday, early evening, December 16

It was after sunset, and Cindy Rice was returning home from work, when her headlights picked up the stranger's car parked beside the road. He'd left it about a hundred yards up from her house, in a wide place which had been plowed out for the school bus to turn around. Cindy slowed to make sure the plate number matched her recollection, and then continued on at a crawl while she thought. She had gone to Boston a few times, a god-awful place, where she discovered that people parked cars everywhere. With so many of them abandoned willy-nilly, it was no wonder that city people thought a car became invisible as soon as it was parked beside the road.

Nothing could be further from the truth on Meadow Road.

Even though Cindy had no proof that this man had poisoned Annabelle, the stranger was from away, which made his guilt more likely. And after all, why else was he hanging around if he wasn't up to some kind of mischief?

She pulled into her dooryard, pleased to see that Jeff had knocked back the snow banks, like she'd asked.

"Where's your sister?" Cindy said as she stamped her boots on the kitchen floor mat.

"Sal's off with Eldon," Jeff replied around a mouthful of Nachos.

Cindy's maternal instinct was troubled by the fact that Eldon had a two-room apartment in Rockland where he and Sally undoubtedly got up to no good.

Cindy reached for the lever action .22, which stood conveniently behind the kitchen door.

"What are you doing?" Jeff inquired.

"Thought I saw a squirrel on the bird feeder."

Squirrel Point had been appropriately named, for the place teemed with the ravenous rodents. Cindy didn't enjoy shooting little animals, but the cost of birdseed, had turned her into a ruthless hunter. Having dispatched countless squirrels to their bushy-tailed nirvanas, she'd become an expert shot. She slid half-a-dozen .22 shorts into the magazine.

"Kind of late for them to be on the feeder, isn't it?" Jeff commented. "It's pretty much dark out there."

"Don't talk with your mouth full," she said, slipping out the door.

Jeff's snowmobile had left a track which ran behind the house before angling away into the woods. Following the track through the gloom, she made her way to a spot where she could see the stranger's car through the underbrush. The Poolers lived diagonally across the road, and they had a string of Christmas lights which glinted red and green on the car's windshield. There would be just enough light.

Cindy levered a round into the chamber. Propping the barrel against a sapling, she took aim and fired. The left rear tire subsided with a hiss.

It's been said that life is like a gigantic web of interconnections, and that plucking one strand of that web can shock the entire structure in ways that cannot be predicted. In her playful vengeance,

Cindy had just given the web of life a hefty yank, thereby setting in motion a series of events, some of which would not be beneficial.

"Jesus, Ma, what are you doing?" Jeff's voice nearly made her jump out of her skin.

"Why the hell are you sneaking up on me like that?"

"You just shot out that guy's tire."

"It wasn't easy either, what with it being near dark."

"You shot his tire just because he parked in the bus turn around?"

"Keep you voice down. And for your information, I shot his tire to do him back for poisoning Annabelle. Anybody who does that deserves punishment."

"Yes, but—"

"Somebody has to stand up for justice in this world, Jeffery."

"But how do you know he poisoned Annabelle?"

"Because he was prowling around there the other day," she replied.

"But are you sure he did it?"

"Damn right I'm sure, and I didn't like the way he talked when I saw him the other day, either."

Jeff stared at the car as it sat lopsidedly in the bus turnaround. "You're sure it's the same car?"

"I remember the plate number."

"Maybe he's visiting somebody."

"Why park here, then? Why not park in front of whoever he's visiting?"

Jeff had no answer for that. "What do you think he's doing here?"

"I think we better check Ziggy's house, is what I think."

"We could call the cops," Jeff said, knowing that wouldn't fly with his mother.

She didn't bother to answer.

They went back to the house, got a flashlight, and crossed the road to Ziggy's shack.

"I don't see anything," Jeff said as they approached the swaybacked building.

"Better check inside."

Jeff opened the door and turned on the single light that hung over what passed for a kitchen table.

"Not much here for anybody to take," Jeff said as they walked around the cramped space. "We brought over all his medical stuff for Annabelle."

"Damn cold in here," Cindy muttered as she looked at the kitchen sink. "You sure the pipes are all drained?"

"I did that when Ziggy had his accident," Jeff replied, sounding hurt.

"If that was an accident, I'm Lady Gaga."

Jeff gave her the kind of look that teenagers reserve for hopelessly ignorant parents. "It was just a drunk, Ma. Going too fast, is all."

"Do you smell something?"

Jeff sniffed the air. "We need to dump Ziggy's garbage."

"That's not what I'm talking about," she said, nosing along the back wall of the building. "Gasoline. Don't you smell it? Come and take a whiff over here."

Jeff was just beginning to smell it too, when there was a muffled thud and a reddish glow in the rear window. They looked at each other for a second and headed out the door.

They found broken bales of Annabelle's hay strewn along the back wall. Flames were exploding up the siding.

"No way we're going to stop that," Jeff said as he reached for his cell phone.

Cindy was still carrying the rifle, and she held it at the ready as she scanned the woods. "Call the cops, while you're at it," she said grimly.

———

It was fully dark as Vince trudged towards Castle-Borofsky. Things could have been worse, he thought morosely. At least Breener's shack was burning enthusiastically when he left, though he would have preferred to stay and watch the building go up.

He would have made a clean getaway if the damn car hadn't had a flat.

He wondered about that tire.

He wondered about the gunshot he'd heard while he was setting the timer behind Ziggy's shack.

He wondered about the quickness with which the Rice woman and her kid had gotten over to the shack.

He wondered if it would become necessary to deal with the pesky woman and her son. Too bad they hadn't been trapped inside Breener's shack.

His own escape had been a close thing, what with the damn tire. As it was, he'd ended up having to hike a good three miles to the Borofsky's, limping whenever somebody drove by.

The limp was an act, of course. Vince knew that anybody who saw him would just see a man, slightly stooped over, limping slowly down the road, and would never remember the clothing, much less the face.

Having to abandon the car was a nuisance, since the police would pick it up. The Rice woman would make sure of that, and would most likely point out the connection to the fire. Needless to say, the cops wouldn't get anywhere with the car, since he'd rented it with a phony credit card and ID. Vince actually had two rentals, each under a different false name. The one with the flat was a throwaway which had never seen the Borofsky's driveway. Normally, except when he went to Meadow Road, the throwaway lived in the Home Depot parking lot in Rockland, where it sat, lost among dozens of other nondescript vehicles.

One could never be too careful.

It did mean, though, that he'd have to take a cab to retrieve his second car.

Vince was cold and tired by the time he made his way up the Borofsky's cobbled driveway and let himself in.

The ostentatiousness of the front hall drew him up short every time he saw it. He stood there for a moment, thinking about the vast emptiness of the place. It would take a lot more than a couple of gallons of gasoline and a few bales of hay to light this place up, he mused. But the dump would sure make a nice bonfire. Speaking of bonfires, he wondered about Sasha Borofsky, and if she might become a problem.

He put the seductive Sasha out of his mind and began to make plans for the next day.

———————

Cindy Rice called about eight o'clock in the evening to tell Ziggy that his house had burned to the ground. At risk of life and limb, Cindy and Jeff had managed to rescue most of Ziggy's clothing and a large cardboard box filled with plastic baggies of herbs and tea.

There was little else to save.

The fire burned so hot and fast, Cindy said, that the shack was pretty much gone by the time Burnt Cove's volunteer fire department arrived on the scene.

"The fire was set on purpose," she told Ziggy. "Somebody piled hay against the back wall, doused it with gasoline and lit it with some kind of time delay thing, is what the firemen said."

Ziggy, his head lowered, said nothing.

"The fire inspector will look at it, and the cops will be up to talk to you tomorrow," she added. "I told them your leg was in a cast and you couldn't travel, so they'll come up later in the morning, unless you tell them different."

After a moment Cindy spoke into the silence, "Are you still there?"

Oliver took he phone from Ziggy's limp hand, and listened grimly as she repeated the story.

The Borofsky's Manhattan penthouse was no less opulent than their Burnt Cove summer cottage. The city lights twinkled in festive glee outside the windows, while in the streets far below, shoppers were bathed in multicolored neon and assailed by thunderous Christmas music as they jostled through their shopping lists.

The atmosphere inside the penthouse was somewhat less festive.

Anton Borofsky sat across the living room from his wife. "Nika told me what happened," he said, his voice strained.

Of course she did, the traitorous little bitch, Sasha thought to herself. "I'm sorry Anton, I'm so sorry," she keened. "I was trying to protect you. I didn't want to hurt you, but he was an animal. He attacked me. I couldn't stop him." She rose to sit on the floor at Anton's feet. "You were right not to trust him."

"It didn't sound like an attack to Nika."

Sasha vowed that the miserable rat would pay for her disloyalty. "Nika has always hated me," Sasha pouted. "And you know perfectly well that she's simple in the head. The woman reads those trashy romance novels and makes things up."

Anton sighed.

"I wish I'd gone with you," she moaned. "I wish I hadn't stayed there, alone with that man. But I never dreamed he'd be violent with Nika in the house." She sobbed against his leg.

He massaged her heaving shoulders for a while, and Sasha rested her chin on Anton's knee, looking up into his eyes adoringly. "You're the only one I really love." She shuddered. "He's an animal and should be shot."

"This has happened before," Anton said sadly as he took her hand.

"Men are such brutes. They keep taking advantage. I hate them." She looked up at him. "Except for you. You protect me. You're my Teddy Bear."

She rose, slid onto his lap with her legs over one arm of the chair and nestled her head under his chin, her willowy body lost against his massive frame. "You're so strong and gentle," she cooed. He put a hand on her hip, pulling her against him. "You're my Teddy Bear," she murmured again.

He squeezed her hip, almost painfully. "Don't worry, my little imp," he said, "I'll see to it that Martell never bothers you again."

"Thank you, my darling," she purred. "I'll feel so much safer."

"I won't have him killed, though," Anton said thoughtfully. "Not this one. That would be going too far."

"Whatever you think is best, my love. You always know what's best."

Chapter 13

Monday morning, December 17

It was warmer, but the early morning sky was a heavy grey, which left the livingroom where the four-legged Annabelle languished, in shadows. She was not doing well, in spite of the warmth and comfort of her quarters. Once in a while she would wander listlessly around the room to sample a taste of food and water, but mostly she just lay on her side, her eyes staring into space.

"I don't think she's getting any better," Oliver said, as he and Sarah leaned over the sheet of plywood that blocked off the livingroom doorway. Wes came over to see what was going on. Wedging himself between his two people, he stood on his hind legs with his front paws over the plywood and stared worriedly at Annabelle.

"Pneumonia," Sarah said. She had decided to spend the night here, mostly, she told herself, because she didn't have a ride home and didn't want to make Oliver drive her. Of course, there was also the fact that Oliver was spending a lot of time with Ziggy's sister.

"She's having more trouble breathing this morning," he said.

Wes whined and nuzzled Oliver's arm.

"I wonder what will happen to Ziggy if she doesn't make it."

"Nothing good. He's having trouble dealing with the problems he has now."

"And that may just be the start," Sarah said. "'Remember Christmas Eve.'"

———————

Ziggy was doing little better than his goat as he sat at Oliver's kitchen table and picked at his breakfast. Two-legged Annabelle sat and scowled at her older brother.

In view of what had happened over past twenty-four hours, Sarah figured that it wasn't surprising for the mood to be somewhat glum as the four of them sat around the breakfast table.

Even here in the kitchen, one could hear the labored breathing of Annabelle-the-goat. Ziggy had tried antibiotics and even some of his special tea on Annabelle, with little effect. He'd explained at length that the pulmonary system of a goat was very different than a human's and more difficult to treat. His actual words weren't as clear or concise as that, of course. He had, in fact, rambled on at length about vacuum cleaner hoses, storks, and inevitably, crows.

Even worse, the house was beginning to smell like a stable, in spite of their best efforts at changing the straw bedding.

"Are you sure you don't want to look at what's left of your house?" Annabelle said to Ziggy as he poked at a slice of dry toast.

He shook his head without looking up.

"You might find something worth salvaging, now that it's daylight," Sarah suggested.

Ziggy slid the toast aimlessly around the plate with his finger.

Oliver put down his coffee cup. "Okay," he said to Ziggy, "it's time for some straight talk."

Annabelle-the-person made a strangled noise that sounded a bit like her namesake.

"The police will be here in a couple of hours," Oliver went on, "and they're not going to be happy if all you give them is a lot of gibberish."

Ziggy ran a finger around the rim of his coffee cup.

"We deserve to know what's going on, too," Sarah added. "First your goat is poisoned, and now your house is burned down. Who is out to get you?"

"People hate crows," Ziggy said.

Coughing sounds came from the livingroom.

"But you must have some idea about who might have done this, and why," Sarah persisted. "Is it because you stand to inherit Myra Huggard's land? Could Anton Borofsky be doing this?"

"I can't see Borofsky burning down Ziggy's house," Oliver said. "After all, it would just make Ziggy move in next door to him that much sooner."

Ziggy continued to study his toast in silence.

Sarah tried a different approach. "Who is Doctor Harry Hastings?"

"Where did that name come from?" Annabelle said.

"The envelope that Cindy found in Ziggy's house had a newspaper photo of a Doctor Harry Hastings in it, and a Christmas card that said, 'Remember Christmas.'"

"It also said, 'Run, and your friends will die.,'" Oliver added.

"Oh, God," Annabelle said, her face suddenly pale. She started to say more, gave Sarah and Oliver a haunted look, and stayed silent.

"I should fly like a crow," Ziggy said, "but I can't. I must stay with Annabelle."

Ziggy turned to his sister. "But you must fly."

"You brought this on yourself," Annabelle said. "If you hadn't gotten those high-powered lawyers, nobody would have known you were here. I can't see why you want Myra Huggard's land anyway. If I owned it, I'd sell the place to Borofsky, or the highest bidder, take the money, and get out of town. Who needs to live next door to somebody who wants you dead?"

"It's what Myra Huggard wanted," Ziggy said.

"Does anybody else besides the Borofskys have it in for you?" Oliver said.

Ziggy busied himself with the toast, sliding it around the plate some more.

Annabelle leaned on the table, cradling her head.

"What are you going to tell the police when they come?" Sarah said.

"I am Contagion," Ziggy announced solemnly.

Annabelle stood and loomed over brother. "Do you want the cops to think you're crazy? That you've fried your brain on drugs?"

"You are all in danger," Ziggy said.

"I figured that from the Christmas card you got," Oliver said. "But if we're all in danger, then we deserve some answers."

"Vengeance is mine, saith the Lord," Ziggy murmured. "I am a murderer."

Annabelle sat down hard in her chair.

After a moment, Sarah asked softly, "Who did you kill, Ziggy?"

"It was so long ago," Ziggy said, his voice little more than a whisper. "It was so very long ago, before I died and was reborn."

"Who was it?" Sarah said again.

"It was so very long ago," Ziggy repeated numbly. "She created Yorick."

"She created Yorick?" Sarah said. "Do you mean Old Nick? Do you mean it was her skull?"

"Life would be easier if it was." Ziggy turned to face Sarah. "No, you have the skull of death."

"He's talking about an old skull I found in the attic of my cabin," Sarah said to Annabelle. "Apparently Doctor Carnell used it for Halloween."

Annabelle sat rigidly in her chair, her fists clenched on the table.

Oliver turned to Ziggy. "I don't think you should tell the police that you're a killer, or mention Yorick. It could give them the wrong impression."

"I think you'd definitely be better off with the fried-brain approach," Sarah said. "It's simpler."

"And more convincing," Oliver added.

Christmas in Midcoast Maine was as likely to be brown as white, with the question of Yuletide snow cover usually remaining up in the air until the last minute. Not so this year, thanks to last weekend's blizzard. Not even the bright sun or the warm southerly wind seemed likely to strip away the two feet of snow in the days that remained before the holiday.

"I thought Ziggy handled the police very well, considering," Oliver said as he and Sarah slowly made their way down Hound Hill road in Oliver's Honda. "He convinced them that he was as batty but harmless, and only talked about flying like a crow one time."

"I guess that means he's not all that crazy, and may be more of a con artist than we think," she said.

"He's enough of a con artist to get a goat into my house."

"Stop stewing over the goat. It's only for a couple more days. The big question is whether Ziggy really did kill somebody."

"Kill somebody literally or figuratively?"

"How would he kill somebody figuratively?" she inquired.

"The same way he became a crow, I suppose."

"The man's gobbledygook gives me a headache," she grumbled. "No wonder his sister yells at him."

Oliver had to stick the nose of his Honda well onto Route One in order to see around the snow banks lining the road. "I have a nightmare scenario where we can't figure out who is out to get him, so he ends up living in my house forever."

"He's not making it easy to help, but there could be somebody from his past, seeking revenge for something Ziggy did before he died—"

"—and was reborn. We shouldn't forget that part."

"Somebody like Doctor Hastings, of newspaper fame."

"Or Yorick," Oliver said. "Annabelle is right, though. Ziggy would be better off if he sold out to the Borofskys."

"At least he'd have one less enemy," Sarah said as they pulled up to her driveway.

Her SUV was plowed in again, in spite of Jeff's efforts. Muttering, she turned away and noticed fresh tire tracks in the snow by her mailbox. Inside it were the usual fliers, fattened by the Christmas season.

Sarah's Christmas spirit was sadly lacking at the moment. "Bah, humbug," she muttered, pulling an electric bill from the junk mail. She was about to stuff the fliers into her the pocket of her parka when she spotted a postcard addressed to "Dr. John H. Carnell."

She looked at the card while they headed for her cabin, and Oliver caught her arm as she tripped going down the steep slope with her eyes glued to the card.

"You'll break your neck if you walk around reading somebody else's mail."

"It's a postcard. Everybody reads postcards. It's from the Night Owl Motel in Rockland."

"That's a pretty sleazy joint for a retired doctor to be staying in."

"According to this, Doctor Carnell left his luggage there, and if he doesn't claim it in the next thirty days they'll dispose of it."

"He sounds kind of forgetful," Oliver commented.

"Why would he give this address?"

"Why not? He does own the place, after all."

"According to this, he was registered for the fourteenth and fifteenth. The fifteenth is when I heard the snowmobiles and shots. What was he doing here in Maine?"

"Visiting friends, doing some Christmas shopping, picking up some lobster?"

"Or riding a snowmobile on Pimm's Pond in a blizzard, and getting shot."

"You can't be serious. You weren't even sure that the snowmobiles weren't a dream."

"I said that I *might* have been dreaming."

"Whatever it is you're dreaming up now, don't do it."

Sarah frowned at Oliver. "I think we should do the old man a favor and pick up his luggage before they sell it out from under him. There could be something valuable that he might want."

Oliver groaned.

"What? We'll be doing him a favor. You said it was a sleazy motel. I'll tell them I'm his daughter and slip a few dollars across the counter."

"And I'll visit you in jail."

Chapter 14

Monday afternoon, December 17

It was two 2 o'clock in the afternoon and Vince Martell was in a foul mood when he returned to the Borofsky place. There was good a reason, of course. He hadn't gotten back from torching Breener's shack until late last night, thanks to the Rice woman and her .22. On top of all that, he'd spent most of the morning taking taxis and busses up to Waterville in order to rent another car to replace the one Rice had shot. Vince made a mental note to pick up some supplies and a burn phone. Before he was done, the pesky broad would need to replace her little Ford shit-box.

As far as he was concerned, the worst thing about living out in the country was having to drive a car everywhere because there wasn't a decent public transit system. That and the fact that there weren't any crowds to get lost in when you did get to where you were going.

Vince was not only in a bad mood, but he also hungry and preoccupied with the Rice woman's meddling as he entered by way of the Borofsky's kitchen door, brown-bag lunch in hand. The front entrance, like the rest of the place, was getting on his nerves.

Tomorrow, he promised himself, he'd ditch this dump and find a motel.

Two men were waiting when Vince entered the kitchen. "Who the hell are you?" he demanded.

"I am Stanko," one of them replied with a gap-toothed smile and a thick accent. "This is friend Karlov. We're, what you say, assistants of Mr. Borofsky."

Great, Vince thought, Russian goons.

The kitchen table, like the room itself, was oversized—a round butcher block affair a good eight feet across. He casually moved to put his lunch bag on the far side of the table from the Russians, as three disturbing thoughts passed through his mind. First, these guys were big, really big. Second, and more worrying, they looked like men who could handle themselves, not that he was a pushover. Third, and most worrying of all, was Sasha.

"Nice to meet you guys," Vince said, trying to bluff along, "but it's late and I haven't had lunch yet, so if you don't mind, I'm going to sit and eat." He casually slid out one of the arch-back chairs. Karlov equally casually sidled a few feet around the table to Stanko's left. Shit, Vince said to himself.

"We not take much of you time," Stanko assured him.

"Yes, we not take long," Karlov agreed.

"Mr. Borofsky is unhappy man," Stanko went on as he shrugged and shifted a bit further around the table. "He wants us to tell you this."

"I'm sorry to hear that," Vince said evenly. "Now if you'll excuse me, I have a busy afternoon." He pulled the chair out further as though to sit down.

"Our message not take long," Stanko murmured.

Vince swung the chair with all his strength into Karlov's face. The man lurched back a step, as blood streamed from his face and pieces of the chair clattered to the floor.

Vince darted away, but Stanko turned out to be remarkably quick for a man the size of an upland gorilla, and he caught Vince's arm, spinning him around.

Vince ducked under Stanko's right fist and punched him in the stomach.

Stanko grunted and rabbit-punched Vince with a left jab. It felt like he'd been hit with a sledge hammer, and Vince would have fallen if Karlov, his face a gory mask, hadn't been there to grab his arm and spin him backwards against the wall like a child playing crack-the-whip. Vince felt the sheetrock give way behind his head.

The room was spinning now as Karlov held Vince so he faced Stanko.

"Not to worry, Wince," Karlov purred in his ear, "we have people come in, fix wall, make place look like new."

Stanko shook his head sadly. "Mr. Borosky wery angry you attack his wife—"

"Are you nuts? She attacked me," Vince gasped.

Stanko drove a fist into Vince's midriff, effectively silencing him. Meanwhile, Karlov used his free hand to punch Vince in the kidney.

"Listen wery carefully, friend Wince. You not welcome in this house," Stanko went on. "You not come back here again, and you go near Mrs. Borofsky, we come back."

"We not be so friendly, if we come back," Karlov breathed in Vince's ear.

The blows kept coming. Vince tried to fight back, land a punch, fend them off, but the blows kept coming. At one point he felt a rib go. He couldn't feel the individual blows any more amid the sea of pain, just his body being tossed around as each punch landed.

In the end, he felt nothing.

———————

"Explain again why I'm aiding and abetting you in this grand larceny?" Oliver said as Sarah drove her Explorer into Rockland.

"I doubt if Doctor Carnell's bags are worth enough to make it grand larceny."

"Okay, petty larceny."

"The stuff may be heavy, and it will easier for two of us carry."

"So now I'm the carry-ape."

"That makes me the brains," she replied smugly. "Besides, two of us being there adds a certain kind of legitimacy—"

"To what must be illegal in a dozen different ways," he grumbled.

"We're doing a favor for a nice old man who is obviously forgetful. It's not as though we're stealing anything. We're just holding his belongings until he comes for them. How can that possibly be illegal? He'll thank us in the end."

"How can he thank us if he's at the bottom of Pimm's Pond?"

"He's *probably* at the bottom of Pimm's Pond, but he might not be."

"In which case he'll be coming back to get his stuff, and it won't be here because we stole it," Oliver said.

"In which case, the desk clerk will tell him where his stuff is, and he'll pick it up and thank us."

"He'll thank us?"

"Like the nice old man he is."

"How do you know he's a nice old man? "Oliver said. "Have you ever met him? Maybe he's a vindictive old goat who takes people to court at the drop of a hat."

"Just because you're having a little goat problem right now is no reason to get all grouchy about poor Doctor Carnell. And to answer your question, I haven't met him. Brian arranged the rental." Brian Curtis, Burnt Cove's Realtor, happened to have shown a romantic interest in Sarah.

"I can't help thinking that you have some ulterior motive for all this. I hope you're not planning to paw through all his stuff."

"The clerk has probably done that already, if the place is like you said. Besides, there might be something that will tell us what happened to him."

"I gather that you've had no luck trying to call the Good Doctor," Oliver said.

"Brian gave me his number, but nobody answered, so I left a message telling him I'd picked up his luggage and have it at his cabin."

Sarah took a short detour as they entered Rockland so they could admire the town's Christmas tree, which consisted of a towering, tree-shaped stack of green, wire-mesh lobster pots. The recent snow had spattered the structure with festive white patches.

"Done your shopping yet?" Sarah teased.

"Bah, humbug."

"Me neither. What with the blizzard and everything else, I'm going to be a last-minute shopper this year." Sarah braked while an elderly couple shuffled across the street. "I know what I want to get for you and Ziggy, but Annabelle has me stumped."

"Carrots," Oliver replied.

"No, I mean Ziggy's sister."

"Exactly. Get a bag for each of them. She likes carrots, too. Just make sure they're organic."

"She probably grows her own carrots."

"Maybe," Oliver said. "I know she grows some of Ziggy's special herbs. Mails them up to him."

"I wonder if they're legal herbs."

"When did you start worrying about legal?"

Rockland's main drag was dressed in its Christmas finery, with lights strung from the reproduction antique street lamps, and the shop windows ablaze with decorations. Between the cars and the pedestrians, traffic moved at a snail's pace.

"You need to get out the decorations, now that you have a tree," Sarah said.

"I don't have any."

"You mean we spent yesterday afternoon cutting down a tree, and you don't have anything to put on it?"

"I gave them all to my sister when I moved up here."

"Why did you do that?" Sarah glanced at Oliver, but he was looking out the window at the storefronts.

"Turn left just beyond the ferry terminal," he replied.

———

The Night Owl Motel consisted of a long single-storey building made up of a row small rooms. "You're right, this place is a dump," Sarah said as they pulled into the narrow parking lot.

"A circumspect dump," Oliver said. "Or so I'm told."

A blowsy, middle-aged woman, the roots of her red hair showing grey, sat behind the counter as they entered.

"Hi," Sarah said brightly, "I'm Sarah Cassidy and this is my husband, Oliver and—"

"Hourly or day rates?"

Sarah tried again while Oliver suppressed a grin behind her. "You don't understand. I'm Doctor John Carnell's sister, and we've come to claim the bags he left here."

"How come he isn't here to pick up his own stuff?" the woman said.

"He was called away suddenly on business."

"You know the way it is with these doctors," Oliver said.

"Yeah, but how do I know you're legit? We have a strict policy here. You leave stuff behind, you have to pick it up in person."

"I have ID," Sarah said reaching into her purse.

"Your ID don't mean nothing to me. This is a high-class motel. We have rules."

"I have the postcard you sent," Sarah said, handing it over.

The woman studied the card as though it was a stock certificate for a defunct company. "How do I know where you got this? We got strict rules—"

Oliver slid a twenty-dollar bill across the counter.

"And he never returned his key either, so now I gotta buy a new one."

Oliver added another twenty.

"Follow me," the woman said, easing out from behind the counter.

"When did I get to be your husband?" Oliver whispered as they followed the clerk outside. "Why didn't you tell me sooner? I must have dozed off and missed the whole thing. Was it a nice wedding?"

"Hush, dear. Don't make a scene," Sarah murmured.

"You owe me forty bucks."

The clerk opened one of the rooms. "I picked up everything he left lying around and put it in the suitcase. It's all there on the bed. It ain't my job to pick up stuff people leave behind."

"He traveled light," Sarah said, looking at the parka and canvas-sided suitcase.

"Most people do around here," the clerk informed her.

"I was wondering when John arrived," Sarah said as the she and Oliver carried Carnell's belongings out to the car under the woman's gimlet eye.

"Got here on the fifteenth, around dark, signed in and went right out again, probably to get supper. Except he never took his stuff before he left."

"Did he bring his snowmobile?" Sarah asked.

"People come here for the peace and quiet, because they know nobody won't snoop on their business," the clerk said piously. "People like their privacy around here, and we provide it."

Sarah removed a bill from her purse. It was snatched from her fingers.

"He didn't have no snowmobile."

"So what's the verdict on Doctor Carnell, now that we have his bags?" Oliver said as they navigated the back roads out of Rockland—a town famous for its one-way streets.

"He and his snowmobile are at the bottom of Pimm's pond."

"What snowmobile? And how do you know this without even pawing through his luggage?"

"Elementary, my dear Watson."

Oliver frowned at her. "Okay, so Carnell signs in to the Night Owl Motel around dark, just as the blizzard is really winding up, and he goes off again in his car—"

"Without his parka."

"Ah, and you think he left his parka in the room because he was wearing something warmer, like a snowmobile suit? But were was the snowmobile? And where is his car?"

"I haven't figure that out yet," she said, "but I'm guessing that he borrowed a snowmobile from a friend, probably a friend with a cabin on the pond, and that's where his car is."

Oliver shook his head. "Why hasn't this friend gotten worried and raised the alarm? Isn't it just as likely that Carnell had a second parka and he took that? Maybe he drove off the road in the blizzard and is at the bottom of a gully somewhere. There are a several quarries in town and people have driven into them before, and those things are deep."

"So is Pimm's pond," Sarah said.

"How do you know he's even disappeared? Wouldn't somebody be getting worried if he had?"

"He was shot and is at the bottom of Pimm's pond," Sarah said stubbornly. "I can feel it."

Chapter 15

Monday afternoon, December 17

Vince drifted in and out of consciousness, surfacing into a dream-like awareness, then sinking back into oblivion. It was after dark before he became fully awake. Even then, it took a while for him to realize that he was sprawled across the back seat of a car.

Slowly, his memory drifted into focus. He remembered entering the Borofsky's kitchen. The goons waiting for him. Their warning. The blows. He tried to sit up. Gingerly. Slowly. Each movement brought fresh waves of pain.

Vince had been beaten up before—it was something that came with the job—but these guys were good, and he gave them a grudging respect for their ability. On a scale of one to five, this was a six. Vince ran a hand over his face and head, assessing the damage. Except for the matted blood on the back of his head from the broken wall, there didn't seem to be much visible damage.

When he thought about it objectively, they had shown a good deal of restraint, considering that Vince was pretty sure he'd broken Karlov's nose with the chair. Like the professionals they were, the goons had been careful to leave bruises where they wouldn't show. His gut, back and legs had taken the brunt of it. And there was also at least one broken rib, down low, which he noticed with each breath.

Vince didn't think of himself as a vindictive man, and he held no grudge against his attackers, who were just doing their job. On the other hand, Anton Borofsky and his vampire of a wife were going to pay a steep price.

Vince had read once about a type of spider that ate her mate after having sex. That was Sasha Borofsky to Vince's way of thinking. But how could he have known that ahead of time? Did the poor male spider know what lay in store?

It was getting damn cold in the car. He looked around, groaning as he did so, but it was after dark and it took a while to discover that he was parked in a shadowy corner beside Hannaford's Supermarket in Rockland. Exploring further, he spotted two trash bags in the front seat. His belongings.

The keys were in the ignition, and Vince summoned his strength, eased painfully out of the car, and staggered around to the driver's side, lurching and weaving like a drunk. His legs and thighs had been thoroughly kicked after he fell down, and they screamed a silent protest as he tried to walk. He hoped nobody was watching and decided to call the cops.

He'd have to find a place to stay and recuperate. Luckily, he knew just the out-of-the-way spot where people didn't ask questions. Slowly, Vince made his way out onto the main road, and headed for the Night Owl Motel.

Ziggy and his sister were in bed by eleven o'clock that night, Annabelle in the guest room upstairs, and Ziggy in part of the living room that wasn't barricaded off for his goat.

Sarah and Oliver were in what had once been the diningroom, but which now contained a drafting table instead of a dining table, and served as Oliver's yacht design work area. They sat in front of Oliver's computer while he Googled Doctor Harry Hastings.

"Annabelle doesn't seem to be getting better," Sarah said in a low voice so she wouldn't be overheard.

"I haven't heard her walking around in there as much today as yesterday," Oliver murmured. "That can't be a good sign."

Sarah glanced at the door. "Ziggy may be a really good doctor for people, but a goat isn't a person," she said in a lower voice. "I wish he was willing to have a vet take a look at her."

"Face it, the guy is stubborn as hell, and we can't force him to call a vet. He's been giving her antibiotics, but she seems to have some kind of resistant pneumonia."

"What harm could it do to get another opinion?" Sarah said. "What if you or I or Annabelle called a vet out here? What could Ziggy do?"

"Fine, but suppose we do coerce Ziggy into accepting a vet and the goat dies while this vet is treating her? How do you think Ziggy would feel about our interfering, then?"

"But Ziggy is worried about her. I can't see why he doesn't want all the help he can get."

"That's not all he's worried about," Oliver said absentmindedly. "Here's something on Harry Hastings. He was a trauma surgeon at Arlington General Hospital."

"Ziggy seemed to know Hastings, judging from his reaction to the picture."

Oliver, who had been working the keyboard, said, "Here's something more. Doctor Hastings died in a home invasion on December 28, 2004."

"Right after Christmas. Maybe that has something to do with the 'Remember Christmas Eve' note."

"But what?" Oliver said.

"Lets check out Doctor Carnell, since we have his luggage."

"Okay, here he is," Oliver said a little later. "Carnell is fifty-three years old, is divorced, lives alone in Boston, and is a Medical Examiner for the state of Massachusetts."

"That's younger than I thought. See who his predecessor was, just for fun."

"Doctor Carnell was hired as ME after Doctor Willard Tierny left and moved to Sarasota, Florida in 2009. Tierny is a widower, is semi-retired, and works as an ME part-time down there. I'm not sure how that helps."

"Tierny is a friend of Ziggy, according to Jeff," Sarah said. "He has a cabin on Pimm's Pond, too."

"Another connection."

"Let's check out Ziggy's bio, while we're at it. He would have been a young Resident then, a lot younger than Hastings."

"Here he is," Oliver said after a moment. "According to this, the rumors are right and Ziggy was a Resident in the Emergency Room at Arlington General up until early 2005. Arlington General isn't that big a place, so I can see how Ziggy could have worked with Doctor Hastings if an ER patient needed surgery."

"Maybe surgery around Christmas, 2004?"

Oliver nodded, working the keyboard. "Wait, this can't be right—"

Sarah stood up and stared over Oliver's shoulder at the screen. "Ziggy committed suicide on January 5th, 2005? There must be a mistake. If that Ziggy is dead, then who is our Ziggy?"

"Could there be more than one Zigfield Follies Breener in the world? Did we just imagine Ziggy's reaction to the newspaper photograph of Hastings? Did our Ziggy come back from the dead, like his goat, in which case this is really Halloween instead of Christmas?"

"Not funny," Sarah said. "When you think about it, though, our Ziggy has kept a pretty low profile over the years."

Oliver nodded. "He has no credit cards or telephone, doesn't drive a car. The man has stayed as invisible as he can get. But what does that mean?"

"It means that there are two Ziggys and ours is a recluse, until his luck ran out when the Boston papers picked up on his lawsuit over Myra's Will."

"Your ex's pro-bono lawyers made quite a splash by upholding the Will."

"And newspapers love to write about underdogs like Ziggy winning against fat cats like Borofsky. So he got his name in the papers and somebody saw it—"

"And that somebody is now out to get him."

"Because he killed a woman, before he died and was reborn."

"Now *you're* talking like it's Halloween." Oliver leaned back in his chair. "Okay, so Christmas of 2004 was a bad time for doctors at Arlington General. First, Doctor Hastings is killed in a home invasion, and then someone named Doctor Breener commits suicide."

"And somebody thinks our Ziggy is the same person who was at Arlington General in 2004, and is out to kill him on Christmas Eve as revenge," Sarah said.

"A stretch, but possible. In any case, I think we need to know more about what happened in the ER that Christmas Eve."

"If you want to know what's going on in a hospital, talk to a nurse."

"Spoken as one who knows." Oliver returned to the keyboard.

They could only find one nurse who had worked the ER during the last few months of 2004, a Violet Tibbs, who lived in Boston's North End. As luck would have it, she was still working at Arlington General. Sarah decided to call the next morning and try to arrange a meeting, combining the visit with some Christmas shopping at the outlet malls in Kittery. For his part, Oliver figured he would pay another visit to the Night Owl Motel.

Chapter 16

Tuesday morning, December 18

The Night Owl's desk clerk seemed almost friendly when Oliver walked up to the counter the next morning. Perhaps she remembered his generosity.

"What do you want today?" she said, eyeing the twenty in Oliver's fingers.

"My wife was wondering if her brother had made a reservation before he arrived," he said, sliding the bill across the counter.

"A reservation? Not hardly. We cater strictly to walk-in customers," she replied as President Hamilton disappeared under her hand. "Besides, it wasn't the kind of weather had enough people out to need a reservation."

"The main road must have been plowed, though, wasn't it?"

The clerk paused for a second, as though trying to decide if that information could be worth another donation. "Well sure, they kept Route One plowed right through," she said, "but the side roads were pretty much shut down by the time he got here."

Oliver thought about that. Apparently, Carnell had checked in and then set right out again into the storm. But where could he have gone with the side roads barely passable? Probably not far. Had he wanted to get supper somewhere? But why hadn't he come back to the motel afterwards? Had he slid off the road into a ditch, and become buried under a snow drift, still unseen and unfound?

On the other hand, what better way to get around in a blizzard than on a snowmobile? If you had one, or could get to one.

Sarah had called Violet Tibbs and set up a meeting in the Arlington General Hospital's cafeteria for one o'clock in the afternoon. With Boston's notorious afternoon traffic—seven months in Maine and she'd already forgotten such things—she arrived a good ten minutes late.

Violet looked to be in her late-thirties, of medium height, with curly black hair showing traces of gray against her chocolate colored skin.

"Sorry I'm late," Sarah said, sitting down at the pedestal table next to Violet.

"I can give you ten minutes, tops," Violet said pointedly.

"I'll try to be quick. I understand you worked in the ER with Ziggy Breener, back in the day."

"Ziggy Breener," Violet said, smiling. "There's a memory for you. He was quite a character, a tragedy what happened."

"Yes it was," Sarah agreed. "The trouble is that he's being stalked—"

"What do you mean he *is* being stalked? The man died years ago."

"Are you absolutely sure? Could there have been some mistake? The Zigfield Follies Breener I know is very much alive, except that somebody is threatening him."

"Of course I'm sure. The Doctor Breener I know committed suicide." She took a swallow of coffee. "Or was driven to it. Simple as that. End of story."

"There must be a mix-up somewhere," Sarah repeated. "Ziggy's sister, Annabelle, is staying with him now."

"His sister Annabelle helped identify the body, or what was left of it after the explosion and fire."

"Explosion and fire? What happened?"

Violet sighed. "He rented a cabin at a motel out in the sticks, Danvers, I think it was—one of those little shoeboxes with a closet-sized kitchenette. Anyway, he stuck his head in the oven and turned on the gas. He must have had a burner or candle or something going because the whole place went up."

"Could Annabelle have made a mistake identifying the body? If there was a fire—"

"Look," Violet interrupted, "it was his car parked there and him who registered. There was a surveillance camera in the motel office, and they got his face on it, big as life. On top of that, there was an autopsy, a DNA test, dental records, the whole ball of wax. That body belonged to Ziggy Breener."

"Could he have been murdered?"

"Murdered? Not according to the cops. What does it matter, anyway? The point is that Doctor Breener is dead." Violet took another swallow of the black, luke-warm brew in her paper cup, and shook her head. "He was just plain full of fun, kind of weird at times, but a really good doctor, and easy to get along with."

"When you say weird, did he kind of talk in riddles, where you had to sort of translate what he was saying into English?" Sarah searched her mind for examples. "Like he always calls me 'Ditch Lady,' because I was climbing out of a ditch when we first met. Or he's talking about flying 'like a crow,' because he's being stalked."

Violet shook her head. "I never had any trouble understanding Doctor Breener. Look, the guy was smart, okay? You don't go through college and medical school on full scholarships without having something on the ball. Did your friend tell you that he was the Doctor Breener who was here?"

"Well, no. At least I don't think he did, but there can't be too many Ziggy Breeners in the world who are doctors."

Sarah wished she'd brought a photo of Ziggy, though he must have aged a lot over the years, considering his life-style.

"All I can tell you is that the Ziggy Breener I knew is dead, so your Breener must be somebody else. It really is as simple as that."

"The trouble is," Sarah said, trying to keep her tongue untangled, "that somebody who *thinks* my Ziggy is your Ziggy is stalking my Ziggy, and from the threatening Christmas card he got, I think it probably has something to do with what happened on Christmas Eve of 2004, when your Ziggy was here."

"Christmas Eve of 2004?" Violet started to get up. "I don't have time for this."

Sarah put her hand on the woman's arm. "Wait, please. Somebody has already been killed. I'm sure of it, and I'm afraid my Ziggy, will be next."

Violet paused, leaning on the table. "I have no idea who your version of Ziggy Breener is." Violet gave Sarah a hard look. "And you have no idea what you're getting into by asking about what happened in the ER that Christmas Eve."

"I know that a woman died, and from what Ziggy said about 'killing a woman,' there probably would have been an inquiry. What happened?"

Violet stood a moment longer before slumping back in the chair. "There was an internal review," she said reluctantly.

"Was he found to be responsible for her death?"

"You could say that. In a way."

Sarah studied Violet's face. "Do you think the finding was wrong?"

"I never actually read it, but from what I was told, the report damned him with faint praise. 'He didn't appear to be impaired at the time,' the report said. 'Perhaps he was overwhelmed by the number of patients,' the report said. Nobody I knew thought Ziggy was using, but it was a high profile case, so there was a lot of pressure to find a scapegoat and Ziggy was the logical choice." Violet sighed. "By the time they were done, it didn't matter which way you went. He was either high and caused somebody's death, or couldn't multi-task and just blew it. There was no smoking gun, no proof of any kind, just innuendo."

Sarah nodded. "And it all led to the same place, that Ziggy wasn't up to the job and a woman died as a result."

"Do you have any idea who she was?"

"I'm hoping you'll tell me."

"Annette Penrose, the wife of Harry Penrose," Violet said, glancing around the cafeteria.

"Penrose, the former mayor of Boston?"

"Yes, that Penrose."

Sarah vaguely remembered the news story. "Wasn't she mugged and killed?"

"She died in the hospital that night, and that was the problem," Violet replied. "Annette survived two hours of emergency surgery, even regained consciousness, more or less, but she had been badly beaten and stabbed multiple times, and she just didn't make it. You said when you called that you had been a nurse, right?"

Sarah nodded.

"Then you know that sometimes the trauma turns out to be too much and a person dies no matter how good the care is."

Sarah thought about Ziggy's impassioned efforts to save his goat. "Did he say anything to you about her death?"

"Say anything to me? Why would he? I was a nobody back then. If he had anything to say about her care, it would have been to Doctor Hastings, the surgeon who operated on her, or one of the other doctors, or one of the senior nurses. And Breener and Hastings are both dead." Violet leaned back in her chair. "Anyway, it didn't matter. Penrose and the hospital wanted a scapegoat and Ziggy was chosen. There was a big insurance policy on her life, and the insurance company wasn't too happy about the lack of a proper investigation, though I guess they paid up in the end. As I said, the whole thing was a hatchet job."

"Why didn't you say anything?" Sarah blurted out.

"What did I tell you? I was just starting out, a single mom with two young kids. You bet I kept my mouth shut. Besides, what could I say? That I thought Ziggy was a good doctor who was being railroaded? Who would have listened to me? I've always regretted not being able to help Ziggy, but what could I have done?" Violet lowered her voice. "I never voted for Penrose and I didn't like the man, but I never saw anybody so broken up about his wife's death as he was. Or so furious. The guy went ballistic. We had to call security to keep him from attacking the staff."

"Would he have physically attacked Ziggy?"

"He didn't get the chance," Violet said. "Anyway, Penrose got his revenge by hounding the man into committing suicide." She scowled at Sarah. "And now you come out of nowhere and tell me that somebody is stalking your friend, who happens to have the same name?" She shook her head in disgust. "I really can't help you with this."

"Have you ever wondered about the fact that both Doctor Hastings and Doctor Breener treated Annette, and both died within weeks of her death? You said a minute ago that you regretted not being able to help your Ziggy Breener," Sarah said. "I'll regret it the same way if I don't do what I can to help the man I know as Ziggy—"

"You know he's not the real thing."

"I know he's my friend, and that's what matters, and the only way I can see to help him is to find out what happened when Annette Penrose died."

Violet toyed with her half-empty cup of coffee, running her thumbnail up and down the cardboard seam. Sarah worried that Violet was going to slice through it and flood the table. "There never was an autopsy on her," Violet murmured.

"I thought an autopsy was mandatory in cases like this."

"Apparently not if you're the former governor and are willing to throw your weight around." Violet looked up. "Hey, let's be fair; everybody has seen those cop shows where the ME breaks open a corpse's chest, peels back the face, saws the top of the head off. Who wants to think about that happening to their loved one?"

"So nobody knows for certain how she died."

Violet stopped the autopsy on her cup and looked up. "I don't see how it would help, but I might be able to get a copy of the inquiry. It won't say much, but it's better than nothing."

"You can do that? Isn't it confidential?"

"Bet your ass it's confidential, but after all those years, I know my way around this place."

There was a thin folder on the table in front of Violet. She picked it up, saying, "Take this and come along with me."

"What is it?"

"Employment application. You were a nurse, so you can talk the talk, right? If anyone asks, you're looking for a job and I'm showing you around."

"You think I'm employable?" Sarah said with a smile.

"Are you still breathing, sweet-cakes?"

Violet set a nurse-on-a-mission pace through the hallways until they reached a small office, where she sat down in front of a computer and began typing. "I'm not exactly a hacker, but I have learned a few tricks over the years."

"Can you really access the inquiry record?"

Violet held up her hands, with their poppy-red fingernails, cocked her head, and gave Sarah an innocent, wide-eyed look. "Oh, I think these magic fingers of mine can handle it," she said in a sing-song voice.

"I don't want to get you in trouble."

Violet stopped typing. "You've stirred up a lot of memories," she said somberly. "Memories that I haven't wanted to think about for years. Maybe this is a chance to make up for the past." She looked at Sarah. "I was too young and too scared to stand up to the big-shots back then, but it's different now. Your Ziggy, whoever he is, deserves better than my Ziggy got. I just hope this helps, though I can't see how it would."

Violet leaned back in her chair a few minutes later, an irritated look on her face.

"It's not there," Violet said.

"Not there, or not available?"

"Deleted, which is not supposed to happen." Violet sighed. "The best I can do is get you Doctor Breener's autopsy."

They left the office a few minutes later, a thumb drive in Sarah's purse containing Ziggy's autopsy.

They had almost made it to the hospital entrance, with Violet prattling on about employment benefits, job descriptions and the like when a tall, white-haired man stopped them.

"What are you doing, Violet?" he said officiously, with a meaningful glance at his watch.

"This is Sarah Cassidy, Doctor Thomas," Violet replied casually. "She's looking for a job and I'm giving her a quick walk around."

"And who told you to go around giving tours? Human Resources has people to do that, and you have other responsibilities."

"I was just leaving," Sarah said in a helpless-little-me voice, "and the hallways are awfully confusing, so Violet offered to show me the way out."

Sarah was given a look of disdain for her trouble.

"Sarah is an old friend," Violet said evenly, "and I'm hoping she will decide to come to Arlington General. It's not as though we don't need more staff."

After some more harrumphing, the doctor walked off.

"There goes a doctor with a real God complex," Sarah said.

"Doctor Thomas has been here forever, is semi-retired, and as near as I can make out, it's his job to wander around making trouble," Violet replied.

"I put my name and number on the application form," Sarah said as the neared the exit door. "Call me if you remember anything that might be helpful."

"Don't hold your breath."

Sarah paused at the door. "Just out of curiosity, did anybody visit Annette while she was here?"

"Her husband was there, of course, and a woman came in later, the vice-president of Annette's company, Athena Associates. I didn't know who she was at the time, but I saw her picture in the paper later, when Annette's company was sold. Edna Bartel. She's running the place now."

Chapter 17

Tuesday morning, December 18

The Rockland police were sympathetic, but reluctant to take much action. First, they pointed out, nobody had reported Doctor Carnell missing. The fact that his bags had been left at the motel wasn't proof of foul play, nor was it proof of any connection to Ziggy's house fire. They did worry about the idea that Carnell's car might have run off the road in the storm and still be buried in one of the many huge snowdrifts which lined the road. They assured him that the possibility would be investigated.

Oliver drove slowly back towards Burnt Cove. Sarah thought that several snowmobiles had been on Pimm's pond the night Doctor Carnell signed into the Night Owl Motel, though she hadn't been awake enough to be sure how many or exactly when. Could it have been Doctor Carnell on some urgent mission, perhaps to warn Ziggy that somebody was out to get him? But why not just pick up the phone? Of course, Ziggy didn't have a phone of his own, but the Rice's next door did.

Oliver had to admit that it was all conjecture, and far fetched at that.

Still, Ziggy, whichever Ziggy he was, had been run down by a snowmobile, his goat poisoned, and his shack torched.

———————

Edna Bartel had a corner office on the fifth floor of Athena Associates. The building was one of several similar boxy structures in a nondescript office park in Chelmsford, just north of Boston.

Edna's secretary escorted Sarah into a spacious and tastefully decorated office.

"Thank you for seeing me on such short notice," Sarah said. She was, in fact, surprised at being able to meet Edna at all, having called from the hospital parking lot less than an hour earlier.

"No problem, Sarah," Edna said, as though they were old friends, "Come in and sit down. I understand you drove down from Maine. Would you like some coffee? I'm planning on it myself." She turned to the secretary without waiting for an answer. "Stephen, bring in some coffee, would you?"

"I have to admit," Edna said when they were alone, "that I was a bit mystified by your call. You wanted to talk about Doctor Breener?"

"You know that we have a man by that name living in Maine?"

Edna paused before replying. "I read a brief article in the *Globe* a couple of weeks ago in which the name was mentioned. Something about a lawsuit, but it's obviously a different Breener." She raised an eyebrow. "Is that why you're here?"

"In a way. Actually, I wanted to ask you about the night Annette Penrose died. I understand you visited her at Arlington General that evening."

"I see—" Edna began.

Just then, Stephen returned with a silver tray holding a bone china coffee service. He placed it on a side table and turned to leave.

"Stay at your desk for a few minutes, Stephen," Edna said. "I have an errand for you to run when Ms. Cassidy and I are through here."

Edna waited until the door had closed behind Stephen. "I have no idea where you're going with this," she said, speaking briskly, "but Harry called me about the attack as soon Annette was transferred to her room from Recovery. I was vice president of the company at the time, and Annette was both my boss and my friend, so naturally I went right over to see her. What does any of this have to do with Doctor Breener's mishandling of Annette's care?"

Sarah had prepared for this response. "My associates and I," she said, hoping to sound convincingly officious, "have reason to believe that the present Doctor Breener is being stalked, and in fact, he has already been physically attacked. Furthermore, we have reason to believe that this attack has something to do with the death of Annette Penrose on Christmas Eve of 2004, so we are reviewing those events." Sarah leaned forward for emphasis. "I think you're aware that the life insurance company wasn't entirely satisfied with the hospital's inquiry, and particularly the lack of an autopsy."

Sarah could tell from the look on Edna's face that her words had struck a nerve. Sarah could only hope that her bluff would shake something loose, some strand that she could grab to unravel whatever was being so carefully hidden.

"What are you, some kind of private detective?" Edna said.

Sarah breezed over the question. "You understand, of course, that this is still a very confidential preliminary review. If we feel this line of inquiry is a dead end, then we'll move on. On the other hand, if we aren't able to put the matter to rest, then we'll have no choice but to turn our concerns over to the proper authorities."

Sarah raised her hands and shrugged in a "what-else-can-we-do?" gesture, then leaned back with an expectant smile.

Edna sat for some time before responding. "I suppose most of this is in the public record," she said in a resigned voice. "I was a nurse in my younger days, so I know the kind of pressure an ER doctor has to deal with. From what I know, Doctor Breener was very capable—though he was just a Resident at the time. There was some talk about drug abuse, but my guess is that he was simply overloaded and missed something, perhaps through inexperience."

"You didn't actually see Doctor Breener while you were there?"

"I was only there for a few minutes, and I didn't see anybody except Annette and her husband. As I say, things were hectic."

"How did Annette seem to you?"

"About what you'd expect. She had just come back to her room, and she was pretty groggy, so we didn't have a real conversation. Harry was there when I arrived, and we sat with her for a while, but as I said, she didn't have a lot to say." Edna shook her head sadly. "It destroyed Governor Penrose when she died. Even if there hadn't been any question of malpractice, it destroyed him."

"It must have been hard for everybody," Sarah said sympathetically.

"I suppose it must have been hard for Doctor Breener, too, considering that his guilt drove him to suicide."

Sarah wondered what had gone wrong that night. She had been a nurse for a while herself, until her first disastrous marriage, and she knew all too well that doctors lost patients in the ER—not to mention the rest of the hospital—all the time without being driven to suicide. What had really happened that made Annette's death so bad?

Sarah changed tack. "Did you know Annette well?"

"She hired me in 1995, when she first started the company, and I came to know her both personally and professionally."

"I remember the papers made a lot of Harry's indiscretions, but Annette stuck by him, so I assume it must have been a good marriage overall."

Edna thought for a moment before answering. "The papers exaggerated, as usual. Yes, it was a good marriage. They were a very devoted couple, in spite of Harry's occasional flings. The only real problems I knew about were money issues around Harry's run for

Congress. It was hard for him when he lost so badly, and I think that may have caused strains."

Sarah nodded. "I know I sound ignorant, but what does Athena Associates do, exactly?"

Edna, on more comfortable ground, visibly relaxed. "Basically, we're investment advisors, but with a different focus. We specialize in providing investment advice and brokerage services aimed at the needs of women." Edna leaned back in her chair. "Studies have shown that women tend to be more successful at investing than men, in the long run. I know that sounds sexist, but the fact is that men often take needless risks when they make investment decisions, looking for a fast buck, whereas women are more conservative and think in the long term, which is where the real money is made."

Sarah nodded. "I remember from the newspaper stories that Annette was very committed to women's issues. I can see how the idea of Athena Associates would appeal to her."

Edna shuffled some papers on her desk. "Annette was an idealist who had very firm ideas of right and wrong, a true crusader for women's interests. The trouble was that she had no business sense, no idea of how to run a company."

"And that was your strength?"

"We worked well together—her vision and my business skills. It was a great loss when she died, but frankly she wasn't all that interested in the nuts and bolts of running a company like this, so I was left with the day to day operations by then. Annette was a fire starter, but not a fire tender, as the saying goes."

"And you're a fire tender."

Edna gave Sarah a thin smile. "That's not as dull as it sounds."

"When did the Ringling Group buy out the firm?"

"A few months after Annette's death. P. Melvin Delroy, who runs the Ringling Group, was a good friend of Governor Penrose, and that may have been a factor in his buying the company, but it was the right thing for the company, I think. We had been strapped for cash from the beginning, and the Ringling Group was able to provide the financial backing for us to grow and prosper. It was a good fit for both firms, and we've done very well, as you can see."

"That's an accomplishment for you, too," Sarah commented.

Edna had thawed considerably by now. "I have good people working for me, and P. Melvin has been very supportive of what Athena Associates stands for."

They talked for a while longer, without Sarah learning anything more. In any case, she didn't dare push her questions any further for fear of reigniting Edna's earlier suspicions.

Edna shook Sarah's hand at the office door.

As soon as Sarah had turned away towards the elevators, Edna stepped over to Stephen's desk. He looked up expectantly.

"I want you to follow Cassidy downstairs and get her license plate number," Edna said.

Stephen stood up.

"Don't let her know what you're doing, okay?"

"No problem," he said, watching Sarah's back as she made her way down the hall towards the elevator bank.

"Scoot, now," Edna said, giving him a gentle push. "Don't let her get away from you."

Sarah was alone in the elevator when Stephen's hand intercepted the closing doors. This was a stroke of luck, she thought.

"Looks like we're headed in the same direction," Stephen said. "Ms. Bartel wanted some papers, and I realized they were still in my car."

"Isn't that always the way," Sarah replied, putting on her most winning smile. Stephen was probably in his twenties, tall and slender, with an earnest expression and an almost stork-like way of walking. With luck, she might be able to get some useful information from him.

Stephen shrugged. "It's a chance to get outside for a few minutes."

"Ms. Bartel seems like a very competent woman."

"Smart," he replied. "The Ringling Group was wise to keep her on when they bought the place; she's built it into a two-hundred-million dollar company."

"I hate to seem ignorant, but didn't Edna Bartel start out as a nurse? Wasn't it a big leap for her to go from there into the investment business?"

"This is a very competitive business, but Ms. Bartel is a very competitive and ambitious person, and she's well suited to it. In any case, Annette Penrose was smart enough to see Ms. Bartel's potential." Stephen shrugged. "And so was the Ringling Group when they bought the company."

The elevator doors slid open, depositing them in the lobby. As they left the building, Stephen added, "Well, I'll leave you here and go off to my car."

———————

Stephen observed that the black Ford Explorer had a good-sized dent in the left rear fender. That would cost her insurance company a pretty penny.

He made note of the license number as he walked away. He also noted that they were Massachusetts plates. Hadn't she mentioned having come from Maine?

Chapter 18

Tuesday morning, December 18

As it happened, Vince Martell had started down the Maine Turnpike not long after Sarah. His destination was the rest stop in Kittery, which he figured was about half way between Burnt Cove and Boston.

The rest stop building was intended to capture the essence of Maine's iconic lighthouses, but to Vince's eye, the round structure emerging from the ground floor looked too chubby to be a lighthouse. Inside, the building had the feel of an old-fashioned railway station: drafty and full of noise. Vince supposed that lighthouse interiors were the same way. In any case, he figured the noisy part was good, since it would be less likely that he and Penrose would be overheard.

The drive had stiffened up his bruised muscles, and Vince walked slowly around the various franchises to loosen up, and find something to snack on.

Armed with a cup of Starbucks coffee and a Danish, he sat at a table under the lighthouse dome. The blustery weather made the seating decidedly cool, and he was glad to see Penrose coming through the door.

"So," Penrose said as he sat down, wasting no time on pleasantries, "what have you got to report?"

Vince had considered that question on the way down, and decided to start with the good news first. "Ziggy Breener has been having a bad week."

Penrose leaned over the table, a look of eager anticipation on his face. "Tell me about it, and don't leave anything out."

Vince described Ziggy's broken ankle, his poisoned goat, his burnt shack, the Christmas card with its warning and photo—each action intended to ratchet up the pressure.

It took half an hour to tell Penrose everything in all the detail he demanded, and by the end if it Vince was thoroughly disgusted, not just with the man's apparent sadism, but with himself for getting involved. Who would have guessed Penrose's thirst for revenge could go so far?

Vince didn't mention that the goat had survived, nor did he mention having his tire shot out by Cindy Rice. He would tell about the Russian goons in due time, since Borofsky might have already told Penrose. Besides, Vince figured that he might be able turn Borofsky's goons to his advantage. He handed over a small plastic bag, containing two paper-wrapped objects. "Here's what you wanted: a coffee mug and a juice glass. They haven't been washed."

Harry placed the bag on his lap. "What about Breener's sister? When are you going to deal with her?"

"I'm working on that," Vince said. "The trouble is, Breener isn't exactly a hermit like you told me, and he and his sister have moved in with one of Breener's friends, so I haven't been able to get her alone yet."

"Surely you can find a way around that."

Vince shrugged. "There's another problem, too," he said, playing his ace in the hole. "Borofsky has hired a couple of Russian thugs, and I'm afraid they're going to make trouble."

"Thugs?" Penrose said blankly.

"Russian Mafia."

"Why did he do that?"

"A misunderstanding. The trouble is that Borofsky is getting impatient with the way we're doing things. He wants Breener eliminated sooner rather than later, and I think he may decide to use his goons to do the job, instead of waiting for us." Vince doubted that Anton Borofsky would actually have Breener killed. No, he thought, Sasha was the killer in that pair. In any case, he hoped the suggestion would distract Penrose.

He was right.

"You can't let him interfere! Breener is *mine!*" Several people seated nearby turned in surprise, in spite of the background noise.

Penrose leaned over the table. *"That man murdered my wife,"* he hissed. "Do you know what it was like to learn that her killer is alive after all those years?"

Vince twisted the knife. "Breener will end up dead, no matter who does it, me or Borofsky."

"I don't just want him dead. I want him to *suffer!* I want him to feel grief and loss before he dies. I swore an oath to myself that my wife's death would be avenged, and I intend to fulfill that oath."

"Understood, but I didn't sign up to take on the Russian Mafia, too," Vince pointed out. "That complication is going to make it harder to do everything the way you want."

Harry sighed. "Okay, do the best you can, but just remember that Christmas is coming and time is running short. I'll be coming to Maine on Friday and staying at the Samoset over the holiday to be on hand." He paused. "Something else has come up that I want you to deal with."

"Before Christmas?"

"Yes." Harry shifted uncomfortably in his chair. "There's a woman, Sarah Cassidy—"

"What about her?"

"The thing is, she's been asking awkward questions."

Vince looked at his companion and wondered what was going on. This was beginning to look like something more than just revenge. "You want me to deal with her, too?"

"Yes. And her boyfriend as well."

"Jesus, Harry, that's a whole new ball game. I can't go waltzing into some jerkwater town and start mowing people down. It attracts too much attention, and it's not my style. You should have hired a hopped up street punk for that kind of stuff."

"I know it will cost more money." Harry slid a bulging envelope across the table. "Down payment, same as before."

Vince looked at his companion suspiciously. "Who's paying for this? Last time, you were talking about being broke, and now money is no object."

"Does it matter where the money comes from? Let's just say I have an associate."

"The same associate who wants the crockery?" At this rate, Vince figured he could retire after this job.

———————

It was close to midnight when Sarah got back from her trip, and she would have gone back to her cabin, except that she wanted to talk to Oliver about the day's events. As it was, she pulled into Oliver's driveway a little before midnight. He was waiting in the kitchen when she entered.

Sarah looked around. "Where are your house guests?"

"They went to bed hours ago," he replied.

"Good. We need to talk in private."

"You look beat. Are you sure this can't wait until tomorrow?"

"No."

"Your phone call did sound mysterious. What did you learn?"

"Violet Tibbs, the ER nurse, confirmed that Ziggy Breener died in 2005. He committed suicide—guilt over losing his patient."

"And she's sure?"

"There was a police investigation, autopsy, DNA test, dental records, all saying that he committed suicide. Annabelle identified the body." Sarah recounted her conversations with Violet. "She was pretty emphatic about him being dead."

"Could Violet be lying?"

"Trying to convince me that Ziggy is dead for some reason? Why would she? Besides, she gave me his autopsy report, not that I've had a chance to look at it yet."

"So, you're telling me that the Ziggy Breener we know and love, the Ziggy Breener whose goat is infesting my living room and whose sister is sleeping in my guest room is absolutely not the real Ziggy Breener?"

"I'm telling you that he's not the Ziggy Breener who was in the ER back in 2004."

"We've been over this before," Oliver reminded her, "but there's still the question of how many Zigfield Follies Breeners, with sisters named Annabelle, there can be in the world."

"Maybe our Ziggy is delusional and just thinks he's Violet's Ziggy."

"Is our Annabelle delusional, too?"

"I'm getting delusional thinking about this," Sarah grumbled. "Remember what Ziggy said the other day about killing a woman in another life, before he was reborn? Well, that woman would have been Annette Penrose, if it was Christmas Eve, like the card he got suggested."

"Should I know who she was?"

"Harry Penrose's wife."

Oliver nodded slowly. "You mean Harry Penrose, the former governor of Massachusetts?"

"That's the one. He tried to run for the U.S. Senate after his term as governor was up."

"He got buried in the election, if I remember right."

"He didn't have enough money," Sarah said. "It must have been hard for him. First he spent a fortune running for Senate and got swamped in the election, and then his wife was killed a month later."

"I remember it all now," Oliver replied slowly. "His wife was attacked while she was jogging one evening after work. Two guys beat and stabbed her."

Sarah nodded. "'The Christmas Killers,' is what the papers called them. They were never caught, in spite of the big manhunt." Sarah sighed. "I can't imagine what it must have been like for Penrose to lose his wife like that on the night before Christmas."

"A possible motive, if he has his Ziggys confused."

"On the other hand, maybe our Ziggy killed a different woman in a different hospital, or not in a hospital at all," Sarah said.

"Did you do anything else down there besides muddying the water?"

Sarah told him about her conversation with Edna Bartel.

"Does *she* think Ziggy is dead?"

"She didn't seem particularly interested in Ziggy, but it doesn't sound as though she ever met him." Sarah rubbed her eyes. "Let's talk about something else before my head explodes."

"I went to the police this morning," Oliver said, "and told them about Doctor Carnell disappearing and the possibility that he ended up on the bottom of Pimm's Pond. And that we have his luggage, such as it is, for safe keeping."

"Why did you do that?"

"Because somebody down in Boston may be wondering where he is, in which case they could decide to call the cops, and they would probably go to your cabin, or maybe the motel. Either way, you could be left trying to explain why you took Carnell's stuff without any authorization."

Sarah glared at Oliver. "So now you're my lawyer?"

"I thought we'd talked about this yesterday."

"We disagreed about this yesterday," Sarah corrected him. "I'm tired and it's past my bedtime." She started to get up. "And I'm going to visit the Borofskys tomorrow morning."

"The Borofskys? What on earth for?"

"I just remembered that Jeff mentioned seeing snowmobile tracks running up their driveway when he plowed it after the storm."

"And you think Borofsky ran down Ziggy?"

"The timing is right, and they certainly have a motive."

"Are you planning to confront them about it?"

"Not directly, but I could pretend to be interested in buying a snowmobile, and ask about theirs."

"I don't like the sound of that, and I don't think you should go there alone. After all, you set fire to their hot-tub the last time you were there."

"I don't like hot-tubs. Besides, it was a small fire, and—" Sarah paused, rocking her head from side to side. "Okay, I'll concede that there was a fair amount of smoke damage, and they had to rebuild the bathroom, but Anton was pretty understanding about the whole thing, and it was a question of life and death. Besides, they were insured." She shrugged. "I expect they've forgotten about the whole thing by now."

Chapter 19

Sarah and Oliver arrived at the Borofsky mansion around mid-morning on a bright and unseasonably warm day, which, in typical Maine fashion, felt more like early spring than Christmas.

They had taken separate vehicles, since Sarah planned to go on to her cabin. She had struggled with this decision today as she had all year. It would be all too easy for her to move in with Oliver, but it was less than a year since her divorce and she wanted to go slow and avoid another entanglement.

Besides, a couple of days of sharing a house with the Breener menagerie was enough to fray her nerves. It was selfish, perhaps, but she needed a day or two of piece and quiet in her own place. Oliver, though unhappy about her decision, had been understanding, and even a bit envious, of her need to escape the zoo which Ziggy had created in Oliver's house.

Sasha Borofsky greeted Sarah and Oliver at the door, saying, "Well, if it isn't the firebug who torched my bathroom."

Oliver coughed discretely.

"It was self-defense," Sarah said.

"That's right," Anton said, as he entered the hall from the study. "Sarah was just trying to escape from that awful Marlee Sue what's-her-name, so we mustn't blame her for doing a little damage to the house." He gave Sasha a peck on the cheek. "Don't forget my dear, this is America. People don't hold grudges in America. That's what makes this such a great nation."

Sasha pouted. "Marlee Sue wasn't all that awful. After all, she did manage to rid the world of Myra Huggard."

"Killing her was still murder," Anton said mildly.

Sarah wondered if Sasha was hoping to rid the world of Ziggy as well. "We were just driving by on the way to my cabin," she said, trying to sound cheerful, "and thought we'd drop by to see how you were coping after the blizzard."

"I was born in Russia, my dear," Anton replied, "so I'm used to snow, and it's nowhere near as cold here as it was in the Old Country."

"We like doing things out in the snow," Sasha added.

"A lot of people have snowmobiles," Sarah prattled. "I'll have to get one myself if stays as snowy as this all winter."

"You should get a snow machine," Anton said. "Sasha and I each have one, and they're great fun, as well as being practical, especially where the roads don't seem to get plowed out properly half the time."

"It was a record-setting blizzard," Oliver said. "It's pretty hard to keep the roads plowed—"

"Especially during the storm," Sarah said. "One would have to use a snowmobile to get around then, don't you think?" She gave Anton an inquiring look.

"I would never go out in a storm like that, unless it was a matter of life and death. Very dangerous." Anton paused. "I did go out the next morning, though. It was beautiful with the fresh snowfall, and I must say that the local snowmobile club does a fine job of grooming the trails, considering their limited resources."

"I don't suppose you noticed anything suspicious when you were out," Sarah said.

"Suspicious? What do you mean?"

"The reason I'm asking is because Ziggy Breener was run down by a snowmobile Friday morning," Sarah said.

Sasha suppressed a quick smile.

"I'm sorry to hear that," Anton said smoothly. "Was he hurt badly?"

"A broken ankle," Oliver said. "It could have been much worse. Jeff Rice found Ziggy, and helped get him to the hospital."

Anton shook his head. "Probably some drunk going too fast. Bad string of luck for him, with his house burning down, too. Anyway, to answer your question, I didn't see anybody 'operating erratically' as they say."

"Just thought I'd ask," Sarah said.

Sasha glared at Sarah. "I hope you don't think we might have injured the man just because he inherited the land next door."

"Goodness, no," Sarah assured her.

"Because that would be an outrageous accusation," Anton said. "Just because the lawyers that your ex-husband obtained for him managed to get Myra Huggard's will upheld doesn't mean that your friend with the broken ankle is out of the legal woods. We will take whatever legal action is necessary to keep him from turning our neighborhood into a slum."

"This is a nice area and we intend to make sure it stays that way," Sasha said.

"I can assure you that we have no need to resort to violence to stop him from using the land inappropriately," Anton added.

"It is Ziggy's land," Oliver said, "and he's got a right to do whatever he wants with it. That's the way it is in Burnt Cove."

"I know all about the typical Maine way of thinking, the rugged individualism, do-whatever-I-want attitude, but we have rights too, and we *will* protect them," Anton said.

"You'd better stick to building boats, instead of trying to tell us what we can or can't do." Sasha said.

"Besides, I can assure you that man has more serious problems than our legal disagreement," Anton said.

Sasha, who had been eyeing Oliver appraisingly, said, "I think we should have Oliver build a boat for us, Anton."

"But you get seasick, my dear."

"Not when the water is smooth. And having a nice motorboat moored out front would be the perfect touch." She sidled over, put a hand on her guest's arm and gazed into his eyes. Sarah noticed that the woman was almost as tall as Oliver.

"You made that rowboat for the Vincents next door, didn't you, Oliver?" she murmured.

It was not a mere "rowboat" Sarah thought disgustedly. It was a classic, sixteen-foot Whitehall pulling boat which she, in fact, had helped Oliver paint last spring.

"Perhaps we can talk about it another time when they're not so busy," Anton suggested.

"I have an idea," Sasha said brightly. She had taken firm possession of Oliver's arm by now. "It just so happens that Governor Penrose will be spending the holidays in Rockland."

Anton frowned at his wife. "I don't think—"

"And we're planning a little cocktail party this Saturday with the governor and a few friends," she went on. "We'd love to have you come." Sasha stepped back and gave Oliver the once-over. "Both of you, of course."

"I'm not sure they would enjoy—" Anton began.

"Don't be silly, darling," Sasha said, "The governor will be delighted to meet some Real Mainers." She turned to Oliver, plastering herself against his side. "We helped fund the governor's run for the Senate, you know. It will be strictly informal. No need to dress up."

While Sarah and Oliver were visiting the Borofskys, Annabelle was confronting her brother. She had spotted Ziggy struggling to put on his jacket while juggling his crutches. "Where do you think you're going?" she said.

"Out to spread Christmas cheer."

"How are you planning to do that, and what do you have in your hand?"

Ziggy had managed to work his arms through the jacket's sleeves without falling or dropping the envelopes he clutched in one hand. "I fly like an eagle to the mailbox," he said sullenly.

"You're going to walk all the way down that icy driveway to the mail box on crutches? You'll fly all right—flat on your back." Annabelle eyed her brother suspiciously. "Why didn't you ask me to take those down for you?" She made a grab for the letters.

Ziggy tried to keep them from her, but his crutches were too big a handicap.

"Christmas cards?" she said with surprise, looking at the envelopes.

"I fly to spread Christmas cheer," Ziggy repeated peevishly. He paused, lost in thought. "I will need tea," he reminded himself.

"Why don't you ever send me a Christmas card?"

"I spend Christmas with you." Ziggy made a fruitless grab for the envelopes.

"A card would be nice, even so."

"Christmas cards aren't always nice," Ziggy said, frowning.

Annabelle looked at the addresses. "Borofsky? You're sending a card to the Borofskys? They've threatened to kill you over Myra Huggard's land."

"Their words were mere flights of fancy."

"And Harry Penrose?" Annabelle went on, her voice rising in volume and pitch. "You know perfectly well that he's out to get you. Just look at the cast on your leg."

"He acts out of ignorance, and the cast was a mere accident. 'Tis the season for forgiveness and good cheer."

"These guys are trying to cheer you right into an early grave." She looked at the last letter. "P. Melvin Delroy? Who is he?"

"He's a friend of Harry Penrose, I'm told," Ziggy said. "He bought Annette Penrose's business when she died, and he has a summer cottage right here in Camden. Perhaps he's in town."

"Whatever you're up to, I don't like it," Annabelle announced. "And you waited until Sarah and Oliver left the house to do this," she added shrewdly.

"I must swoop like an eagle before the postal person arrives."

Annabelle sighed. "I've half a mind to keep these, but you'd probably sneak out and mail more."

"Christmas is coming, the goose is getting fat, and there's no time to lose."

———————

"I don't have anything to wear to a fancy party," Sarah said as they stood beside her Explorer in The Borofsky's driveway. "All my good clothes are down in Sudbury."

"Sasha said it was informal," Oliver replied.

"That's fine for you. All a man needs is a suit and tie."

"When in Maine, dress like a Mainer."

"That's exactly what I mean. I have no intention of being the token Maine native at a millionaire's gala, especially when my house is in Massachusetts."

"I don't have a problem with being the token Maine native," Oliver said mildly. "Maybe we could bring Ziggy along as our guest. Somebody there might know who he really is."

"I'm not sure you should go at all, if you're going to have that attitude. Besides, I'm not sure you'll be safe there."

"*Me* not safe? You're the one who wants to nose around a bunch of big-shots, looking for trouble."

"This is a heaven-sent opportunity to learn some more about Penrose's wife, and what happened," she said. "Anton as much said that Ziggy had other enemies besides him, and we know Penrose has a good motive to be stalking Ziggy."

"I think you should be really careful about messing with somebody like Penrose, or Anton Borofsky, for that matter."

Sarah shot a glance at Castle-Borofsky. "I think you should be careful with Sasha."

"Sasha?" Oliver said blankly.

"Oh, come on. Don't pretend you didn't see her ogling you like a side of beef. And right in front of her husband, too."

"Don't tell me you're jealous," he said, suppressing a grin.

"That woman gives me the creeps. She's a predator when it comes to men."

"A predator?"

Sarah looked at him pityingly. "Wasn't it obvious? It must be a hormone thing that makes men so blind to women like that."

————————

Sarah and Oliver stood on the deck of her cabin a little later. The deck had been shoveled clear of snow by the ever-industrious Jeff Rice, and they watched the activity on the far side of the pond as a snowmobile was maneuvered through a hole in the ice. While this was happening, a crew of divers were descending into the water.

Sarah shivered. "I told you that I'd heard snowmobiles on the pond during the blizzard. It looks like the divers are looking for a body."

"That should tell them how he died, assuming it is Doctor Carnell."

"He was shot," Sarah said. "I heard it."

The noon sun was strong and warm on their faces, warm enough to melt the few patches of snow that Jeff had missed.

"I'm freezing out here," Sarah said. "I need to go in and get something hot to drink."

Oliver looked at her, concern on his face. "Are you sure you want to stay here alone?"

"I've told you before that I'll be fine." Still shivering, she turned to go back inside.

"What about those footprints around your windows?"

"I'll be fine," she repeated.

"Damn these stubborn Irish," Oliver grumbled as he followed her inside.

Chapter 20

Wednesday midday, December 19

Sarah and Oliver ate an impromptu lunch, consisting of leftover squash soup and Asiago Focaccia, in her cabin. It was a welcome change to be free from the constant noise of Ziggy, his sister, and his goat. That, together with the warmth of the noon sun beaming in through the slider, heat from the woodstove, which Oliver had stoked enthusiastically, and the hot soup, combined to fill her with a feeling of contentment and tranquility.

Plus, she had carefully seated herself so she couldn't see the rescue workers out on the pond.

They ate in silence while Sarah studied Ziggy's autopsy report on her laptop.

"What's the verdict?" Oliver said when she finished.

"The body was so badly burned that I can't imagine how Annabelle would have been able to identify him."

"Did she lie about recognizing the body to protect him somehow? Could that explain why she was so upset about Ziggy's contagion comment?"

"Maybe, but they had DNA and dental records that all said the body was Ziggy's. I don't see how it could be anyone else. Her ID really didn't matter."

"So Violet is right, and our Ziggy isn't her Ziggy."

"Except that somebody thinks he is," Sarah said, "like Harry Penrose, who blames him for Annette's death."

"I wonder about the Borofskys, too."

"The Borofskys?"

"I'm not a lawyer," Oliver replied, "but what happens to Myra's Will if our Ziggy is a fraud? Does he still inherit if he's an imposter using a phony name?"

"Maybe that's what Anton Borofsky meant this morning when he said Ziggy wasn't out of the legal woods. I can check with Claude on that." Sarah started to slide the laptop over to Oliver, and noticed the Medical Examiner's name on the autopsy. She slid it back in front of her. "Wait. The ME who did the autopsy was Doctor Tierny."

"And he's a friend of Ziggy." Oliver shook his head in frustration. "All this is just leading us around in circles. Violet is right; The simplest explanation is that our Ziggy had nothing to do with Arlington General's Ziggy, and our Ziggy killed some other woman, maybe on Christmas Eve, somewhere else."

"Except that our Ziggy knew Doctor Hasting, judging from his reaction to the newspaper photo. And our Ziggy knows Doctor Tierny. That's a lot of connections."

––––––––––––

Ziggy Breener flitted around the edges of Violet's mind, like an obnoxious tune that wouldn't go away. Of course, people died in the ER all the time—that's just the way it was, and one had to learn to live with it. But she'd been young then, and just learning how easy it was to blame oneself for some real or imagined oversight that might, or might not, make the difference between life and death.

Perhaps it had been her youthful innocence, but at the time Doctor Breener had seemed too competent, too assured to make the sort of mistake that would cause Annette Penrose to die. Violet remembered that Annette had seemed to be stable after her surgery. They had breathed a sigh of relief and turned their attention to the more serious cases. Another life saved.

And then, suddenly, Annette Penrose was dead.

At the time, it had never occurred to Violet to think that Ziggy might blame himself for what happened.

On the other hand, not every patient was the wife of a powerful Boston politician. A powerful and very angry politician, who might be irrational enough to seek revenge on anybody who happened to be named Ziggy Breener.

Violet had dreamed about Annette last night. The woman had been lying dead on her bed, a huge four-poster affair with heavy Victorian hangings and embroidered silk sheets. There were garlands of lilies framing her alabaster face, which was smeared with blood. Violet was standing there, wondering how Harry Penrose had managed to fit a bed that size into a hospital room, when the corpse called out to her in some foreign language that Violet couldn't understand. She woke up with a start.

It was the last straw.

Violet was a pragmatist, rooted in the-here-and-now, and she had little patience for dreams, especially dreams whose occupants babbled in a foreign language. If a dream was her sub-conscious mind's way of communicating to the conscious, than at least it could have the courtesy to speak English.

It was all the Cassidy woman's fault for stirring up those long-buried memories, not to mention the foolish notion that Doctor Breener was alive. Cassidy was like poison ivy, leaving an itch that demanded to be scratched.

She remembered how outraged Doctor Tierny, the ME, had been at not being allowed an autopsy and how he had snatched away Annette's paperwork immediately after her death, pending an inquiry as to how the former governor's wife could die in the hospital from apparently non-life-threatening injuries. And now, all that information was gone.

Violet had been scouring her memory of that night ever since Sarah's visit and had come up with scraps and bits of recollection, but how accurate were they after all this time? So many patients, and so many years had come and gone…

She sat in her tiny office before going home at the end of her shift, doodling notes on a lined pad.

Her musings were interrupted by the arrival of the officious Doctor Thomas at her door. Violet gave an involuntary start.

The pesky doctor was in his early seventies, tall, gray and stooped. He looked at her thoughtfully through rimless glasses for a moment before asking, "Catching up on your paperwork?"

"Just some odds and ends before I head out."

Thomas was normally easy going, if a bit meddlesome, and he seldom lectured her, out of deference to her years of experience. He was, after all, smarter than the average bear, and knew the value of somebody with her knowledge and skills. Even so, he looked to be in a lecturing frame of mind now. "You've been here for more than ten years, haven't you?" he began.

"About that," Violet replied, wondering what her latest transgression was.

"Your work record in that time has been exemplary," he went on, "with the possible exception of being, shall we say, independent and outspoken at times."

Busted, Violet thought with disgust. Aloud, she said, "I'm trying not to get carried away so much."

Thomas cleared his throat. "I'm sure, with all your years on the job that I don't need to tell you that a patient's records are strictly confidential." He paused for effect. "Giving out such information is a serious violation of our rules."

Violet nodded.

"A *serious* violation," he repeated. "A cause-for-termination violation. I would not like to think that you were giving sensitive information to somebody like, for instance, the Sarah Cassidy woman you were talking with yesterday. And even more especially when it's records pertaining to a patient of, let's say, Annette Penrose's stature."

"I would never give out privileged information inappropriately," Violet said, especially since there didn't seem to be any information on Annette Penrose to give out.

Doctor Thomas studied her face for a moment, clearly reluctant to push the issue.

Violet was relieved by his uncertainty, but how in the world did he know about Cassidy asking questions? Somebody must have told him, but who? She would need to be much more careful from now on.

———————

It took almost an hour for Violet to track down Sean O'Malley, the first cop on the scene of Annette's attack. She still remembered him coming into the ER, shivering, looking half frozen, and holding Annette's hand as she was wheeled in. She'd had to pry their fingers apart and drag the big Irishman to the waiting area where she piled on two more blankets.

"I don't know if you remember me," Violet began, "but I met you in the ER on the night you came in with Annette Penrose. I'm the one who escorted you out to the waiting room."

"I never forget a pretty face, especially after you damn near suffocated me under all those blankets. Are you still at Arlington General?"

"Yes, and I'm reviewing some of our records. We do that periodically with old cases that haven't been closed, and I don't believe hers was ever resolved." Violet figured she could kiss the blarney stone as well as anybody. "The thing is that I've run across a minor detail that I wanted to check up on, just to fill in the blanks—"

"I retired three years ago," Sean interrupted tersely, his voice noticeably cooler.

"I understand, but you were at the scene, and I was hoping there might be something—"

"It's all in the report."

Violet gave a helpless sigh. "I'm just trying to see if anything was missed, like any conversation you had with her, or anything that seemed odd and didn't get written down."

"What the hell is going on here?"

"This is purely routine."

"Look, I was with her from the beginning until they wheeled her into the ER, and she was unconscious the whole time. Didn't say a word."

"Was there anything about the attack itself, anything at all, that seemed strange?"

"Are you at Arlington General now, Violet?"

"Yes."

"I'll call you back through the switchboard." With that, O'Malley was gone.

She picked up the phone a minute later. "You're not trying to con me, are you?" O'Malley said. "You're not planning to write some kind of tell-all book, are you?"

"Absolutely not," Violet replied stiffly. "As I said, I've been reviewing the records on the off-chance that something was missed that might help the police track down the muggers, and I'm hoping you can help."

There was a long silence on the line. "Some cases really stick in your craw, and that was one of them. I'd love to get my hands on the punks who did that to poor Mrs. Penrose."

"Is there anything you can think of?"

"It's probably nothing," he said tentatively, "but they didn't take anything when they mugged her, and that's always bothered me. Maybe it was because I came along and interrupted them before they could actually rob her, but she had a fanny pack they could have got off her in a second when they first spotted me. It was like all they cared about was hurting the poor woman." He paused. "I suppose they were high on acid or some damn thing."

———————

Violet called Sarah that evening. "Hey, Buttercup," she said when Sarah answered.

"Violet?"

"I've got tomorrow off," Violet said briskly, "and I was wondering if you'd like to meet me in Freeport to do a little Christmas shopping. No big deal, just two pals cruising the outlet stores and talking about old times."

"I'd love it," Sarah said, wondering what Violet was up to. "I'm going to a party for a bunch of fat cats, and need to get something to wear. Something that will make a statement."

"You want *me* to help you find something that'll make a statement?" Sarah heard a snicker. "I bet we can do a helluva lot better than that outfit you had on the other day." Violet paused. "Just for the record, you aren't some kind of a reporter for one of those sleazy tell-all tabloids are you?"

"God no," Sarah assured her. "I'm just who I said I was."

"That's what I figured, 'cause you don't seem sneaky enough to be one of those creeps."

"Thank you, I think," Sarah replied.

"I wouldn't ask, but somebody around here knows that you're poking around down here, and they don't seem too happy about it."

"I hope my visit didn't get you into trouble."

"I've told you before that trouble is my middle name. Can you be in front of Bean's at ten o'clock?"

"I'll see you then."

"Bring your track shoes, 'cause I move fast."

Chapter 21

Thursday morning, December 20

Thursday morning was cloudy and cold when Sarah and Violet began their shopping at L.L. Bean's. Unlike Sarah, who tended to browse at random until something struck her fancy, Violet had armed herself with a list and marched off with paper and pencil in hand while Sarah wandered around to look at the variety of Bean's iconic boots.

Sarah was checking out the selection of insulated gloves—boots and gloves are kind of similar after all—when she noticed an elderly man in a green parka and black knitted cap shuffling painfully down the aisle. He looked vaguely familiar, and it took her a moment to remember that he'd been standing outside the store.

"Let's check out Bean's outlet store, next," Violet said when they joined up a little later. "Then we can see about a decent dress for you."

They were seated in Freeport's Corsican restaurant shortly after noon with shopping bags piled at their feet, like the booty of a pair of Viking raiders.

"You don't think that dress is too much, do you?" Sarah said.

"You've got a good figure for an old broad, so why not flaunt it? Bright and tight. You can't go wrong with that combination. Trust me, your boyfriend will love it." Violet eyed Sarah shrewdly. "Or is this a jealousy thing? Is there another woman out there, some competition?"

"No." Sarah sampled a spoonful of her clam chowder. "Well, there's Annabelle. And there's Sasha, who's a vampire with a reputation, but they're not the real reason for the dress."

"Of course not. Silly of me to ask. So, is your boyfriend a live-in?"

"No."

"Do you want him to be?"

"When the time is right."

"I'm not going to spoil my lunch by getting into that," Violet commented. "Does your boyfriend want to live with you?"

"Oh, yes."

"Okay, so let me get this straight," Violet said between mouthfuls of lobster stew. "You're going to shimmy around your boyfriend in that new do-me dress and then send the guy home where Annabelle and the vampire lady can sink their fangs into him? You're a strange woman, Cassidy."

"That's ridiculous. The vampire lady turned up just the other day, as far as I know. Besides, Ziggy and Annabelle are staying in Oliver's house, so it's crowded enough without me cluttering up the place."

"Annabelle is living in your boyfriend's house?" Violet's spoon hovered in mid-air.

"It's not the way it sounds."

"Jesus, woman, you'd better rein in that man before it's too late. We're gonna have to buy you some hot lingerie."

"Stop trying to get me confused," Sarah whined.

"Trust me, getting you confused is like shooting fish in a barrel."

"Thanks a lot. Now it's your turn. What about your boyfriend?"

"He bailed out fourteen years ago and left me with two kids, a boy and a girl, who are both in the military now."

"Nobody on the horizon?"

"There will be, when the time is right," Violet replied, echoing Sarah's earlier comment.

They concentrated on eating for a while before Sarah said, "The main reason I want the dress is because there's somebody I want to pump for information." She paused. "Harry Penrose."

Violet took some time swallowing a spoonful of her lobster stew. "I Googled you the other day," she said at last, "and you've been involved in several murders over the past year. Are you some kind of private eye, or do you just like sticking your nose into hornets' nests?"

"It's more like hornets' nests falling on my head."

"Here's a genuine Violet Tibbs safety tip: stop walking under hornets' nests."

"I'll keep that in mind for the future, but right now—" Sarah pulled a snapshot of Ziggy Breener from her purse and handed it to Violet. "Does he look familiar?"

"This is your version of Doctor Breener?" Violet studied the photo. "Who can tell with that beard covering most of his face, and that scruffy watch cap on his head? Does he live on the street?"

"He had a shack, until somebody burned it down last week."

Violet looked more closely, tilting the photo towards the light. "This guy looks too old."

"I don't think the last ten years or so have been easy for him."

"His eyes and the shape of his face look right, but it can't be Doctor Breener, because he's dead. Have you checked to see if he has a brother?" Violet returned the picture. "This guy may look like him, but he's not the real thing. You need to let go of the idea that your Ziggy Breener is the same person as mine. It's just too bad for your Breener if somebody has him confused with my Breener, but coincidences happen all the time. Two people with the same oddball name."

"What about Annette?" Sarah said, shifting gears. "Did she say anything in the ER?"

"Does it matter?"

"Probably not, but if there was something funny about the attack, she might have mentioned it."

Violet filled Sarah in on her conversation with Sean O'Malley. "As far as I can tell, she didn't say anything about the attack to anybody, except maybe Edna or Harry."

"But O'Malley thought there was something odd about the mugging?"

"I got the feeling it was a sort of cop's instinct thing." Violet paused. "Something else is bugging me, though. Somebody knew I was looking through the computer records on Annette. Doctor Thomas gave me a hard time about it."

"But the records had been deleted."

Violet nodded. "I know she was a high profile case, but to delete all the records, and flag anybody who looks for them seems a little over the top."

"The thing is, if Annette was murdered—"

"Of course she was murdered, for chrissake."

"I mean in the hospital," Sarah said.

"In the hospital? I suppose you think JFK was assassinated by the Cubans, too. I don't know why I'm talking to you. Life was so much simpler before you came along." Violet began to ferociously spoon stew into her mouth.

Sarah waited a few moments before saying, "Why did the inquiry try to blame it all on Ziggy? Sure he was on duty, but there was the surgeon, Doctor Hastings, too. Why not spread the blame around?"

"You're a piece of work, Cassidy. First of all, it was Christmas Eve, and there weren't a lot of Doctors around. Breener and

Hastings were the ones who handled Annette's case, and with Doctor Hastings dead, Doctor Breener was the only one left to blame."

"And I suppose nobody wanted to besmirch the memory of a senior surgeon like Doctor Hastings when there was a junior Resident handy."

"Look, the name says it all: Zigfield Follies Breener. His parents were hippies, and he was a little odd himself. Maybe he smoked some pot. Whatever it was, I don't know, and I don't care. But you can see how the Suits would look at this oddball, and decide that he must have been high and screwed up."

"It gets them off the hook."

"The man was a damn good doctor."

"One of a kind," Sarah murmured.

"Don't even think about going there."

Sarah looked up and saw the green-parka-man sipping a cup of coffee across the room. "Don't stare," she said to Violet, "but the old man sitting behind you in the glasses and green parka has been following us all morning."

Violet heaved a sigh and shot a glance over her shoulder before turning back. "I remember seeing him in the chocolate store, which means he likes chocolate. Doesn't everybody?"

"He was in Bean's, the North Face, and Brooks Brothers, too."

"Did he follow us into the dress stores?"

"I don't think you're taking this seriously enough."

"I think you're taking it way too seriously," Violet said. "I don't think he's as old as he looks, though. My guess is that he walks like an old man because he had a car accident, or got banged up somehow. I see it in the ER all the time—stiff and sore from taking a shot to the gut."

"I can't be sure, but I think there was somebody else following us, too," Sarah said. "Tall and thin in a black windbreaker."

"Christ almighty, Cassidy, you've got to be the most paranoid, aggravating broad I've ever met. No wonder people try to kill you all the time."

"You need to come and meet my Ziggy."

Violet dropped her spoon into the stew. "Your Ziggy Breener is a goddam fraud. There's no way I'm getting sucked into your fantasy."

———————

While Sarah and Violet were shopping, Cindy and her daughter were sitting around the Rice's kitchen table, along with Oliver and Eldon.

"How is Ziggy?" Cindy Rice asked Oliver.

"He's learning to get around pretty well on crutches, but he's not supposed to put any weight on that ankle for a while. Tending to Annabelle is the only thing that's keeping him halfway sane."

"How is Annabelle?" Sally said.

"The goat? Better today, I think. She doesn't sound quite so much like a piece of paper stuck in a vacuum cleaner hose when she inhales," Oliver replied. "Those are Ziggy's words, not mine."

"Tell Oliver what you told me," Eldon said to Cindy.

"I saw the man who burned out Ziggy," Cindy said. "He came nosing around the day before the fire. I went out and talked to him and got a good look. I told the cops about it, too, but they don't give a damn about some shack being torched down here."

"That's why I figured you should hear this," Eldon said.

"What did he look like?" Oliver said.

Cindy tapped a cigarette out of the pack and lit it. "I'd guess he was in his forties, medium height, beefy guy, curly brown hair." She blew out a cloud of smoke. "Had glasses on, but I think they was phony."

"What do you mean, phony?" Oliver said.

"Like they was window glass. You know how, when you look at somebody wearing glasses, around their eyes looks a little warped, kind of like a fun-house mirror? Around this guy's eyes was like looking through window glass."

"Okay," Oliver said, unconvinced. "Was there anything else?"

"Damn right," Cindy replied triumphantly. "He had a phony limp, too."

"A phony limp?" Sally said incredulously. "How could you tell it was phony? Did you kick him in the shins?"

Cindy blew a cloud of smoke at her daughter. "It was plain as day. He was walking around like his right leg was all stove up, but I saw out the window when he got here, and he didn't have no trouble hopping out of his car. A limp like that, he'd have had trouble driving a car, much less hopping in and out of it like a spring chicken."

"So, you saw a guy in his forties, medium height, beefy, with brown hair, maybe wearing phony glasses, and maybe walking with a phony limp," Sally said. "That's not much to go on, Ma. You sure he wasn't wearing a wig, too?"

Cindy took an irritated drag on her smoke. "You think I can't spot a wig, smart-ass? It may not be much, but it's a helluva lot better description than what you had before."

"How do you know that was the same man who torched Ziggy's place?" Oliver asked.

"Because it was the same car parked by the road the next night," Cindy said triumphantly. "I took the plate number, and double-checked before I shot out his tire."

"Did you tell the police?" Sally said.

"I ain't fool enough to tell them about the tire, but I figure it must be the firebug's car, 'cause otherwise he'd have come back to fix the flat and take the car away. He probably stole it. Anyhow, I gave the cops the number, not that they'll do anything with it."

Oliver figured that Cindy was underestimating the police. "If this guy is any good, he won't leave anything useful to turn up."

Eldon nodded. "Probably used a phony name."

"To go along with his phony limp," Sally added.

Cindy glared at her guests. "Jesus, you clowns ain't any help at all," she grumbled. "Looks like I gotta do every goddamn thing myself."

Chapter 22

Thursday morning , December 20

Oliver left the Rices and headed over to drop in on Pearly Gaites at his boatshop. Like many Mainers, Pearly believed in the wisdom of being especially thorough when it came to clearing the first snowfall of the winter, on the theory that one should leave room to plow the next storms, because they were bound to come. As a result of this thinking, the parking area between Pearly's weather-beaten shop and the cove it sat beside was well clear of snow.

The cove was empty of boats, and the steely grey water was troubled by a damp, cold wind that added to the overall feeling of desolation.

It was warmer inside the shop, where a half-finished, thirty-six-foot yawl occupied most of the interior, its newly planked hull filling the air with the smell of cedar.

Pearly may have given Eldon a few days off for Christmas, but not himself. As a result, Oliver found him working on parts of the boat's interior, much of which he assembled on the shop floor and then placed in the boat.

Pearly, who was bent over the workbench planing a six-foot-long mahogany board, looked up. "I hear you've opened a hospital for goats," he said. "How's that working out?"

"The goat with the broken ankle is driving me nuts, and the one with pneumonia is turning my livingroom into a stable, but at least she seems to be getting better. It's damn slow, though."

"It just seems that way," Pearly said. "Ziggy's sister still there?"

"Yes, and her goal in life seems to be to needle Ziggy."

"Getting your goat, are they?"

"The corn-ball jokes never end with you, do they?" Oliver grumbled. "I saw your cousin Charlie, the sheriff, helping pull that snowmobile out of Pimm's Pond yesterday."

"People never learn, no matter how many warnings they see on TV," Pearly said, disgusted. "Going out on the ice this time of year, and with the warm fall weather we've been having lately, too. Hell, there was open water on that end."

"How did they know there was anything in the pond?"

"Somebody called it in yesterday. Anonymous tip."

"Did they recover a body?"

"Yeah."

"Do you know who it was?"

"They haven't notified the next of kin yet," Pearly said as he sighted along the board.

Most parts of a boat are curved, and a series of short pencil ticks marked the curve that Pearly was shaping the board to. Oliver could see that it was curved not just along the board's length, but across its width as well. "Did Charlie tell you who it was?"

"They haven't notified the next of kin yet," Pearly repeated, returning the board to the bench vise and picking up the plane.

"Is it somebody from around here?"

Pearly kept his tools razor-sharp, and the plane rolled out a long, thin spiral of wood. "Nope."

Building a boat, with all its complex shapes, required patience, Oliver reminded himself. "Anybody we know?"

Pearly studied the board again. Oliver figured that his friend would probably spend another half-hour getting it shaped, and that it would fit perfectly when he was done. No point in climbing in and out of the boat more often than necessary.

"It depends on who you know," Pearly said reasonably.

Oliver rolled his eyes, and rolled the figurative dice. "Was he a doctor?"

"What is this, twenty questions?"

"I'm just trying to figure out what's going on with Ziggy, and maybe keep him from getting hurt worse." Oliver figured he'd hit pay dirt from Pearly's reaction. Sarah was right, it had to be Doctor Carnell.

Pearly ran the plane over his board again, looked at the result, grumbled in irritation, and turned to Oliver. "Some of us aren't like you, with stock options and stuff like that to help pay the bills, so we have to work for a living instead of pestering people."

The target of Pearly's comment had worked for an engineering firm before moving to Maine. He admired the half-finished boat in silence while he waited for Pearly's outburst to pass.

"Yes, it was a doctor," Pearly said at last. "Now, let me get back to work, for chrissake."

"A surgeon?" Oliver could be as patient with his questions as Pearly was with his plane.

"No, smart ass."

"A dentist?" Oliver inquired, feeling like one.

Pearly looked for a moment as though he was about to plane a slice off Oliver's nose. "No, you goddam pest, it was a dead-person doctor. Now will you let me get back to work?"

"A dead-person doctor?"

"Are you going to torment me now just because I can't pull the right word off the tip of my tongue? You know who I mean, dammit. The guy who cuts open dead bodies to see what killed them, like on TV."

"A Medical Examiner?"

"Yes," Pearly growled as he sighted along the board again. "Jesus, you're worse than Chinese water torture. Can't a man have peace and quiet in his own shop? Yes, a Medical Examiner, and before you start trying to screw it out of me, his name was Willard Tierny. You happy now?"

"I won't tell anybody except Sarah, Pearly. Sorry if I got your goat."

"You're the idiot with a houseful of goats."

It was almost dark by the time Sarah got back to her cabin. Carrying her shopping bags, she gingerly made her way down the snowy slope to the cabin door, thankful that she'd had the foresight to leave some lights on.

It wasn't as though she was nervous about the man, or men, who may or may not have been following them around Freeport, or the man who had been looking in her windows. Still, the shadows that lurked around the cabin's edges made her nervous. She hurriedly unlocked the door and dumped her shopping on the kitchen table. It was entirely possible that the stalkers, if that's what he or they were, had been tailing Violet, not her. The woman clearly had a mind of her own and wasn't afraid to speak it. Who knew what sort of enemies she might have collected?

She put the shopping bag with her new dress to one side to try on later, once she had the cabin warmed up. Even if the green parka had been following them, he was much too crippled to be a real threat, and she wasn't really sure if the black windbreaker had been tailing them at all.

Sarah hung up her coat and closed the curtain across the slider. Maybe Violet was right and she was paranoid. Maybe she really was taking the whole business with Ziggy too seriously and imagining something that wasn't really there. This Ziggy had nothing to do with Violet's Ziggy—a weird coincidence and nothing more.

She filled the woodstove and lit it. Her day had been fun, but more important, Violet's pragmatism was making her rethink her assumptions. Maybe she was right about her relationship with Oliver. Maybe she was pushing him away, or letting him get away.

And he was spending a lot of time with Annabelle.

She put the kettle on to boil. Renting a place of her own for the winter had seemed reasonable last fall—a chance to try out Maine, and Oliver, without entanglements or commitments.

But as Violet pointed out, that worked both ways. She remembered her reaction last week when she called Oliver's house and Annabelle answered. Sarah figured that Ziggy's sister must be a lot younger than Oliver, but maybe he liked younger women, Sarah thought, remembering her ex's underage girlfriend.

———————

Vince lay on the battered bed in his room at the Night Owl Motel and nursed his aching body with a beer. Since his meeting with Penrose the other day, Vince had been driving by Cassidy's cabin late every evening and early every morning, trying figure out her schedule and find the safest time to get her alone. He'd followed her this morning when she took off early to go shopping. Tailing Cassidy and her colored friend around Freeport was tedious, but all that walking had worked out some of the soreness.

Vince thought of himself as a hunter, and like any good hunter, he took pride in learning about his prey, their habits and ways of thinking. But it was more than that. He'd read somewhere that Native Americans used to pray for their quarry, communing with them, before the hunt. It was a show of respect, he supposed. Vince thought of himself like that. Sarah Cassidy was his quarry now, just like Annabelle and Ziggy.

He was pretty sure that Sarah had spotted him and knew she was being watched. To Vince's mind that was an important part of his personal ritual—that the victim should know the fear of being hunted. Like Ziggy Breener.

It had been three days since he got tuned up by Borofsky's goons, and he still tired easily. That was bad, since Christmas was coming fast, and there was a lot to do, a lot of accounts to settle.

Including Anton Borofsky's pet apes.

Chapter 23

Friday morning, December 21

The morning was cloudy, the air heavy with a cool dampness that smelled of snow when Sarah left her cabin right after breakfast with a grocery list in her pocket. She would pick up some food for the next few days before going on to see how Oliver and his house guests were doing. She also wanted to talk to him about yesterday's shopping trip with Violet.

She was just about to get into the car when a UPS truck pulled up. The driver looked unhappily at the icy ski slope that led down to her door, and beamed with delight when she took the package.

It was a small box, with a return address saying, "Wilber's of Maine," the chocolate shop in Freeport. Sarah smiled to herself. Violet must have ordered it yesterday while they were shopping and had it delivered. A sticker on the side said, "Open now!" Just like Violet, Sarah thought. She put the gift on the Explorer's seat to share with Oliver later.

She pulled into his driveway around mid-morning. As she approached the back door, Sarah could hear Annabelle exclaiming loudly, "Enough is enough! I can't go on like this!"

An abrupt silence descended when Sarah entered the kitchen.

She wondered if the constant verbal sparring was a normal part of their relationship, or the result of Ziggy's present difficulties.

"Where is Oliver," she said, breaking the tense silence.

"In the barn," Annabelle replied.

"The boatshop," Ziggy corrected her.

Annabelle-the-goat gave a juicy cough from the livingroom.

Sarah left the scene.

Oliver's boatshop, which had, in fact, once been a barn, was cool in despite the valiant efforts of an outdoor wood furnace located beside the building.

Sarah knew that Oliver and Pearly were both working on the interiors of their respective boats, and she wondered at times if the two men were having an informal race to see who could finish first—though they would never admit to such a thing.

Wes, nestled in a quilt-lined box, leaped out to greet Sarah as she entered. Sarah knelt to say hello to him, and stood up to kiss Oliver.

"What are the daffy duo fighting about now?" Sarah asked.

"Basically, she's trying to persuade Ziggy to go into hiding until the stalker gives up."

"And he won't do it?"

Oliver perched on a convenient sawhorse. "I think the thing that's really keeping him here is the Christmas card he got with the 'Run and your friends will die' message."

"So he's going to sit around here and wait to be killed? That makes no sense. What can the stalker do if Ziggy and Annabelle go into hiding, knock off half the people in Burnt Cove?"

"The stalker wouldn't have to go that far," Oliver said softly. "The idea of one person being killed, let's say Cindy Rice, for example, would be enough to stop Ziggy from running. He tried hiding once already, and look what happened to his goat."

"We need to call the police."

"Neither Breener will go along with that."

"But somebody ran him down, and sent him a threatening

Christmas card," Sarah said. "Why on earth not go to the police?"

"Partly because Ziggy keeps saying that he's a murderer, which wouldn't be very helpful." Oliver paused before going on. "It sounds strange, but I have a feeling that the main reason he won't call the cops is that he feels he deserves whatever happens."

"For God's sake, why?" Sarah said, exasperated. "Nobody deserves to be murdered. How can he just wait around for somebody to kill him?"

"Annabelle has been asking that all day, and he just keeps saying that it's not Christmas Eve yet." Oliver sighed. "It is his life, after all."

"Does he really think somebody will kill him on Christmas Eve?"

"Who knows what Ziggy really thinks?" Oliver said. "We don't even know for sure who the somebody is."

"Harry Penrose and his mistaken identity."

"Probably, but maybe not." Oliver shrugged. "Anyway, you're just in time to help install your galley."

The galley in question was a cabinet about four-feet long with a small sink and space for a portable stove on top, and storage underneath. Sarah looked at it proudly, having built it in Oliver's cellar workshop. Her father had been a carpenter who specialized in custom cabinet work, a skill she had picked up, to some extent, from helping him as a little girl.

"You finished it," she said, her feelings hurt.

"Annabelle and I finished it yesterday."

"You and Annabelle finished my galley?"

"You weren't around, and she volunteered."

"How did you get it out of the cellar?" she asked. The thing weighed over a hundred awkward pounds.

"Annabelle helped me this morning. Gave her break from trading barbs with Ziggy. She's a lot more fun when you get her away from her brother, and the woman is stronger than she looks."

Sarah cast a critical eye on the galley. It hadn't needed all that much work, really, she supposed: some trimming, sanding and paint. Still, it rankled. "Being a farmer makes you strong, I guess. God knows what she grows."

"Organic vegetables and herbs, from what she told me."

"I wonder what kind of herbs."

"Some of them are the kind that end up in Ziggy's magic teas."

Oliver had managed to get a lot more information out of Annabelle than she had. "Does he sell his tea, assuming it's legal?"

"Not a chance," Oliver replied. "Those potions are a labor of love." He shrugged. "If you get in the boat and guide the galley in place, I'll use the chain falls to hoist it up to you."

There was no deck yet, which made it much easier to install the cabin's interior. Even so, it took some jockeying to lower the galley in place and make sure its back fitted properly against the hull.

"How was your shopping trip?" Oliver asked as he began fastening the galley in place.

"I got a new dress for the Borofsky's party tomorrow. Violet called it a 'do-me' dress. I think you'll like it."

"I can't wait to get a look at a genuine do-me dress." Oliver wiggled his eyebrows suggestively in a good imitation of Groucho Marx. "Sounds like the trip was a success."

"Violet was fun and we had a good time, but I'm not sure I learned anything new about Ziggy's problem, though I think she had a bit of hero worship at the time."

"Mmm. The brilliant, personable young Resident. That would be natural, I suppose," Oliver said. "Did you try the snapshot of Ziggy on her?"

"He didn't have a beard when she knew him, and he's aged a lot over the last ten years or so. Living in a drafty shack and riding around town picking cans off the roadside must put the years on."

"So, she wasn't much help."

"She thinks I'm paranoid, especially when I told here that one, and maybe two, people were following us around Freeport."

"People were following you around Freeport?" Oliver sounded incredulous. "Why would anybody do that? Are you sure they weren't following Violet?"

"She didn't think so, but she didn't think anybody was following either of us. She just thought I was crazy."

Oliver had his head was inside one of the cabinet doors, and he observed a small gap where the curve of the galley didn't quite fit against the hull. It was a very small gap, and nobody but a contortionist would notice. Still, he suspected that Pearly Gaites would pull the galley out and plane it fit better.

"I dropped in on Pearly this morning," Oliver said, "He was working on his boat, and I irritated him by breaking up his concentration."

Oliver, his head still buried in the cabinet, held out his hand, which Sarah supplied with another screw.

"The body they pulled out of Pimm's Pond wasn't Doctor Carnell, by the way," he said, as he drove the screw home.

"Who was it, then?"

"I had to weasel it out of Pearly and nobody is supposed to know yet, but the body was Doctor Tierny."

"The Medical Examiner who did the autopsy on Ziggy? That's irritating. Why wasn't Doctor Carnell in the pond? Not that I wanted him dead or anything, but now we have a new body and Carnell is still missing."

———————

A strained silence filled the kitchen when Sarah and Oliver entered. Annabelle was at the stove, where she appeared to be making a large pot of soup, while Ziggy sat morosely at the table.

"There's a shopping list on the counter," Annabelle told Oliver. "You'll need to pick those things up tomorrow morning. And for heaven's sake buy organic food, not the trash you've been eating."

Sarah shot a glance at Oliver, but he seemed to be taking Annabelle's instructions in stride. Having brought in Violet's box of chocolates, Sarah opened the outer box with the help of Oliver's jackknife.

"I thought we might have some of this now, to brighten up the day."

The inner box was wrapped in shiny red paper. Wes trotted over and sniffed at the package hopefully. "Guess he likes chocolate," Sarah said.

"He does," Oliver said, "though I don't give it to him because chocolate is bad for dogs. Actually, what he really loves is opening presents."

"Opening presents?" Sarah said.

"Hold the box down so he can reach it."

Wagging his tail happily, Wes worried at the bow with his teeth, and then went to work on the wrapping paper. Sarah laughed at the dog's industrious enthusiasm, and even Annabelle and Ziggy peered at the goings-on.

With the ribbon and paper removed and thoroughly shredded, Wes pawed impatiently at the box.

"Opening the box is your job," Oliver told Sarah.

The alluring aroma of chocolate filled the room as Sarah lifted the lid. "Wes is going to want a piece," she said.

"Just a small one," Oliver said.

Annabelle handed over a paring knife and Sarah cut off a corner, handing it to Wes.

Wes gave a sniff and backed away.

"That's odd, he loves chocolate—" Oliver began as Sarah raised the piece to her mouth.

Ziggy reached across the table, snatched the candy from Sarah's fingers, and grabbed the box.

"Hey!" Sarah said.

"Now what are you up to?" Annabelle demanded.

"Always heed animal wisdom," Ziggy said, clutching the box to his chest.

It was Annabelle who broke the startled silence. "Damn it, look what you've gotten them into!"

Ziggy sniffed at the piece of chocolate Sarah had been about to eat. "I must do a test," he said as he struggled to his feet, the candy and its box in one hand and a crutch in the other.

Annabelle opened her mouth, but Oliver put his hand on her arm to cut her off.

Ziggy hobbled to the diningroom, where he'd set up his trunk of pharmaceuticals.

The others stayed in the kitchen, silent.

It didn't take long before Ziggy returned, his face grim. "Cyanide," he said.

"And you can tell that, how?" Annabelle said.

"I had test strips for testing water. Chocolate with almonds and cyanide. Most unhealthy."

"I told you from the start that your damnfool antics would get us killed!" Annabelle howled.

"Shut up!" Sarah yelled, her mind churning with questions and doubts. Annabelle and her brother collapsed into their chairs.

Oliver spoke into the lull. "Are you sure Violet sent it?"

"Not really. We were in the store, so she had the opportunity, but I can't see why."

Annabelle opened her mouth. Oliver held up a warning hand and she shut it.

"Besides, she'd be an obvious suspect," Sarah said.

"If you were still alive to accuse her," Oliver pointed out.

"If *any* of us were still alive to accuse her." Sarah shuddered. The Breeners sat frozen in place.

"I think you should call your friend," Oliver murmured.

Sarah looked at him.

"Just in case she got a box, too."

Sarah glanced at Ziggy's ashen face. "I'll call from upstairs."

"Your box of chocolates arrived first thing this morning," Violet said. "They smell yummy. Thanks."

"You haven't eaten any, have you?" Sarah said, her heart suddenly beating overtime.

"Not yet. I brought them into the ER—I'm on the night shift, dammit—and I was going to hand a few around."

"Whatever you do, don't touch them. They're poisoned."

"Yeah right, almond-flavored truffles, laced with poison—"

"Cyanide."

"Of course, what else could it be? You've got to stop reading those cheap mysteries, Cassidy."

"This isn't a joke, dammit! I got a box, too, and Ziggy tested the candy and—"

"Let me get this straight. This weirdo, who you claim is Ziggy Breener, who died back in 2004, just tested your truffles and found they were dosed with cyanide. Shouldn't you be taking some kind of medication?"

"The bottom of each truffle has a tiny needle hole," Sarah said slowly, emphatically. "Look at one and you'll see what I mean."

"I'm on duty, Cassidy, and I don't have time for this shit."

"Just promise that you won't eat any of the candy."

"Whatever," Violet muttered. "I'm hanging up now, but maybe I'll call you later, when you're a little calmer."

Chapter 24

Light snow had been drifting down for most of the evening, just enough to cover the ground with a fresh dusting of white. The snow stopped by midnight, and it was calm and still at two o'clock in the morning, with just enough moonlight filtering through a filmy overcast to show Vince the way down Meadow Road. He had parked well away from the Rice's place, just in case somebody was awake.

He was forty-eight, an age when one begins to ponder life and the future, and he'd begun to think about retiring from his present profession, especially after his encounter with Barofsky's goons. The hard fact was that he hadn't bounced back from that experience as fast as he would have ten or fifteen years ago.

Vince liked dogs in general, and it seemed to him that a nice hunting dog would be an ideal companion in his later, less strenuous, years. He could go off and shoot some birds and not have to deal with nut-cases like Penrose.

The only problem with dogs was that they were light sleepers, and they barked. He'd made it his business to find out which houses on Meadow Road had dogs, and he gave those places a wide berth.

Luckily for Vince, the Rices were dog-less.

A large, inflatable Santa Claus was moored to the front lawn of a tired-looking cottage. A faint breath of wind brought Santa to life, and his pudgy plastic arm waved to Vince as he passed by. Next door, a battered single-wide had a string of lights along the front.

Vince figured that a lot of these people didn't have two nickels to rub together, but that didn't stop them from spending what they had on blow-up Santas, or the huge inflato-snowman across the way.

He came to a plastic crèche in front of a small prefab. Somebody had used a few scrap boards to make a crude roof over the crèche, tucking a string of Christmas tree lights under the roof. Vince paused to take in the scene. He had never thought much about the religious side of Christmas, Santa Claus, yes, baby Jesus, no.

Vince knew that murder was one of the Seven Deadly Sins, but he figured that God was pretty understanding when it came to letting Vince kill off the sort of low-life he usually dealt with. He figured that he was, in fact, doing God a favor.

This flash of insight only served to increase his dislike of Harry Penrose. It was one thing to rid the world of a lowlife thug, but killing some kook who lived in a shack in Maine? And to torment the kook beforehand? Vince hadn't liked the idea from the start, and he liked it even less now.

Except for an occasional breath of air, the night was utterly still, with only the faint crunch of his footfalls breaking the silence.

He came to a tiny, three-room cottage with a scraggly pine tree, about Vince's height, growing in the front yard. Somebody had tossed a short string of lights over the branches, and the multi-colored bulbs reflected their holiday hues on the fresh snow. Again, he stopped for a moment before moving on.

Yes, Vince thought, he would fulfill his contract with Penrose out of professional pride, but after that, perhaps he would move to a place where he could spend his time with a shotgun and a good bird dog.

He came to the Rice's house and stood, looking and listening. A glance across the road revealed the patch of ground—it's blackened surface now hidden under an inch of white—where Ziggy's shack once stood. Satisfied that he was unobserved, Vince stepped quickly over to Cindy's Ford Escort, slid a gift-wrapped shoe box under the rear end, and walked quietly away. He was well clear of the area when he took out his burn phone.

An explosion and a ball of flame lit the night behind him, and Vince turned to admire his handiwork. There was something special about a good bonfire that appealed to him, a cleansing purification. He stood and watched the flames as long as he dared before hurrying off into the night.

———————————

It was not yet dawn when the fire trucks left, and Burnt Cove's deputy sheriff pulled up in front of the Rice's house.

"Where the hell have you been?" Cindy demanded. "I bet the law would be here a lot quicker if people had more money around these parts."

Charlie Howes knew Cindy and her temper from past encounters, which was why he'd dragged his feet in getting here. "What happened?" he said.

"What happened? Jesus, ain't it obvious? The firebug who torched Ziggy's place did the same to my car, is what happened."

"Are you sure it's the same person?" Charlie said.

"It ain't rocket science, Charlie. And I know who done it, too."

"She thinks she's seen him around here before," Jeff said. He was wisely standing out of his mother's reach.

"I can give you a description of him, too," Cindy said defiantly.

Jeff rolled his eyes.

Charlie caught the eye roll. "You gave me that description before, but why would the person who torched Ziggy's house want to burn up your car?"

Cindy paused for a second. She didn't dare tell the law, even if it was just Charlie Howes—who had grown up in town and didn't really count—that she'd shot out the perp's tire last week, and that was probably why her car had been destroyed. "Because he knows I can finger him, that's why," she said.

Charlie looked at her skeptically.

"I've got his footprints where he walked up to my car, too. Took a picture of them with my cellphone before everybody stomped all over everything." She held out her cell triumphantly.

It was a nice sharp picture. "They're L.L. Bean boots," Charlie said. "Name's on the sole, and they look new." He returned the phone. "There are a helluva a lot of people wearing Bean boots, Cindy."

"I don't give a damn about helluva a lot of people. I want you to go and arrest the damn firebug before he torches the whole neighborhood! Jesus, I've never seen such a wuss. What's the matter with you? I gave you his description, now go issue an APB, or whatever the hell it is, and pick up the sonofabitch!"

———————

About the time that Cindy was giving Deputy Sheriff Howes his marching orders, Sarah's cell chimed from her jeans pocket. The jeans were located on the far side of the room from Oliver's bed, and it took her several seconds to summon up the will to get up and cross the icy room to the cell. Being clad only in one of Oliver's oversized T-shirts made it a more difficult decision. She finally made a dash for the jeans and leaped back under the covers.

Wes, inspired by these signs of life, hopped onto the bed and lay on Sarah's stomach.

"Did I wake you up?" Violet said.

"It's barely dawn," Sarah protested, frowning up at the ceiling.

Half awake, Oliver rolled over, mumbling, "Who the hell is that?"

"Violet."

"Am I interrupting something?" Violet said.

"Most people I know don't usually call this early."

"Early for you, late for me. By the way, the lab is interested in where those chocolates came from. I told them I didn't know."

"You had them tested?"

"You really aren't awake yet, are you? Of course I had them tested. I work in a hospital, after all."

"And they were poisoned?"

"All six of the little bastards. Cyanide in almond-flavored truffles. What will they come up with next?"

"Sometimes the old ways are the best," Sarah replied.

"I don't suppose you've heard the morning news?"

"What do you think?"

"A body was found in a pond in Burnt Cove, Maine the day before yesterday, and it's been identified as being Doctor Tierny," Violet said.

"I knew that yesterday, and the pond happens to be right outside my cabin."

There was a pause before Violet went on. "I'm beginning to think you may not be a paranoid nut-case after all."

Sarah had shifted the phone to her other ear so Oliver could listen in. "Thanks for the vote of confidence."

"I want to meet this friend of yours who claims to be Ziggy Breener."

"He doesn't claim to be your Ziggy," Oliver said. "In fact, it's possible that he's a quack with a fake diploma."

"At last, the voice of reason," Violet said. "Is that your boyfriend?"

"Who else would it be at this hour?"

"Listen to what the man says. Has he seen your new dress?"

"Not until we go to the party tonight," Sarah said. "And our Ziggy *is* a real doctor. I just don't know who else he might be."

"Getting anything out of Ziggy isn't as easy as you might think," Oliver said.

"We'll see about that," Violet replied. "How long does it take to get there from here?"

"About three to three-and-a-half hours, depending on how fast you drive," Sarah replied. She gave Violet directions to Oliver's house. "We won't tell Ziggy you're coming, so he won't get upset."

"Upset?"

"He's stranger than usual right now," Sarah said.

"Thinks he's a crow," Oliver added.

"So he's nuts?"

"Maybe," Oliver replied. "The weirdness could be an act, the way he switches it on and off. All I know is that he's been like this, off and on, ever since I've known him."

"Don't tell him about Tierny, either," Violet said. "It'll take me a little while to arrange things, but I should be there by ten o'clock or so."

"Be careful," Oliver said to Violet, "just in case our friend with the truffles decides to try something else."

"You be careful, too," Violet replied. "After all, we're both on this guy's Christmas-candy list."

Chapter 25

Saturday mid-morning, December 22

Sarah and Oliver met Violet at the door and escorted her into the kitchen, where Annabelle and Ziggy were seated.

Sarah made the introductions, telling them only that Violet was an old friend who came up for a visit. Meanwhile, she studied Ziggy's face for any sign of recognition. Was there a tiny widening of his eyes, an ever so slight tightening of his mouth beneath the unkempt beard? Frustratingly, it was impossible to say. She glanced at Violet and received a tiny shrug.

There was a coughing noise from the livingroom, followed by the scrabbling of little hooves.

"What's that?" Violet said.

"Annabelle," Sarah replied.

"I thought *she* was Annabelle," Violet said, nodding at Annabelle.

"Annabelle-the-goat lives in the livingroom," Oliver explained.

"You have a goat in the livingroom?" Violet frowned slightly. "Doesn't this town have a health inspector?"

"We're pretty loosey-goosey up here in Maine," Oliver replied.

"Violet works in the ER at Arlington General in Boston," Sarah said, tossing her comment into the silence.

Ziggy looked at Violet blandly.

"Sarah tells me that you're a doctor," Violet said, "and you look a little bit like a Doctor Breener I used to work with years ago."

"There are many Ziggy Breeners in the universe," Ziggy replied in a vague, dreamy voice, "and I am only a few of them—"

"I have no idea what the hell you just said," Violet replied.

"Perhaps I was a doctor in another life, but as you know, it can be difficult to remember one's previous existence."

"Is this some kind of reincarnation bullshit?"

Ziggy's gaze sharpened on Violet's face. "I am known as the Can Man, professor of pop bottles, connoisseur of cans, doctor of deposits, and nothing more."

"That's an interesting career," Violet said, "but I wonder if you're related to the Ziggy Breener who used to work in the ER at Arlington General."

"I fly like a crow, straight and true."

"Okay, but crows can be deceitful, too. In fact, they're known for it."

Ziggy frowned. "A crow may steal in order to survive, but it's honest thievery."

"If there is such a thing as honest thievery." Violet paused before adding casually, "Did you know that Doctor Tierny's body was pulled from Pimm's Pond last Wednesday?"

Ziggy seemed to shrink in his chair.

"He was a friend," Violet's words were a statement, not a question.

"A true friend in a dark hour."

"What dark hour?" Violet said.

"When I died."

"This is bullshit," Violet said.

"I must fly like an eagle." Ziggy murmured.

An eagle? Sarah wondered where the crow went. She glanced at Oliver, and noticed him staring at Annabelle. Sarah had been so absorbed with Violet and Ziggy that she hadn't noticed the expression on his sister's face. An expression of ashen fear.

A few fruitless minutes later, Violet turned to Sarah and Oliver, saying, "Could we talk in private?"

"What do you think?" Sarah said after she and Oliver had ushered Violet out to the boatshop.

Violet heaved a frustrated sigh. "He's the right height, build, hair, eye color, and his voice sounds about right, as near as I can remember. His face is the right shape, but I can't tell for sure with that Gabby Hayes beard he's wearing. He sure looks a lot older than my Ziggy."

"As I said before, he doesn't claim to be your Ziggy," Oliver said.

"One thing bothers me," Violet said. "My Ziggy was good friends with Doctor Tierny, and your Ziggy took it pretty hard when I told him Tierny was dead."

Sarah nodded. "'A true friend in a dark hour,' as he put it."

"What about your Ziggy?" Oliver said. "Did he talk like that?"

"It's like I told Sarah, I was new in the ER, and I only knew Doctor Breener for a few months before he killed himself. I remember that he used to say some kooky things, but it was like a joke for him. Not like he was serious, just a way to relieve the tension. We used to laugh."

"I don't think our Ziggy's way of talking is a joke," Oliver said. "A riddle, maybe, but not a joke."

"Did you see Annabelle's expression?" Sarah said. "She looked scared to me."

"Scared of what?" Oliver said. "Has she been covering up for Ziggy, and now she realizes the cat is out of the bag? Is she afraid that Violet will go off and tell everyone that this is the real Doctor Breener, the man responsible for Annette's death?"

"That's not going to happen," Violet said. "The fact is that I never saw Annabelle when she ID'd Ziggy's body, so I can't even tell you if she's the real thing."

Oliver tried a different tack. "Would anybody have screened Annette's body for poison, even if there was no formal autopsy?"

"Not likely. Besides, Cyanide poisoning isn't a pretty way to go. We would have noticed that, for sure."

"There are other kinds of poisons," Oliver said.

"Like Annabelle-the-goat," Sarah said. "Harry Penrose was broke after he lost his run for Senate, and Annette had a big life insurance policy."

"Maybe his grief over her death was an act to cover up his part in the killing," Oliver said.

"It was quite an act," Violet said.

"Even so, it would explain why he prevented any autopsy," Sarah said. "To cover up the poison."

"I remember that Tierny was madder than hell when Annette's body was snatched before he could do an autopsy," Violet said. "He could be one hard-ass SOB about things like that."

"Do you think he was suspicious?" Sarah said.

"Mostly, I think he was goddam frustrated at the breach of protocol."

Just then, a UPS truck rumbled up the driveway.

Oliver took the small flat package, and brought it into the shop.

"It's addressed to Ziggy," Sarah protested, as Oliver began opening it.

"Which Ziggy?" Oliver said.

"And to think that you're the same person who gave me a hard time over reading Doctor Carnell's postcard."

Oliver shook his head sadly. "Look what you've done to my sense of right and wrong."

"What if it's a bomb?" Sarah suggested.

"Why didn't you say that before I got it open?"

Inside was a framed photograph and another Mistletoe Christmas card. Violet glanced at the photograph. "Speak of the devil, that's Doctor Tierny."

The card had a note, saying, "Remember Christmas Eve."

"Rubbing more salt in Ziggy's wound?" Sarah said.

"That's not a comforting sort of message, even if it isn't exactly a threat," Violet commented.

"Ziggy thinks it's a threat and so do I," Sarah said.

"Your friend is running out of time, in that case," Violet said.

"The trouble is that he won't do anything about it," Sarah said.

"Ziggy doesn't need to see this," Oliver murmured.

"Look, I'm sorry not to be more help with this," Violet said, "but I can't see any way to help your friend, especially if he doesn't want any help."

They talked a while longer, to no avail, and Violet left just after noon, declining an invitation to lunch.

———————

"Borofsky called while you were out," Cindy told Jeff, as he sat at the table, gorging himself on lunch like a starving hyena.

"Wha'd he want?" Jeff managed around a mouthful of the Hero sandwich that he'd picked up at Skipper's store.

"They're having a big party this evening, and he wants somebody to wing out the road and his driveway for all the cars."

"He'll have to wait 'til later this afternoon."

"That's what I told him. He said anytime before four was okay."

"I'm not getting much of a Christmas vacation," Jeff muttered.

Cindy smiled to herself as she fired up a coffin nail. "Why don't you stay here and let me wing him out? It'll give you a break, and I gotta borrow the truck anyhow to pick up some groceries. He's right on the way, and it won't take a minute to wing the shit out of that little driveway of theirs."

Jeff looked at her with alarm. "You'd better let—"

"I've done my share of plowing, young man, and I can wing out a road as well as anybody."

"But he's got a bunch of fancy shrubs and stuff in there—"

"I can handle it." Cindy's offer wasn't made simply out of concern for he son's welfare. She had given the matter considerable thought and decided that here was a perfect chance to do a little detective work, since the cops were just sitting on their hands. She harbored deep suspicions about the Borofskys, not just because they were filthy rich, or Russian, but because they had a grudge against Ziggy. By Cindy's logic, anybody who had it in for a friend of hers must have friends who were her enemies. Enemies who might torch her car.

Besides, there were those snowmobile tracks in their driveway after the storm.

And so it was that Cindy made her way to the Borofsky estate, where she dutifully winged out the road and driveway, destroying a few unlucky shrubs in the process. There were no clues to uncover, nor did she expect any. Her return trip on the way home was when she hoped for enlightenment.

Chapter 26

Saturday afternoon, December 22

While Cindy was busy winging out the Borofsky's driveway and pruning their shrubbery for the impending festivities, Sarah was also getting ready for the party. She hadn't been able to persuade Oliver to let her go back to her cabin alone—not even long enough to get dressed for the Borofsky's gala. She had argued that a poisoned truffle wasn't the mark of a violent killer. She had threatened that he'd have to sit around for at least an hour while she got dressed. It was all to no avail.

"I could help," he'd suggested.

"You can bring a book."

In the end, Sarah, feeling sullen, parked in front of her cabin with Oliver's Honda close behind. Still open for debate, at least in her mind, was where she would spend the night after the party. It was four o'clock in the afternoon, and the sun was sinking below the trees as they made their way down the steep path.

Deepening shadows were closing in around the cabin, making Sarah almost glad to have Oliver with her. It was even conceivable, she supposed, that he was right and whoever was behind the truffles could resort to violence if poison didn't do the job.

Sarah wondered about Violet, so certain that she was perfectly safe and could take care of herself. She was probably alone in her apartment by now. Sarah put the key in the lock, turned and kissed Oliver. "Thank you for coming with me," she said, to his astonishment.

———————

Sarah's upbringing had included strict parental dress codes, so she felt a certain amount of trepidation as she modeled her new dress for Oliver.

"Wow," he said appreciatively.

"Wow? Is that your only comment?"

"Bow wow," he added, wiggling his eyebrows.

"You don't think it's too much?"

"It is definitely not too much. It's perfect, and you look really good in it. You'll be the hit of the party."

"Are you sure?" she said. "I would never have gotten something quite so—"

"Hot?" he suggested.

"—if Violet hadn't egged me on."

"Violet did good," Oliver assured her.

"I hope the Borofsky's house is warm, or I'll freeze to death."

"Don't worry, the men will be plenty warm once we arrive."

"You're not being much help."

"It'll do the Borofskys good to see that we Maine hicks don't always go around in sweatshirts and jeans."

"It is just a cocktail party," Sarah waffled, "I could put on the suit I have."

"I thought the whole point of the dress was to, umm, loosen Penrose's tongue, so to speak. He being such a ladies' man."

"So long as that's all of him that gets loose. Which reminds me: you're pretty hot in that suit, so watch out for Sasha."

"Now *I'm* getting nervous," he said.

"Then we'd better go before we both chicken out."

———

"Lots of money here," Oliver said as they pulled into the Borofsky's driveway amid a collection of top-end luxury cars.

"My ex-husband used to entertain people like this."

"Lucky you. I thought this was supposed to be a small cocktail party. There must be a hundred people here."

"Look on the bright side," Sarah said. "Maybe one of them will want you to design and build a boat."

"Sasha wants me to build a boat for her."

"I've already warned you about Sasha. That woman is trouble."

"She seems harmless enough."

"It's amazing how clueless men are when it comes to the opposite sex," Sarah replied, taking his arm.

They were greeted at the door by a large, beefy man whose tuxedo strained to enclose his bulky frame. He welcomed them in heavily accented English, relieved them of their coats, and directed them to the ballroom.

"That gorilla was definitely not one of the men who were following Violet and me around Freeport," Sarah whispered as they headed for the ballroom door.

A dozen people were milling around the vast entryway, admiring the sweep of the grand staircase and the opulent chandelier which hung from the ceiling far over their heads. Sarah looked up at the glittering glass, remembered Marlee Sue, crushed beneath its predecessor, and shuddered.

"Maybe the gorilla has a smaller friend who was following you," Oliver suggested, breaking into her morbid thoughts.

Sasha glided over, a little unsteadily, as they entered the ballroom. "Well," she said, eyeing Sarah's dress, "I guess our house is safe tonight. You couldn't hide a book of matches in that outfit."

"Have I set fire to this house before?" Sarah purred. "There have been so many that it's hard to remember."

Anton Borofsky was obviously keeping a watchful eye on his wife and he hurried over. "Do mind your manners, darling," he scolded Sasha. "Speaking of firebugs, I hear the Meadow Road arsonist has struck again. Apparently, he set fire to Cindy Rice's car last night."

"My God," Sarah said. "Was anybody hurt?"

"No," Anton replied. "Fortunately, they were in bed asleep. It's a tough neighborhood down there." He shrugged. "At any rate," he told Sarah, "there's somebody who is anxious to meet you."

"Oh, good," Sasha said. "That will give me a chance to spirit Oliver off to a quiet corner so we can talk about the boat he's going to build for me."

"Er, yes," Oliver said uncertainly.

"Meanwhile, I'll take the lady and find her a drink," Anton said. "Just be sure you don't keep the poor man tied up all evening, dear." Anton escorted Sarah away.

The ballroom was filled with what looked to be nearly two-hundred people, but Anton skillfully guided her through the crowd towards a second muscle-bound waiter, who was wandering through the guests carrying a silver tray loaded with Champagne flutes. The man's face was heavily bruised, and his nose was bandaged, as though he'd lost a heavyweight boxing match.

"Thank you, Karlov," Anton said, taking a glass for Sarah. "Poor Karlov had an automobile accident the other day," he said as they turned away. "The roads aren't very well plowed here. Very slippery."

Sarah spotted Harry Penrose, standing off to one side, engaged in an earnest conversation with a man she didn't recognize. "I know Governor Penrose from newspaper pictures, but who is the other man?" she asked Anton.

"That's P. Melvin Delroy," Anton replied in a voice that conveyed a sense of awe. "He runs the Ringling Group." He noticed Sarah's uncomprehending face and added indulgently, "It's one of the biggest private equity firms in the country. The man is

worth billions. He poured a lot of money into Harry's run for the
Senate in 2004 at the start, but they had a falling out. In the end, of
course, Harry lost, mostly for lack of money. In any case, they seem
to be back on good terms now."

Sarah's antennae twitched. "A falling out?"

"Over a woman, according to rumor. It's often the way with
hot-blooded men. It must have been an epic confrontation, since
neither one of them will take 'no' for an answer."

Sarah remembered Edna Bartel referring vaguely to strains in
Harry's marriage to Annette. "Men, women, and money can be a
bad combination," she said.

Anton beamed at her.

"I heard that he collected life insurance on Annette," Sarah said.
"Did that help Harry's financial situation?"

"I'm sure it helped some, but he's made a great deal more
money as a lobbyist, after losing the election."

"A lobbyist?"

"One of the advantages of the political system in this country.
His political connections make Harry valuable to people like P.
Melvin Delroy." Anton glanced at Harry and P. Melvin. "I expect
Harry is trying to persuade P. Melvin to help fund another Senate
run."

Sarah scanned the room, and caught a glimpse of Sasha clinging
to Oliver's arm and speaking in his ear.

She turned away as Anton introduced her to Harry Penrose.

"So, you're Sarah Cassidy," Harry said after the introductions.
"Weren't you married to Claude Johnson at one time?" His gaze
wandered over Sarah's dress.

"We were divorced a year ago," she said, surprised. Harry
Penrose obviously did his homework.

"Claude is a good man, a very capable tax attorney." He turned
to his companion. "You know Claude Johnson, don't you, P.
Melvin?"

"Of course. He did some work for me a while back. An excellent legal mind."

Feeling no need to discuss the quality of her ex's mind, Sarah sidled up to the appreciative ex-governor. "It's such a pleasure to meet you," she gushed. "I hope you're planning to try for the Senate again. We need men of your stature running the country."

"Would you vote for me if I ran?" he said coyly.

"Of course," Sarah cooed, resting her hand on his arm. Harry Penrose was a lot like her ex, she reflected. She could see the man practically melting as he ogled her. Tearing his eyes away, Harry turned to P. Melvin, saying triumphantly, "See? I do have supporters."

P. Melvin gave Harry a pained look. "If you'll excuse me, I'm going to rustle up some more of that excellent Champagne."

Harry escorted Sarah to a quiet corner. Once there, his demeanor turned decidedly cooler. "I understand that you've been asking around about Annette."

Even though Sarah had prepared herself for this sort of question, she was momentarily taken aback by the change in tone. That and the disconcerting fact that he'd known that she had been looking into Annette's death. Who had told him?

"Someone is stalking a friend of mine named Ziggy Breener," she said, noting the abrupt tightening of Harry's face. "I think it's a case of mistaken identity, because I gather there was another Ziggy Breener, who was a doctor—"

"—whose negligence resulted in my wife's death."

"So I hear. Anyway, I was just looking into my friend's past to see who might be stalking him and why, and your wife's name came up. I'm sorry to open old wounds," Sarah said, resting her hand on his arm again. "Especially so close to Christmas Eve."

"It is a difficult time of year," he said, his tone softening.

"You must have been very close." She patted his arm, feeling like a rat.

He rested his hand on hers. "Thank you for your understanding. You know the worst part? It's not that it happened on Christmas Eve. It's that I wasn't there when she died."

"I thought you and Edna were there."

"Not when she died. Annette was dozing, so I went to the cafeteria to get something to eat. Ten minutes. Edna had me paged, but it was too late."

"My God, that must have been hard," Sarah said with real sincerity. Nothing ventured, nothing gained, she thought as she said, "I can understand why you wouldn't have wanted to allow an autopsy on top of everything."

Harry's expression hardened and his mind seemed to snap instantaneously from past to present. "You have a hell of a nerve if you're suggesting that I might have been trying to cover anything up." He glared at her. "There was no autopsy because the hospital made a clerical error, typical of a place that employs incompetent doctors. It was all in the inquiry, along with a rather miserly settlement."

So there was a settlement, probably confidential and probably sizeable, Sarah thought. Did Arlington General delete the inquiry into Annette's death to cover up its clerical error? If so, it would explain their quick reaction to Violet's prying.

One thing was certain: her dress wasn't doing any good with Penrose now. "I'm sorry," she said, yet again.

"And I hope you aren't suggesting that I might be stalking your friend, or having him stalked," Harry said, reining in his temper.

"Of course not. The idea never occurred to me."

"You cannot possibly imagine what her death—her pointless death—did to me. But it all happened long ago, and I've managed to move on. Perhaps your friend has other enemies."

———————

Cindy arrived at the party late. She hadn't had much shopping to do, nor could she afford to spend much, what with Christmas emptying her pocketbook. In any case, she had dawdled long enough to pass by the Borofsky's a little after five o'clock, by which time the festivities appeared to be in full swing, and a good number of cars were parked in the driveway and along the road.

Cindy parked, got out her flashlight, and walked slowly along the line of vehicles parked beside the road, looking for footprints in the freshly plowed snow. She had grown up tracking game in the woods and her keen eye soon picked up the marks left by a pair of new L.L. Bean boots. She carefully compared the image on her cell with the spoor in the snow, and concluded to her satisfaction that she had found the perp. After all, how many people wear L.L. Bean work boots to a fancy party? Satisfied, she returned to the truck.

Justice comes in many forms.

Backing up to get a good running start, she lowered the plow blade to half-staff and proceeded at a good clip. A twitch of the steering wheel created an impressive furrow from stern to stem in the offending vehicle's side—a car that had looked almost new, until now.

A good hunter has patience, and Cindy, well endowed with that virtue, parked a hundred yards up the road and hunkered down to await developments.

"Sarah looks quite ravishing tonight," Sasha said. "It's not often that a woman her age can look good in an outfit like that."

"Yes, she does," Oliver agreed, trying to rise above the age comment. "Who is that man talking to your husband? He was with Harry Penrose a minute ago."

"That's P. Melvin Delroy. He's a multi-billionaire, and that's his wife, Janet over there, the skinny brunette in the green dress. She's anorexic, poor thing."

Oliver didn't know what to do with the anorexia comment, but was saved from the need to reply as Sasha went on, leaning over to whisper in his ear. "Janet is a very jealous woman, and keeps the poor man on a short leash."

Oliver could feel her breath on his ear, along with the aroma of Champagne in his nostrils.

"I've heard that she has a prenup." Sasha breathed.

"A prenup?"

"Rumor has it that P. Melvin has mixed business and pleasure with some of his female employees."

"I see," Oliver said, pondering the lives of multi-billionaires and gossip queens.

Sasha relinquished possession of Oliver's ear and crooked a finger at the hovering Karlov, who worked his way over and replaced their empty flutes.

"Poor Karlov got into a fight," Sasha commented as Karlov lumbered away. "He has a short temper."

"P. Melvin seemed to be having quite a conversation with Harry Penrose," Oliver said, relieved to have some breathing room between Sasha and himself.

"P. Melvin helped bankroll Governor Penrose's last run for Senate, which was a total disaster."

Oliver nodded.

"The governor is probably looking for money for another try. The man spends money as fast as he gets it," Sasha said, taking a hefty swallow of her drink. "He's already tried to squeeze money out of Anton and I, but he won't get any from us."

"Oh?"

"Personal reasons," Sasha said, taking another swig of Champagne. "Oh, look, Sarah is talking to Harry now. My, she does get around. He's quite a yachtsman, you know."

"Maybe I should talk to him and see if he's in the market for a new boat."

"I thought we were going to go off and talk about *my* new boat."

"We could do that later, after you introduce me to Harry, and we have more time."

"Harry already has a big sailboat. He had it custom made here in Maine somewhere."

"An extra boat can never hurt," Oliver informed her, solemnly.

"All right, but let me put my empty down on the table over there first," she said, taking his arm. "Besides, we don't want to waste that sprig of Mistletoe hanging over the doorway," Sasha murmured, as she tugged at his arm.

To Oliver's relief, the sound of shattering glass and a muffled explosion shook the room. Shouts of "Fire! Fire!" erupted from the kitchen.

The crowded room quickly turned into a maelstrom of confused people pushing towards the door.

Karlov tossed his tray onto a nearby table, yelled something in Russian to the other waiter, and they bolted for the kitchen.

"Everybody remain calm!" Anton shouted above the crowd. "It's just a small kitchen fire! The automatic fire extinguishers will take care of it. Make your way into the hall and out the front door. There's no need to hurry."

Oliver managed to reach Sarah's side as they worked their way towards the front hall. "The firebug seems to have moved to the ritzy side of town," he said.

Suddenly, Sasha appeared. "You're behind this!" she screeched in Sarah's face, raising her hand as though to strike out. "I know it!"

Sarah put up her hand to ward off the blow, but Anton stepped in, grabbing his wife's arms. "You know perfectly well who started the fire," he snarled, giving Sasha a shake that rattled her teeth. "It was Vince Martell, your latest fling, only this time your little game has gone too far."

Sasha sagged in his arms, her huge eyes fixed on his face. The image of a bear confronting a fawn flashed through Sarah's mind.

Or perhaps a bear and a lynx.

Sarah and Oliver moved towards the entryway where they could hear Harry Penrose exhorting the crowd to make an orderly exit.

Chapter 27

Saturday evening, December 22

Floodlights illuminated the Borofsky's back terrace, leaving deep shadows beyond the edge where Vince stood and watched the Borofsky's kitchen door as smoke and flames billowed from a broken window. The terrace had been cleared of snow for reasons that escaped him. At any rate, the Borofsky's compulsiveness made life easier for him.

Vince had decided on the way over here to deny Penrose all the petty little vengeances the ex-governor wanted. Vince felt good about that. He'd already looked at Oliver's house and figured out how to deal with the Breeners. Fire was the ultimate cleansing element.

As he expected, the two mastodons came thundering out the kitchen door. Vince tightened his grip on the length of iron pipe in his hand as one of the thugs turned to the left and the other towards Vince's hiding place in the darkness.

It was the luckless Karlov.

Karlov noticed fresh prints in the snow and started to speak just as Vince stepped out and struck his battered face with the pipe, shattering his jaw. Vince hit him again in the ribs, felt bone breaking, doubled him over with a shot to the gut, and drove him to the ground with blows to his back.

Stanko was coming fast now, heading for the sounds of struggle, but half-blinded by the floodlights. He looked down at Karlov's writhing form, looked up just in time for Vince to crack his skull with the pipe. Incredibly, Stanko managed to stay on his feet and swing a wild roundhouse punch. Vince dodged the fist, backhanded Stanko in the ribs with the pipe and dropped him with a blow to the kneecap.

He turned as Karlov began rise, and kicked Cossack's legs out from under him.

He turned again to find Stanko trying to get up.

Vince felt like he was playing a game of wack-a-mole with a pair of elephants for a while, but finally it was over and the Russians were subdued.

He didn't want to kill the bastards, who he admired for their professionalism, but he intended for them to remember this night. And to be out of commission for several days to come.

Cindy's patience paid off sooner than she'd expected. A man came sprinting down the road, a flashlight bobbing and weaving in his hand. He paused for a second beside his damaged car, the flashlight scanning the carnage. The driver's side door wouldn't open, so he darted around to the undamaged side and slid in behind the wheel.

Cindy thought this behavior was peculiar. Why didn't he take a minute to look at the damage?

A hubbub from the house answered her question. This guy didn't have time to admire wrinkled tin. He was making a getaway.

Or so he thought.

Cindy followed at a discrete distance as her quarry, whose driver-side headlight was out, made his way to Route One and headed North to a back corner of the Home Depot parking lot in

Rockland. Here, she watched as the man exited his rumpled car and drove off in another.

Cindy looked on with delight. This was just like the spy movies she loved to watch on TV.

Only the spy wasn't getting away this time, because Cindy Rice, ace detective, was on his tail.

———————

A pimply-faced intern looked intently into Violet's eyes. "Hello," he said. "I see you're awake. Can you tell me your name?"

"Oprah Winfry."

The intern nodded encouragingly. "And who is the president of the United States?"

"George Washington?"

How about counting to five for me."

"Five."

"You're not being very helpful."

"What happened to me?"

"What do you remember happening?"

Violet closed her eyes and tried to take an inventory of her body. Everything hurt, but in a vague, drug-dulled way. God, she was tired. She opened her eyes to find the intern still peering down at her. He looked to be in his early teens, which wasn't true, of course.

"I was driving down Route One, just south of Damariscotta. It's a divided highway there—"

Violet closed her eyes again. It couldn't have been more than a few seconds, though, because the intern was still there when she reopened them.

"You can go back to sleep now, if you want, Oprah."

"My name isn't really Oprah," she murmured, closing her eyes.

"I know, Violet," he said.

"Oh, God." Violet's eyes flew open. "A truck. It came out of nowhere. It sideswiped me. In the rearview mirror, I saw him hit the back end. My car. It started to skid, around and around. I couldn't control it—" She began to twist and turn in the bed.

"It's okay," the intern said gently. "Get some rest and you'll feel better soon."

"What happened to me?" Violet's voice took on a steely edge.

"You were pretty banged up."

"How banged up?"

"You are one lucky woman to be alive," he replied. "Compound fracture of the left arm, four broken ribs, fracture of the right leg. You're in the recovery room at Miles Memorial Hospital in Damariscotta after two hours of surgery to patch you up and set the breaks. You'll be fine, but it'll be a while before you're ready to waltz down the halls of Arlington General Hospital."

"My kids—"

"We've notified them, and also Arlington General. Is there anybody else you want us to call?"

"Give me my cell."

———————

With his two thuggish butlers missing, and a smokey haze beginning to fill the entry hall, Anton Borofsky was reduced to carrying armfuls of outerwear from the coatroom for his guests to grab on their way out. Good hosts to the bitter end, Anton and Sasha bid gracious, if hurried, farewells to the departing revelers, even as the first Burnt Cove volunteer fire truck pulled up to the door.

———————

"You have to admit that the Borofskys know how to throw a party," Oliver said as they pulled onto Squirrel Point road. "Too bad Sasha blamed you for setting the fire."

"She was just drunk. You heard what Anton said to her. They both know the firebug is somebody named Vince Martell."

"Probably the same person who torched Ziggy's place, and Cindy's car."

"And if so, why?" Sarah said, checking her cell. There was a text message from Violet, saying, "Call me ASAP, V." Sarah decided to deal with her later. "And here I was, thinking we'd have a nice Christmas party, without needing to worry about crows, sick goats, and a man who is either a fraud, crazy, dead, or all three of the above."

Oliver sighed.

Sarah put her hand on his knee. "Why don't you drop me off at my place so I can change, and I'll follow you up to your house?"

"You don't have to do that."

"I know that, but I want to."

Oliver waited in the Honda while Sarah made her way down to the cabin. She waved at him as she unlocked the door and he blinked his lights before pulling away.

Sarah hurried into the bedroom to change out of her skimpy dress. It was deliciously warm in the cabin compared to the night outside but even so, her jeans and sweater were a welcome improvement.

Sarah looked around for her overnight bag. Hadn't she left it on the bed when she brought it down from Oliver's place? The evening's excitement must have gotten to her, because it was right there on the floor beside the bed. Being only half unpacked, it only took a few minutes to refill it.

Ready to go, she decided to see what was on Violet's mind, sitting on the bed to make the call.

"You're home early from the party," Violet said, her voice sounding as though she'd just awakened. "How did the dress go over?"

"The house caught fire."

"You've still got it, babe."

"No, I mean the house caught fire, as in smoke and fire trucks."

There was silence on the line.

"Where are you?" Violet said, sounding much more awake.

"In my cabin."

"Alone?"

"Yes."

"Where's your boyfriend? You flash that dress and he goes home? You need to turn him in for another model." Violet's voice sounded oddly flat, in spite of her words.

"He dropped me off a few minutes ago, so I could grab some things before I drive up to his place," Sarah said.

"Do it fast."

"What do you mean by that?"

"I mean somebody ran me off the road and tried to kill me."

Sarah looked around the room, a sudden foreboding filling her. "Were you hurt?"

"I'll be in the hospital for a few days, from the sound of it. I'll expect a visit."

"Where are you?" Sarah said, thinking somewhere in New Hampshire or Massachusetts.

"Right next door in Damariscotta. Miles Memorial Hospital, or something like that. I only came around a couple of hours ago."

A couple of hours ago? Violet must have been hurt more badly than she was letting on.

"Now I'm thinking," Violet said, "that those people you saw following us at Freeport were real after all, and if they're trying to kill me, then they may be going after you, too."

"You're sure it wasn't just an accident?"

"You think I can't tell when somebody rams the side of my car and runs it into the ditch?"

"I'll come down and see you tomorrow morning, and we'll talk about this."

"Get out of that cabin, now."

"I'm just leaving. I'll see you tomorrow." Sarah broke the connection.

She made her way down the hall to the front room, where Oliver must have forgotten to turn out the lights before they left earlier.

She walked down the short hall slowly. Had Oliver really left the lights on in there? Had the pile of magazines on the table been moved, or was it her imagination? Suddenly, the room seemed alien.

In all the excitement, she had made a foolish mistake. She had unthinkingly let Oliver leave her here alone. At the last instant, even as she started to turn away at the threshold, momentum carried her forward.

A man was seated in the easy chair. He looked to be in his fifties, muscular, grey-haired, and ominous in the shadowed room.

Chapter 28

Saturday evening, December 22

"What are you doing in my house?" she demanded, trying to put up a good front.

"Actually, this is my house," the stranger replied mildly. "Come in and sit."

"You're Doctor Carnell? We thought you were dead for a while. The police are looking for you."

"Among others," he replied. "I saw my bags in the guest room. Thank you for rescuing them from that fleabag motel."

"Where have you been all this time?" Sarah said.

"Here and there." Doctor Carnell replied. "You have something of mine. I want my skull back. I've searched the cabin, and it's not in the attic where I left it."

"That's because the attic window blew in during the blizzard and I brought the skull and some papers down stairs to dry them out."

"And I suppose you left it out in plain sight where everyone could see it."

"From what I hear, you were using it for a Halloween decoration."

"That was then, when things were different. Where is the skull now?"

"Underneath the kitchen sink." She got up, opened the cabinet door, and reached inside.

"It's gone," she said, peering into the darkness. "Somebody must have taken it."

He scowled at her. "Do you have any idea what you've done?"

"I'm beginning to."

"That skull may be the only thing that can keep Ziggy Breener alive."

"This is all about DNA and dental records, isn't it?" Sarah said. "That's why you kept the skull for all these years. It's about testing it to prove that Ziggy Breener is dead, just in case something like this happened."

Doctor Carnell shook his head sadly. "You know just enough to be a danger to yourself and your friend."

"What is the truth, then? Is that the real Ziggy Breener's skull?"

"As far as you're concerned, Doctor Breener is dead."

"What about Doctor Tierny?" Sarah said, exasperated by his non-answer. "He did the autopsy on Ziggy, and he was killed. How is he involved, and why did somebody kill him? And what about Doctor Hastings? He operated on Annette Penrose, and was killed," Sarah paused. "How much longer can you keep hiding out in one of those empty cabins before somebody catches you? After all, Jeff checks a lot of those places."

She sensed uncertainty in his eyes. "I can help if you'll trust me," she said softly.

"Only your friend can stop what's happening, and his time is running out." Doctor Carnell rose and moved to the sliding door. "Christmas is coming, after all."

"I know where the skull is," Sarah said.

Doctor Carnell paused.

"You haven't called Jeff or Ziggy lately, have you?" she said. "I know of only three people who have keys to this cabin: you, me, and Jeff. And Jeff knew where I'd put the skull."

Doctor Carnell stared at Sarah for a moment as though unsure what to do. Finally, he sat down. "I was on the pond with Will Tierny when he was killed."

"I thought I heard more than one snowmobile."

"There were two."

Sarah nodded. "What happened?"

Doctor Carnell looked at Sarah again, as though trying to decide how far to trust her. Finally, he said, "Will Tierny was in Florida, and got an anonymous phone call."

"What did the caller say?"

"That Ziggy Breener would die for killing Annette Penrose, and that Will would die for covering it up. That was all. Will tried to warn Ziggy, but he didn't seem to take the threat seriously at the time—"

"He did later, when his goat was poisoned and he realized that his friends were on the hit list, along with him." Sarah sighed. "I know what you mean, though. It's almost as though he does blame himself for her death."

"He has no reason to, as far as I can see, but Ziggy has a mind of his own. Anyway, Will called me, anxious to get the skull back. He'd given it to me as a souvenir when he retired."

"Did he say why?"

"As far as I knew at the time, it was just a skull that Will had filled with red cellophane. It turns out that he had put something else in there too, and he wanted it right away."

"What was it?"

"All he would tell me was that it had to do with Annette Penrose's death. Apparently, he'd suspected all along that something was fishy about her death, and he'd gathered whatever evidence he could at the time, which wasn't much with the body gone."

"And he hid that evidence in the skull?"

"It can't have been hard proof of wrongdoing or Will would have turned it over to the police, for sure. At any rate, he must have thought the information was worthless by the time he gave me the skull."

"Suspicions and suppositions? Something he was saving in case more evidence turned up?" Sarah said.

Doctor Carnell nodded. "Something he didn't want to leave in a filing cabinet where the wrong person might come across it."

"Hiding it in plain sight."

"These are powerful and dangerous people."

"And then Ziggy was discovered, and things changed," Sarah said. "But if there's no real proof of Annette's murder hidden in the skull, how can it help Ziggy?"

He gave Sarah a wry smile. "He was bringing proof with him to go along with whatever was in the skull."

"Additional proof to go along with whatever is in the skull?" Sarah echoed as understanding dawned. "To prove she was murdered, and Ziggy had no part in her death. And what was the 'proof' he was bringing?"

"Who knows? A bloodstained pad gathered while they were trying to resuscitate her? An IV needle? Whatever he could conjure up that would look convincing."

"Like the proof he created for Ziggy's autopsy," Sarah said, with a hint of disapproval. She wondered if Doctor Tierny had diddled other autopsies in his career.

"You make it sound as though Will was being dishonest—"

"Wasn't he?"

"Will and Ziggy were good friends. He was just trying to keep Ziggy alive, and it's not as though he was framing somebody for the murder."

Sarah could see no point in arguing over Doctor Tierny's ethics, so she said, "Did you find anything in his cabin after he died?"

"I turned the place upside down. No luck."

"So there's no proof, real or faked, that Annette died of poison or some other cause, instead of Ziggy's error?"

John Carnell nodded.

"What happened that night?"

"We'd agreed that I needed to be there to collect the skull—it is my cabin, after all, and why would you let a stranger paw around in the attic? Anyway, Will had gotten to his cabin just before the blizzard shut down the back roads, but I had to work and couldn't get here until late Friday evening. I could barely make it to Rockland at that point, much less to Will's place.

"Anyway, I called him and said I was stranded, so we arranged to meet at the Rockland ferry terminal, and we rode back together on his snowmobile." Doctor Carnell shook his head. "I'd brought a snowmobile suit, just in case, but I was never so cold in my life, even with it on."

"You were coming to my cabin for the skull that night?"

"God, no. He wasn't in that much of a rush. We were going to come over Saturday morning."

Sarah nodded. "What went wrong?"

"I think somebody must have been watching Will's cabin and followed his tracks into Rockland."

"A stalker."

"Yes, a stalker." Doctor Carnell sat for a while, as though reluctant to relive the experience. "He attacked us when we got back to the pond. It had begun to snow hard again, and he came out of the snow, going like hell, and took a shot at us. Will swerved, trying to get away. I was so cold and numb that I couldn't hang on and fell off." He stared out the slider into the darkness. "The fall knocked me out and by the time I came around, they were both gone. All I could do was hope that Will had gotten away."

"Instead, the killer herded him out onto the thin ice."

Doctor Carnell sighed. "It took almost an hour to find my way back to the cabin, and it was the middle of the next day before I thawed out."

"Then what?"

"I didn't dare to stay there, so I broke into one of the other cabins that I knew had a snowmobile. That's how I got here."

"And you've been there ever since?"

"No. I went back to Boston for a couple of days to see what I might find in Annette's old files that might help show that Ziggy wasn't negligent in her care."

"Any luck?"

"No."

"Not even a copy of the hospital's inquiry?"

"No. And it's not easy to make that much material vanish so completely. It takes a lot of clout to manage that."

So, Carnell confirmed Violet's experience. Sarah nodded. "But you think there's a copy in the skull?"

"That's why I'm here."

"But what good will it do? You said there's no hard proof."

"Damned if I know, but I can't think of anything else." Doctor Carnell got up and went to the slider.

"Where are you going?"

"What I should do is get my car and go home. I've already taken too much time off from work."

"And leave Ziggy in the lurch?" Sarah said.

"What else would you suggest?"

"At least call Ziggy and make sure gets the skull. Tell him what happened."

"I can't see what good it will do him now."

Sarah didn't see what good it would do either. "It can't make things worse," She said as Carnell eased out the door.

Carrying a flashlight in one hand and her tote in the other, Sarah hurried up the slope to her Explorer. Darkness closed in around her, and shadows danced in the flashlight's beam.

———————

While Sarah was entertaining her visitor, Cindy was stalking her quarry through the streets of Rockland, and eventually to the Night Owl Motel, where Mister Matches was obviously staying.

Cindy parked across the street and lit a cigarette while she pondered her next step. It was virtually unheard-of for Cindy Rice to ask advice from anybody, but this was an extraordinary situation. She had run the damn firebug to ground, but now what?

She could call the police, but what would they do besides hassle her for following the guy around? Even worse, they'd probably end up arresting *her* for dinging up the firebug's car. That was not the eye-for-an-eye justice she craved after the destruction of her beloved Ford Escort.

Who could she talk to safely? It had to be somebody who knew about Ziggy's problems. Eldon was a good kid, but too young for this sort of thing. Sarah Cassidy would be a possibility, if she weren't from Massachusetts. Deke Pooler, who lived just down the road from her, was always glad to offer help and advice—except that he was dumber than a bucket of shrimp. Pearly Gaites was a possibility, except that his father had feuded with the Rices back in the days of Prohibition. Cindy thumbed through her mental rogue's gallery some more, pulled out her cell, and called Oliver Wendell.

"I've found the firebug, and he just raised hell at the Borofsky's party." She told him about the footprints, tagging the perp's car, and her pursuit.

"Where are you now?"

"Outside the Night Owl Motel. It looks like he has a room there. And don't tell me to call the cops."

"Are you sure he didn't see you following him?"

"Not a chance."

"According to Anton Borofsky, the firebug's name is Vince Martell, and I think he was hired to kill Ziggy."

"Well he ain't no friend of Borofsky, that's for sure."

"Not any more," Oliver agreed. After a pause, he added, "If I were you, I'd make an anonymous call to Borofsky, and let him handle it."

———————

It was midnight, and Anton Borofsky was a very long way from the Christmas Spirit as he stood in the water-stained entry hall of his house. The firemen had left, but the aroma of smoke lingered on. As did the man Anton blamed for the catastrophe.

"What the hell did you tell that hoodlum of yours to do?" he snarled at Harry Penrose.

"I just got off the phone with him," Harry replied, "and he told me that your two goons beat him up last week. The way I see it, he was getting his own back."

"I don't suppose Martell bothered to tell you *why* Stanko and Karlov roughed him up."

A crash and a screech of rage echoed from the kitchen. It was bad enough, Anton fumed, that his house was trashed and his wife was stamping around in a blind fury, but what was worse, their great gala, the first one in their new house, the chance to make a good impression on the carefully selected glitterati, had turned into a disaster that would live on in the memories of their guests.

"That animal, Martell, started it by assaulting my wife. *My wife!* If we were in my country, I'd have him beaten to death."

Harry took a deep breath. He knew all about Sasha Borofsky's reputation. "I'm not going to get into a discussion about what might or might not have happened between your wife and Vince. I'm concerned about—"

Anton balled his fists. "Stop talking like a goddam lawyer! You know damn well what happened!" Anton caught himself. The fact that Sasha had problems when it came to men wasn't exactly a secret. Penrose was undoubtedly aware of that, and could make a good guess as to what had probably happened between her and

Vince. He changed direction. "Why the hell did he set fire to my house?"

Harry was nothing if not a good politician, and he knew when to back off and look for compromise. "Look, I'm sorry about the fire. The fact is that Vince went overboard with that, and I've talked to him about it. The important thing for both of us is to deal with Breener."

"You damn well better get Martell under control, or I'll do it myself. He put Stanko and Karlov in the hospital."

"Vince was worried that they'd jump the gun and kill Breener before Christmas, so he decided to discourage them, that's all." Harry gave a weak smile and shrugged. "Maybe he went too far, but I had emphasized the need to wait until the proper time. I'm sorry if he took my instructions too seriously and they ended up in the hospital."

"Do you think I can't replace Stanko and Karlov if I want? I can have half a dozen men up here by morning. I can have Breener taken care of tomorrow, if I like."

"Don't you understand why I'm staying in this God forsaken place over the holiday?" Harry leaned into Anton's space. "It *has* to happen on Christmas Eve."

Anton shrugged "I don't give a damn when that man is disposed of, so long as you keep Martell away from me and my wife. Otherwise, he'll be the one who ends up dead. Your obsession with this whole Christmas business is going to get you into trouble." The words had just left Anton's mouth when his cell chimed. He quickly moved out of Penrose's earshot.

Chapter 29

Saturday, Around midnight, December 22-23

Vince Martell was pissed. It had been satisfying to pay the Russian goons back for the beating they'd given him. So what if he'd tossed a Molotov cocktail into the kitchen to flush them out? It had seemed like poetic justice at the time. After all, Molotov had been a Russian, hadn't he?

Penrose hadn't seen it that way when he called a few minutes before midnight. "What the hell were you trying to do?" he'd demanded. "I'm not paying you to start some crazy vendetta with the Russian Mafia."

"Tonight was on me," Vince had said. "It's about respect. His goons caught me by surprise and beat me up the other day. My reputation is dead meat if I let people think they can get away with something like that."

"But this is the Russian Mafia for God's sake! Anton Borofsky is connected!"

"I can handle it," Vince assured him.

"Three suspicious fires in a week? The police will be all over this."

"Jesus Christ, what did you expect? Talk about vendettas; you're the one who came up with this crazy idea to torment Breener before you finish him off. If you don't like the way I'm doing things, then do the job yourself."

The conversation had gone down hill from there.

The problem was, Vince reflected after he hung up, that Penrose hadn't thought his plan through, hadn't realized that he had no stomach for the consequences of his crazy scheme. He just didn't understand the sort of cold-bloodedness you needed for this kind of revenge, and didn't realize there was bound to be collateral damage. Penrose was a wimp who'd gotten in over his head, and now he was panicking.

It never paid to work with amateurs.

Vince finished packing and looked around the motel room to make sure nothing had been left behind for the Russians to find. There were a lot of places around Belfast where he could stay inconspicuously.

He had no intention of becoming collateral damage himself.

A furtive knocking on the door interrupted Vince's gloomy train of thought. He eased the 9mm Glock out of his suitcase.

No way it could be the Russians, who were probably still in a hospital somewhere, and it would take Borofsky hours to bring in reinforcements.

Besides, the Russians wouldn't bother to knock.

The visitor began pounding on the door.

"Who is it?" Vince said, the Glock in his hand.

"Sasha Borofsky. Let me in."

Vince thought about ignoring her but she'd probably just make a scene out there. He opened the door a crack. "Get the hell away from me."

"Let me in. I don't want to be seen out here."

Vince didn't want her to be seen either, so he let the woman in. "How did you find me?"

"Somebody called Anton half-an-hour ago and told him where you were. Stanko and Karlov will be coming as soon as they get out of the ER. They're really mad at you. They're going to kill you, Vince."

The damn goons were a hell of a lot tougher than he'd imagined. "They won't go after me until I've killed Breener for your husband."

"How many times do I have to tell you? Anton doesn't care about killing that bum. He just wants him out of the way."

"The only way to do that is to kill him," Vince said. "Now that you've warned me, go away, and stay out of my sight."

Unfortunately, Sasha wasn't ready to depart. "I think it was wonderful what you did to Stanko and Karlov," she breathed. "They're brutes and deserved it for attacking you." she paused. "I wish you hadn't set fire to the kitchen, but I sort of understand why you did it."

"Get out."

"You're all packed," she said, glancing at his suitcase and taking a step closer. "I'd hoped we could see more of each other."

"Do you know how much trouble you've caused me?"

"I'm sorry," she said contritely, her slender, delicate hand brushing his cheek. "Let me make it up to you."

Vince grabbed Sasha by the arms, spun her around and pushed her towards the door. "You can make it up to me by disappearing."

"But I can help you."

"If you aren't out of here in the next ten seconds, I'll wring your neck." He opened the door and gave her a shove.

Vince watched the vampire-lady get into her car and vowed to never again contract for a hit on Christmas Eve.

Sasha was gone when Vince got to his car, suitcase in his left hand, the Glock held close by his side in the other. He looked around carefully, but there were only a pair of anemic floodlights, which did little to push back the shadows.

He was about to open the car door when two apparitions stepped out of the gloom, looking like a pair of gory escapees from a grade-B horror movie. Karlov's jaw was heavily wrapped with bandages, his right eye a mere slit. The rest of his face was swollen and purple, and blood had seeped through the wrappings around his head. Stanko was no better. Both walked with staggering limps, Stanko half dragging his right leg. Both men's breathing was noisy and labored.

"We are wery, wery angry Wince," Stanko rasped.

Vince stood for a moment, frozen in place by a combination of awe and terror. Jesus Christ, he marveled, what did it take to put these monsters down? He threw the suitcase at Stanko, darted towards the front of his rental, and fired at Karlov.

A bullet tore through Vince's side as he rolled behind the car's front end.

Civil disturbances were common at the Night Owl Motel, and the 911 operator didn't need directions to find the place. Bertha, the motel's night clerk was also familiar with disturbances, and she appeared at the office door in a dressing gown and holding a shotgun.

"The cops are on the way, you sonsabitches!" she bellowed over the gunfire.

Her warnings went unheeded, since the three men were already biting the dirt and nursing assorted bullet wounds.

Cindy Rice didn't know it yet, but she had done far more than avenge the destruction of her elderly Ford Escort. Thanks to her detective work, Vince would be entering early retirement instead of serving as Harry's Santa Claus.

Chapter 30

Sunday morning, December 23

"I met Doctor Carnell last night, after the Borofsky's party," Sarah told Ziggy, as the two of them sat around the breakfast table in Oliver's kitchen. They were alone, since Oliver and Annabelle had disappeared amidst secretive whisperings, as though they were a pair of lovesick teenagers. "He came to my cabin looking for the skull, which I assume you asked Jeff to take. I told him to call you here. Did he do it?"

Ziggy looked at her gravely for a while before saying, "Doctor Carnell must fly before he's discovered."

"That's why he's been lying low in one of the summer cabins along the pond."

"He must fly," Ziggy repeated, defeat in his voice.

"He wants to help, Ziggy. He just doesn't know how."

"The eagle must fend for himself, Ditch Lady Sarah, and I have cost too many lives already," he said heavily.

"Promise me that you won't do anything foolish."

Ziggy studied her face as though trying to memorize it. "The time for promises is past," he said, his voice little more than a whisper. "What will be will be. Christmas is almost here, and death is in the air."

"Hey Ma, get a load of this," Jeff said from his seat in front of the TV, where he was eating breakfast.

Cindy, who was having trouble waking up after last night's excitement, put down her coffee mug and turned to the screen, which was showing the Night Owl Motel's parking lot. Three men, she learned, had been arrested and hospitalized after a shoot-out that had brought out most of the Rockland Police Department. An investigation was on-going, and mob-connected violence was suspected.

Cindy ground out her cigarette and muttered, "I guess he won't be firebombing anybody for a while."

Jeff looked at her suspiciously. "You were out pretty late last night. Did you have anything to do with that?"

"Where's your sister?" Cindy replied.

"Not up yet."

"Go pound on her door or she'll be late."

Jeff grumbled and got up. "I hope you don't get yourself arrested."

Cindy threw her coffee spoon at him.

"So, who do you think is behind all this, lady detective?" Violet said. She was sitting in the hospital bed, with her arm in a cast, looking bruised and sore.

"I don't know, but it's probably my fault that you got hurt," Sarah said contritely. "I was just trying to help Ziggy, and instead, I stirred up more trouble."

"Trouble, hell. The way I see it, I wouldn't be in this bed if I'd been a good girl and eaten my truffles."

"If at first you don't succeed," Sarah murmured.

"I'm thinking that our problems began when I started looking for that missing inquiry on Annette Penrose's death. Doctor Thomas was onto me right away, and probably other people, too."

"Could he have made the inquiry disappear?" Sarah said.

Violet shook her head. "It would have to be somebody a lot higher up than that.

"Like upper level administration?" Sarah said, telling about Harry's accusation that clerical error had quashed the autopsy.

"The hospital trying to cover up its own blunder," Violet said. "That makes sense, but it still doesn't tell us how Annette died or who killed her."

"There's a lot of poison going around," Oliver mused.

"There was opportunity, too, as far as Annette was concerned," Sarah said. "According to Edna, Harry was at the hospital alone with Annette for a while before she got there, and according to Harry, Edna was alone with Annette for a while just before she died."

"So either one could have done it, depending on the poison used, and how fast it acted," Oliver said.

"*If* Annette was poisoned, which we have no way of proving," Violet said. She shifted uncomfortably in the bed. "Being a nurse is okay, but being a patient sucks," she grumbled. "I've been lying here thinking about that night when Annette died. Not much else I can do in this place."

"And?" Oliver prompted.

"And nothing, not a damned thing. It's like I said before, we didn't talk, like having a conversation. She just kind of babbled a few words as she was coming around after the surgery. Sometimes, people will say the craziest things at a time like that, without being conscious. It can be embarrassing sometimes."

"What did she say?"

Violet shrugged, winced. "She just mumbled about seeing the pearly gates. You know how people have these near-death experiences? I remember thinking that's what was going on with Annette."

Sarah leaned forward in her chair. "She said she was seeing the pearly gates? Were those her exact words?"

"Hell, that was a million patients ago. You want me to remember her exact words?"

"I could be important." More likely it was pure foolishness, Sarah thought, but still...

"I have no idea what her *exact* words were, but it was something like, 'I see the pearly gates.' She mumbled it a couple of times. Is that good enough for you?"

"Did she say, 'I see *the* pearly gates,' or just, 'see pearly gates?'"

"You're enough to drive a woman to drink, Cassidy."

"It could be important if she said, 'see Pearly Gaites,' because Pearly Gaites is a person."

"As far as I'm concerned, the pearly gates are where Saint Peter hangs out with this humongous big book, and he raps you up-side the head with it for everything you did wrong on earth. I know, because I've been thinking about the pearly gates since yesterday afternoon."

"Pearly Gaites is a boatbuilder here in Maine, and Harry Penrose is a sailor," Sarah said.

"Are you actually taking this pearly gates shit seriously?"

"It is pretty thin." Oliver said.

"Do you have anything better?" Sarah retorted.

"All I have is the headache you've just given me," Violet said.

"You're welcome," Sarah said. "The thing is that Governor Penrose loves classic, wooden boats—the kind that Pearly Gaites builds. I remember the Boston papers giving him a hard time over his 'elitist' boat."

"Pearly is pretty well known as a boatbuilder," Oliver said. "It wouldn't be all that unreasonable for Penrose to have him build a boat, and Sasha said at the party that Harry had a boat built in Maine."

"I think we need to visit Pearly," Sarah said.

"I think you two are blowing smoke," Violet said. "And I don't see where Doc Tierny fits into any of this."

"I thought he was killed to keep him from getting the skull," Oliver said.

"Assuming the killer knew about the skull and knew Tierny was coming to get it," Sarah said. "But if so, why didn't the killer break into my cabin that night and look for the skull?"

"Maybe he didn't know you had it," Violet said, "or he didn't want to wake you up from your beauty sleep."

"That would have been unusually thoughtful for someone who was trying to kill me."

"Maybe there's some other motive and the skull doesn't matter to the killer," Oliver said.

Violet looked at her guests. "We need to do something to put an end to this foolishness before somebody else gets hurt."

———

"I hope Violet knows what she'd doing," Oliver said later, as he and Sarah made their way up Route One towards Pearly Gaites' boatyard.

"There's no stopping her," Sarah replied. "She's got the bit in her teeth after being nearly killed twice."

"I just wish you two would give some thought to the possibility that the killer might succeed this time."

Chapter 31

Sunday noon, December 23

Pearly Gaites was seated by himself in the tiny office, which was tacked like an afterthought to the side of his boatshop. The space was just big enough for a desk with an ancient computer, a small drawing table, a pair of chairs, and a tired Naugahyde sofa. A sandwich in one hand and a steaming mug of coffee in the other, Pearly looked up as Sarah and Oliver entered.

"This looks like trouble," Pearly said by way of a greeting.

"I think you're ahead of us with your boat," Sarah said, peering through the inner door at the half-finished boat which occupied much of the shop's floor space.

"That's because I have to work for a living, instead of gadding around like you two," Pearly explained.

"We have some questions," Sarah said.

"You and your disreputable friend aren't going to weasel any more confidential information out of me. Besides, I haven't talked to Charlie, so I don't have any more scandal to share."

"This isn't anything confidential," Sarah assured him. "We were just wondering if you ever built a boat for a Harry Penrose."

"It would have been around 2004," Oliver said.

"Harry Penrose? Yeah, I remember him. He used to be governor of Massachusetts, ran on a goodie-two-shoes ticket and ended up being investigated for miss-use of campaign funds. Typical Massachusetts pol."

"That's the one," Sarah said.

"I never forget a boat, or who I built it for," Pearly informed her. "It was a forty-seven foot yawl, and 2004 sounds like the right time. It was after he got out of office, anyhow." Pearly stared off into space as though conjuring up fond memories of Harry Penrose's yawl. "I had old Den Cooley working for me back then." Pearly turned to Oliver. "That was a little before your time. Den was one hell of a worker. Of course, Eldon was still in school, at UMO."

Pearly sipped his coffee. "That boat was some nice, top of the line. They say Penrose is a crook, but he always treated me fair. I wouldn't mind building another boat for him. Best of all, he paid cash on the barrel, no haggling, no bitching, no cutting corners." Pearly paused. "Well, not cash, cash," he corrected himself. "He didn't walk in here with a suitcase filled with hundred-dollar bills, like a drug dealer. He was too classy for that, paid by check."

"Okay," Oliver said to Sarah, "so Pearly built a boat for Penrose, but I don't see why Annette would mumble about talking to Pearly. She must have known about the boat."

"That was just after Penrose lost his run for congress, and was having financial problems," Sarah said. "I wonder how he paid for the boat."

"Maybe Annette was wondering, too," Oliver said.

"You know the old saying," Pearly said, "follow the money."

"What kind of check did Penrose give you?" Oliver said.

"The kind that doesn't bounce."

"A personal check?"

"What, you want copies of Penrose's checks?" Pearly said.

"Well—"

"Because I can get them for you," Pearly crowed triumphantly. "I'm not some ignorant yahoo, Ollie," he said, using Oliver's least favorite nickname. "I'm computerized all to hell-and-gone in here, everything scanned in like gangbusters. I can print out copies of anything you can think of," he added, leaning over the computer's grimy keyboard.

There were a series of checks: a down payment, three progress payments, and a final check on completion of the boat.

"They're all company checks, drawn on the Ringling Group's account," Oliver said.

"That's very generous of the Ringling Group," Sarah said.

"They're an investment company," Pearly said, "probably investing in the ex-governor."

Sarah looked at the checks displayed on the screen. "They were investing a lot of money in Harry Penrose."

"Damn right," Pearly said. "They must have wanted something expensive."

"It may look like a lot of money to us, but maybe not so much for the Ringling Group," Oliver said.

"What's the date on the first check?" Sarah asked.

"November 30," Pearly said.

"Three weeks before Annette was killed." Sarah said.

"A tough couple of months for Penrose," Oliver said. "First he spends most of his fortune running for the U.S. Senate——"

"And losing, big time," Sarah added.

"And then his wife is killed."

"According to Violet, Annette had a big insurance policy on her life," Sarah said.

"Big enough to make him a millionaire?" Pearly said.

"I doubt it. But at least big enough for the insurance company to want details on her death," Sarah said, "and make a stink because there was no autopsy."

"Penrose didn't have it that bad," Pearly pointed out. "After all, I built him a boat that somebody else paid for."

"That may be the key," Sarah said, "if Annette started asking awkward questions about who was paying for Harry's new boat, and why. Did she talk to you?" she said to Pearly.

"Nope."

"Maybe because she died, or was killed, before she had a chance," Oliver said. "Can you Google the Ringling Group?"

Pearly muttered about people interrupting his lunch hour and went to work. In a moment he had the corporate home page spread across the screen. "P. Melvin Delroy is the big high mucky-muck," he said.

Oliver nodded. "He was at the Borofskys' barbeque. The guy is worth billions."

"I should have charged more for the damn boat," Pearly said.

"If the Ringling Group spent a pile of money on Harry, then it stands to reason that something good must have happened to them about the same time," Oliver said.

"You have a weird mind," Pearly commented.

"Do a little Googling," Oliver suggested.

"What am I going to put in there, smart ass? 'Good things that happened to a filthy rich billionaire in 2004?'"

"How about checking the Ringling Group's company news?" Sarah said. "Maybe something will connect to Harry Penrose."

"Most of this is just the usual stuff," Pearly said after a while. "They sure did buy a lot of companies and dice them up."

"Loot them for their assets, is more like it," Oliver said.

"Wait," Sarah said, looking over Pearly's shoulder. "There's a piece on Athena Associates."

"Who are they?" Pearly said.

"It was run by Annette Penrose."

"According to this announcement, the Ringling Group suspended its efforts to make a hostile takeover of Athena Associates on November second," Pearly said. "I don't see why Delroy would pay Harry Penrose for that."

Pearly scrolled on. "Here's something about a bill the Massachusetts Legislature passed, that according to this report, will make it easier for takeover artists like the Ringling Group to do their thing."

"When was it passed?" Oliver said.

"Late October. I can picture Penrose being given a boat for pushing that through," Pearly said.

"Would he have had the time, though?" Oliver said. "After all, he was in the middle of his run for Congress"

"I'm not sure what we can make of all this," Sarah said, after a few more minutes of searching, "except that a lot of these things could have been influenced by an ex-governor who knew how to pull strings."

"Or they might not have been," Pearly said.

"One thing we can say is that Penrose and Delroy were thicker than thieves," Oliver said, "until some time in the fall of 2004 before the election, when, according Sasha, they had a falling out."

"What kind of falling out?" Sarah said.

"She didn't say, but she hinted that there may have been a problem between them involving a woman, and apparently P. Melvin stopped donating to Harry's campaign."

"Maybe he bought Penrose a boat, instead," Pearly said. "I don't see how does any of this explains who is after Ziggy, though."

"Harry Penrose," Sarah said. "I think he's confused our Ziggy with somebody else."

"So all you need to do is straighten Penrose out," Pearly said.

"We're not getting any help with that from Ziggy," Oliver said.

"Merry Christmas," Pearly said.

Chapter 32

Sunday, early afternoon, December 23

Sarah and Oliver returned to his house and were greeted by Wes with more than his usual doggy enthusiasm when they entered the kitchen. Even Annabelle-the-goat made welcoming noises from the livingroom.

"Where is everyone?" Sarah said.

"Annabelle borrowed my car to pick up some groceries."

"We could have done that for her," Sarah said.

"No we couldn't. She's strictly organic. The last time I bought groceries, she threw most of them out because of all the chemicals. She and Ziggy are probably scouring every natural food store on the midcoast for healthy food."

"They must make an interesting pair on a shopping trip. Can Ziggy get around well enough to do that sort of thing?"

"He can hobble along with the best of them at this point," Oliver assured her. "The guy is tough as nails."

Just then Annabelle entered with her arms full of shopping bags. "At least we can finally eat some decent food," she announced.

"Nuts, green mush and lawn clippings," Oliver muttered darkly.

Annabelle gave Oliver a friendly rap on the arm. "Stop teasing. I know you really like my cooking." She put her shopping bags on the kitchen table and looked around. "Where's Ziggy?"

"I thought he was with you," Oliver replied.

"Why in the world would I take him grocery shopping? ZIGFIELD! Where are you!?" she bellowed in a voice that made Sarah wonder if the woman raised pigs on her farm. There was no reply. "Have you searched the house?" she said with growing alarm.

"We only just got back ourselves," Sarah said.

Oliver turned to Wes. "Wes, where's Ziggy? Fetch Ziggy."

Wes cavorted around the kitchen and nosed the door, whining.

"He's probably out in the barn, setting up a pen for the goat," Oliver said hopefully.

Ziggy was not in the barn, or the house, or anywhere else they looked.

The man had vanished.

Annabelle did not take the discovery well. "He's probably wandering around in the woods—"

"On crutches? In three feet of snow?" Sarah said.

"Oh, God, he's probably fallen into a snowbank, and we won't find him until spring," Annabelle said, imagining the worst.

"I didn't see any footprints out there," Oliver said. "My guess is that he called a cab."

Annabelle gaped, a dawning horror disfiguring her face. "He's run away again," she moaned.

"He wouldn't run away after getting that Christmas card," Sarah pointed out.

"Besides, he talked about being an eagle when he heard about Doctor Tierny," Oliver said, "and eagles don't hide. Crows maybe, but not eagles."

"He's going to do something crazy, then. He's going to sacrifice himself to save us," Annabelle said in a voice of doom.

Sarah thought about her conversation with Ziggy that morning, and his gloomy talk about having cost so many lives. Oliver and

Annabelle had missed that conversation, hadn't heard the despair in Ziggy's voice. Was Annabelle right? Had he gone off to let himself be sacrificed? She didn't have the heart to say anything.

Oliver shook his head. "Eagles are hunters. They strike their prey from above without warning."

"The man is crazy as a loon," Annabelle moaned. "He's going to do something dumb and get himself killed!"

"Don't underestimate Ziggy," Oliver replied, trying to sound reassuring.

Yes, Sarah thought, but how much did Ziggy know? Did he realize how useless the skull was without Doctor Tierny's faked evidence? How did the Ziggy-eagle plan to strike? Did he know who his enemy really was? Did he even have a plan?

The woodstove made a faint, cooling ping as the coals began to die out. Clearly, it had been a while since the stove was last fed, which meant that Ziggy had been gone for some time—long enough to be well along with whatever scheme he'd hatched. Oliver got up and put in a few pieces of kindling to revive the fire.

"Where would he go?" Sarah said.

"He sent some Christmas cards the other day, to the Borofskys, Penrose and somebody named Delroy," Annabelle said.

"P. Melvin Delroy?" Sarah said.

"It was a Camden address," Annabelle said. "And he muttered something about needing tea."

"Tea?" Sarah said.

"I think you should look around outside some more," Oliver told Annabelle. "Search the house and the boatshop again. Sarah and I will take the car and check some other possibilities."

"Like what?" Sarah said.

"Possibilities," Oliver repeated, taking her arm and walking her to the door.

———

While Sarah and Oliver were looking for the elusive Can Man, Violet Tibbs was lying in her new hospital bed at Arlington General Hospital in Boston. A watery, mid-afternoon sun cast vague shadows on the wall. It had been a tiring and painful three-hour ambulance ride from Maine, but she was in a private room—one of the perks that came with a nurse who had seniority in her own hospital. Violet was more exhausted from the trip than she had expected, and try as she might to stay awake, her eyelids were getting heavier with each passing minute.

Edna Bartel, dressed in a white blouse and skirt, could have passed as a nurse to the casual observer. She appeared at Violet's door just after three o'clock in the afternoon, and looked tentatively into the semi-darkened room. Violet was asleep, snoring faintly.

Edna entered the room and stood at Violet's bedside for a moment before reaching for the syringe in the pocket of her skirt. She took a quick glance into the hallway before inserting the needle into the IV line's port and depressing the plunger.

A handful of seconds, and the empty syringe was safely capped and back in her pocket.

She stood at the bedside a while longer, and watched Violet's breathing become slower and slower.

"How's our patient?" A voice at the door nearly gave Edna a stroke.

"Doctor. You gave me a start. I just dropped in for a short visit, but Violet is sleeping and I don't want to disturb her." Edna shifted to block the doctor's view of Violet's still form, and read the name on the doctor's tag.

Doctor Thomas nodded. "Sleep is a great healer. Perhaps we should leave her to get some rest."

"Yes, and I do have to get back to work. I gather she's doing well?"

"Up and about in no time," Doctor Thomas assured her.

Edna doubted that prognosis.

Doctor Thomas returned to Violet's room ten minutes later to find the patient sitting in her bed talking to Vanessa, the duty nurse. A security guard was at Thomas's side.

"She had the syringe in her pocket," Thomas said. "Talk about red-handed."

"I don't think Edna was wearing gloves, so there should be prints on it," Violet said.

Doctor Thomas looked solemn. "You know how very reluctant I was to go along with this bizarre scheme of yours—a serious breach of protocol—but I must admit that you were right." He shook his head. "That plumbing trick you did with the second IV bag hidden under the covers was a stroke of genius. You collected the evidence?"

"Every drop," Violet replied. "I was just afraid that she might be conscientious enough to check under the covers and make sure the IV needle was inserted into my arm properly. That little security camera you put up must have gotten the whole thing."

"I don't ever want to see you pull a stunt like this again," Doctor Thomas said sternly. "And don't go off on your own to play detective again."

"What about Edna?" Violet said, suddenly feeling exhausted again.

"Security has her under lock and key, and the police are on the way. We'll turn everything over to them. I think Ms. Bartel will sing like a bird to make a deal. From what you told me, attempted murder is just the start for her."

"Save some of the evidence, just in case," Violet said nodding at the IV bag. "Some pretty powerful people will want to make this go away, and they obviously have access to the hospital's computer system." Violet paused. "And you'd better warn the police that those same people will want Edna to go away, too."

Doctor Thomas gazed at her for a moment. "Yes, nurse," he said. "Do you have any other instructions for me," he added, with no hint of irony.

"Yes. I need to make a phone call."

Chapter 33

Sunday afternoon, December 23

"Tea?" Ziggy inquired of his guests. He was sitting in the room's only armchair with his plaster-encased leg stretched out, and his crutches close at hand. Doctor (or not) Ziggy Breener (or not) seemed completely at ease, which was surprising, considering that at least one of those present wanted to see their host planted in the frozen ground.

The woodstove gave a cheery warmth to the room, a warmth that was distinctly lacking in the eyes of Anton Borofsky, Harry Penrose, and P. Melvin Delroy.

Doctor Carnell poured tea into mismatched cups and handed them around the chilly gathering, along with a plate of brownies. Having completed his hosting chores, Doctor Carnell took his seat in a straight chair beside the slider, where the hazy afternoon sun did little to warm his back.

"Did you put something in this tea?" Penrose said suspiciously.

Ziggy took a swallow from his cup by way of an answer. "This is good tea, for good people," he said. "Maybe not so good for bad people."

Harry Penrose got up threateningly.

"For God's sake, Harry, the man is playing with your head," P. Melvin said. "Sit down and relax."

"First, I want to thank my good friend, Doctor Carnell for letting us use his cabin for this festive event," Ziggy began. "But I suppose you're wondering why I've asked you here."

"Just skip the damned foolishness," Anton Borofsky said.

"I have no idea why you invited me, of all people," P. Melvin said.

"It's the Christmas Season," Ziggy replied, "so there should be three Wise Men, and you're the wisest men I know."

"But you don't know me," P. Melvin pointed out.

"Your reputation precedes you like a bird on the wing," Ziggy said, "and I thought you might like to be here with your good friend, Harry Penrose."

"What are you talking about?" P. Melvin said with a frown.

"Ignore him," Anton advised. He turned to Ziggy, and using a voice one might apply to a slow child, said, "The Wise Men bring gifts, and I have come to offer you a Christmas gift. I know that you're a man of simple needs who prefers to live modestly." He took a sip of tea. "I have no desire to see you harmed if it can be avoided, but I think it's in the best interests of everybody for you to stay on Meadow Road among your friends."

He cast a glance at Harry and P. Melvin. Harry glared back while P. Melvin sipped his tea and gazed out at the pond.

"These men aren't your friends, Mr. Breener," Anton said. P. Melvin raised an eyebrow at this. "I'm proposing to be your friend and buy you out. I'll pay generously for your land on Squirrel Point and I'll even donate part of the property for a small nature preserve, with restrictions, of course." Anton looked at Ziggy expectantly. "You'll have more than enough money to build a comfortable new house on Meadow Road with no hard feelings on my part."

Ziggy sipped his tea. "That is generous," he said dreamily. "A nest among my friends. I could have a SPA, and splash like a duck in the water."

"I have Christmas present for you, too," Harry Penrose said, "and it's payback for killing my wife." He turned to Anton, adding, "And you'll get yours for putting Vince Martell in the hospital."

Anton bristled. "You're the one who started all this by hiring a professional hit-man and letting him run amok."

"And I suppose your goons are choir boys?"

"For God's sake you two, stop that kind of talk," P. Melvin said. "The place could be bugged for all you know, and Breener is as slippery as an eel."

Harry gave Ziggy a look of pure hatred and turned to P. Melvin. "Tell him what you learned."

"I come here as a friend, just like Anton," the multi-billionaire said, "and I've brought a gift as well. It's the gift of truth. I have evidence which proves that you are the Doctor Breener who treated Annette Penrose on the night she died." He took another bite of brownie. "This is really excellent, by the way."

"Stop eating that stuff," Harry said. "It probably has some kind of poison in it."

"Harry, Harry, Harry," P. Melvin scolded. "You're far too gullible for your own good. The Three Wise Men don't get poisoned in the Christmas Story, and Doctor Breener has no need to harm us. Besides, I'm telling the truth." He turned to Ziggy. "I read your autopsy, and there's nothing in it that mentions any fingerprints."

"Of course there's no mention of fingerprints," Carnell said. "The body was too badly burned to recover any."

"Sad, but true. Nevertheless, Harry's employee, Vince Martell, was kind enough to recover our host's fingerprints from his shack before it burned down."

He smiled benevolently around the room. "It also happens that Zigfield Follies Breener was indiscrete enough to get caught with a controlled substance on his person, back in his college days." P. Melvin waggled a scolding finger at Ziggy. "Of course, such indiscretions are all too common for a youthful student. At any rate, fingerprints were taken upon your arrest—the only official prints on record, amazingly enough." He gave the kind of complacent sigh that the extremely rich are particularly good at. "It was hard work for my operatives to track you down, Doctor Breener."

"The fingerprint proof confirmed what I already knew," Harry said to Ziggy. "Doctor Tierny was your best friend, wasn't he? It's too bad the phony autopsy he created didn't help you in the end. I suppose he used a stray cadaver, someone who gave his body to science, for your scheme. How does it feel to know that your friend paid the ultimate price for his deceit?"

"Careful, Harry," P. Melvin warned.

Harry took a bite of brownie and leaned back in his chair. "Doctor Tierny's death is on your head."

"Justice will be served," Ziggy said in a flat voice. He paused, gazing at Harry Penrose. "Remember, it's not Christmas Eve yet."

Harry's face turned an ominous purple. "You can babble all you want for all the good it will do."

Just then, Sarah and Oliver walked into the scene.

"Why does everybody keep breaking into my house?" Sarah demanded.

"Sorry to be late," Oliver said. "I hope we aren't interrupting anything."

"What are they doing here?" Harry said.

Ziggy gazed at the newcomers. "They come as doves amongst a flock of hawks. No matter, you're just in time to hear the reading of my Last Will and Testament."

Anton Borofsky shrank lower in his chair with a resigned sigh.

"You wrote a Will?" Oliver said.

"It seemed wise, since I may not be on this astral plane much longer." Ziggy pulled a crumpled sheet of paper from his pocket and cleared his throat. "My estate comes in five parts. The first part consists of my medical supplies, including my collection of medicinal herbs and recipes, which I leave to my good friend and colleague, Doctor John Carnell." The recipient of this boon, his face shadowed by the grey light at his back, nodded in appreciation. "Sadly, the recipe for my Red Tag Tea was lost in the fire." The Can Man paused thoughtfully. "Perhaps it will come to me before it's too late."

P. Melvin rolled his eyes. "Is this going to take much longer?"

Ziggy went on. "The second part of my estate consists of the land I inherited from the late Myra Huggard, my good and esteemed friend."

"Land that you plan to sell to me," Anton prompted.

Ziggy stared at the ceiling for a moment, his lips pursed in thought. "Perhaps," he replied, "if I live long enough to change my Will."

Anton Borofsky's gaze fell heavily on Harry Penrose's livid face. "You may be assured, doctor, that nobody will be allowed to harm you."

"I've got two men coming up tonight, so don't threaten me, you goddamn fishmonger!" Harry yelled.

"GENTLEMEN!" P. Melvin's voice boomed out. "Don't you see he's toying with us, trying to get us to fight with each other? This is the Christmas season. Surely we can be civil while he plays his little game." He turned to Ziggy, adding, "Go on, Doctor."

Ziggy cleared his throat again. "In the event of my death, half the land will go to the Spruce Cone Center for troubled teens to be used as a camp and recreation center. The other half will go to the town of Burnt Cove for a park where people— not just rich people, but ordinary people—can dig in the clam flat, enjoy swimming, boating, running jet skis, having picnics and barbeques. And perhaps a rock concert or two."

P. Melvin put a restraining hand on Anton Borofsky's arm.

Sarah had been watching Ziggy as he talked. He seemed changed from the way he'd been all week, wacky still, but with fewer birds and no crows flying around in their funereal black. She noticed as he started to speak that his eyes—dare she think it—were like those of an eagle studying its prey, namely his guests. Sarah followed his gaze.

"The third part of my estate is a skull which the late Doctor Tierny gave to Doctor Carnell some years ago, and which Doctor Carnell was kind enough to give to me."

Ziggy paused dramatically. "I leave the skull to Mr. Harry Penrose for his edification."

"Why the hell would I want a skull?" Harry said, baffled.

"One can learn a lot from the study of a skull, if one has an open mind," Ziggy replied mildly. He eyed each of his guests in turn. "And forensic science has come a long way since 2004, so findings that weren't possible then are commonplace today."

"What are you talking about?" Harry said, still looking confused.

P. Melvin turned to Ziggy. "Go on with your Will."

Ziggy cleared his throat yet again. "The fourth part of my estate is a letter which reveals much skull-knowledge. I leave this letter to my friend, Ditch Lady Sarah Cassidy, who may someday need the insurance the letter contains."

"Could we wrap up this foolishness?" Anton said.

Ziggy's gaze roamed around the room. "The fifth part of my humble estate is a vial of blood, stored in a hospital freezer."

Harry Penrose's face paled, his mouth gaped.

P. Melvin's eyes narrowed.

Anton Borofsky looked bored.

John Carnell's face was lost in shadow.

Sarah could only imagine her own expression. "You saved a vial of Annette's blood?"

"Annette's blood? What are you talking about?" Harry said.

"Shut the hell up, Penrose," P. Melvin growled.

Ziggy raised his hand for their attention. "Now that my affairs are in order, and you have heard my Will, it is time for me to make a confession." He paused to scan his guests' faces. "The fact is that I am responsible for Annette Penrose's death."

Chapter 34

Sunday afternoon, December 23

Harry Penrose lurched to his feet. "So you admit that you killed my wife!" He advanced on Ziggy, his face purple with fury.

"Hear him out," Oliver said to Harry, holding him back.

Ziggy sighed. "I should have done more at the time, but I was young and ran like a rabbit when I should have stayed and fought like a tiger. I am responsible for her death being what it was: an unjust death."

Ziggy turned to Harry. "Even worse, I realize now that I'm also responsible for your life being what it is."

"You're not responsible for what happened," Sarah said. "The fact is that Annette was poisoned, and judging from what was used, nobody could have saved her."

"Poisoned?" Ziggy said.

"Two men were stalking us while Violet and I were shopping in Freeport last week," Sarah told Harry. "One was your hired killer, Vince Martell, and the other man was tall and slender, and looked vaguely familiar. I couldn't place him until later, after Violet was run off the road, and I'd talked to her in the hospital. Then it came to me that he looked just like Stephen, with his slightly stork-like gait. My guess is that he arranged the attempt to poison Violet and me, and ran Violet off the road."

"Who is Stephen?" Harry said.

"Edna Bartel's assistant."

"Are you saying that Edna poisoned my wife?"

"Yes, and no," Sarah replied.

Oliver turned to P. Melvin. "You wanted Athena Associates in the worst way. The company was starting to take off and it would be a perfect addition to your little empire."

"Of course I wanted to buy her company. It was a good investment."

"Unfortunately, Annette was too stubborn to sell it to you," Sarah said, "so you took the hostile takeover route, as you had with so many other companies."

"The thing that confused us was that you suddenly gave up on your takeover efforts," Oliver said, "which seemed very uncharacteristic for somebody with your reputation as a ruthless manipulator, who doesn't take 'no' for an answer. Why did you give up like that?"

"I'm sure you have some hare-brained theory," P. Melvin said dryly.

"I think you found a better way to achieve your goal," Sarah said. "At first, when we learned that you had bought a boat for Harry just before Annette was murdered, we thought that perhaps you'd paid off Harry with a boat to kill his wife so he could sell you the company and make a fortune."

Harry Penrose stood in an apparent state of shock, his jaw gaping.

Sarah went on. "The trouble was that Harry's grief seemed too real to me to be an act. Besides, if it was an act, and he was involved in Annette's murder, why he would go to such lengths to threaten Ziggy after all those years had gone by? Why risk digging up the whole affair after it had been safely buried?"

"On the other hand," Sarah said to the frowning billionaire, "if Harry wasn't involved in Annette's murder, then why did you give him a boat? We thought about the possibility that the boat was a payoff for some sort of lobbying effort on your behalf, but there didn't seem to be anything in the Ringling Group's company reports that might warrant that kind of payment. In fact, the biggest piece of company news having any direct connection to Harry was the abandonment of the Ringling Group's takeover attempt of Athena Associates, which hardly seemed like good news for you. That's when it dawned on us that perhaps you weren't paying Harry to do you a favor, but instead you were paying him because he was blackmailing you."

Harry nodded silently, his eyes fixed on the floor.

"Your wife is a very jealous woman," Sarah said to P. Melvin. "I think that Harry learned you were working closely with Edna under the table, so to speak, in his effort to take control of Athena Associates, and he suspected that there was more than met the eye in that relationship. I suspect that Harry hired a Private Eye to get the goods on your affair with Edna, and blackmailed you to save Annette's company, and the boat was just an added bonus."

"And why shouldn't I blackmail Delroy?" Harry said. "Annette needed the company more than he did."

"You're a total idiot, Penrose," P. Melvin growled. "Nobody can prove any of this slanderous lie."

Oliver turned to Harry. "I don't suppose you told Annette about the blackmail in order to protect her, but she must have wondered how you were suddenly able to have Pearly Gaites build a boat for you. Where was the money coming from? She probably wondered if there was a connection between the boat, her company, and the aborted takeover attempt." Oliver shook his head sadly. "Unfortunately, you underestimated P. Melvin's ruthlessness when you assumed that he wouldn't find another way to get control of Annette's company."

"Since Harry had forced you to abandon your takeover, you had to go to plan B," Sarah said to the tycoon. "You knew that Harry would sell Athena Associates to you, if Annette was out of the picture. After all, building him a boat was good, but it wasn't the same as cash, and he still needed money, so all you had to do was get Annette out of the way."

"I hope you're not going to say something stupid," P. Melvin warned her.

Sarah ignored him. "Perhaps Harry let slip that Annette was in the habit of taking an afternoon jog around the Arlington reservoir, or maybe you had her followed to learn her routine. In any case, you hired a pair of thugs to kill her and make it look like a mugging gone wrong—"

"Do you have any idea how much trouble you can get into spouting that kind of slander?" P. Melvin said.

"Let her go on," Harry growled.

"Thank you," Sarah said. "Unfortunately for you, she survived the attack and ended up in the hospital."

Oliver took up the narrative. "It can't have been too hard for you to persuade Edna Bartel, with money and the promise that she could run Athena Associates, to come in on Christmas Eve, look in on Annette, and slip something into her IV. Her training as a nurse made things a lot easier."

"How do you proposed to prove a wild story like that?" P. Melvin said.

"I just got a call from Violet Tibbs," Sarah replied. "You know, that pesky ER nurse who has been asking awkward questions about Annette's death?"

P. Melvin scowled. "What about her?"

"She just called to say that Edna Bartel tried to kill her an hour ago. Poison in her IV."

P. Melvin glared at Sarah. "So she tried to kill this nurse? What makes you think I had anything to do with that? The woman was overly ambitious, panicked, and lost control. So what if she took it on herself to kill Annette in hopes of running the company? You can't prove that I persuaded her to do it."

"That's not going to fly," Sarah said to P. Melvin. "Think about it from Edna's perspective. The whole thing must have been an emotional roller coaster for her. First, she acts as a spy—as well as a lover—helping you in your hostile takeover effort, in return for the promise that she'll run the company, and Annette will be left in the cold. Then you drop the takeover, and Edna's left in the lurch. And finally, you persuade her to kill Annette. Poor Edna must have thought she had it made when you put her in charge of the company—a job she turned out to be quite good at—to keep her quiet. And with Ziggy dead, there was nobody to threaten her."

"This is a pack of lies," P. Melvin said.

"Shut up, Delroy," Harry growled.

Sarah went on. "I can imagine what Edna must have thought when she learned that Ziggy Breener apparently was alive and well, and living in Maine after all those years. And then I turned up, asking questions. On top of that, Violet started poking around in the old files. A guilty conscience is a wonderful thing, and I can picture what disasters Edna imagined. So she went to her weapon of choice, and sent out the poisoned truffles."

"A wondrous tale," Ziggy murmured.

Sarah went on relentlessly. "At first I thought it might be Harry, but he was fixated with killing Ziggy on Christmas Eve, and there was a good chance that he would end up eating one of the truffles before then, which would never do."

"I doubt if Edna will take the fall for Annette's murder alone," Oliver said. "My guess is that she'll sing like a bird about how you wanted Annette out of the way so you could take over her company."

"Let her sing," P. Melvin sneered. "Without any proof, it's just her word against mine. You have no idea who I am and what I can do."

"I've met Edna," Sarah said, "and she strikes me as being a lot tougher that you give her credit for. I suspect she has more proof than you think."

Oliver turned to Harry. "P. Melvin isn't just a stock manipulator; he manipulated you and Edna, too. I think his contacts in the hospital were feeding him information which he shared with Edna so she could deal with Sarah and Violet. At first, I doubt if he wanted you to stir things up by going after Ziggy. But when he saw that you were going ahead regardless, he decided to make the best of it and went to the trouble of finding proof that this is the real Ziggy, and making sure you knew it. After all, it was possible that Ziggy could make problems for him after all those years, so he made sure that you would do his dirty work while he remained safe."

Sarah looked at Harry sadly. "Killing Ziggy now won't avenge Annette's death; it will only serve P. Melvin's purposes."

Harry turned, looming over the seated P. Melvin. "You've been lying to me all those years, laughing behind my back."

"Don't listen to them, Harry."

"That's why you were so quick to 'help me out' by buying Annette's company after you had her killed."

"God knows you needed the money, and buying her company helped both of us. After all, this whole revenge thing was *your* obsession. I just pointed you in the right direction."

With a screech of fury, Harry grabbed the teapot, the closest weapon, and leaped on P. Melvin, beating him about the head with it.

"Where are the rest of our guests?" Ziggy said.

"I warned you this might happen," Doctor Carnell said as he opened the slider to admit two men. The first wore a cap with the words, "Deputy Sheriff," on it. The cap, recently purchased by the town of Burnt Cove after an extended debate at the last Town

Meeting, had cost all of thirty dollars. Looming behind him was
Eldon Tupper.

"I thought it was beginning to sound rowdy in here," Charlie
Howes said from beneath his new cap.

"You called in this hick sheriff? Is this some kind of joke?" P.
Melvin said.

"Are you P. Melvin Delroy?" Charlie said.

"Is this more of your foolishness, Breener?" P. Melvin
demanded.

"I am but a humble dove of justice," Ziggy said serenely.

"And I am the deputy sheriff in town, and this is my special
deputy, Eldon Tupper," Charlie said in his best official voice, as
befit his new cap. "I'm here to inform you that the State Police are
on the way, and I've been instructed to detain you until they arrive."

"You? Detain me? I could buy this whole goddam town and
bulldoze it flat if I wanted. And you're going to detain me? Do you
have any idea who I am?"

"According to the call I got while we were waiting outside,
you're a really rich guy who paid somebody to kill a woman and
bamboozled some dumb politician into trying to kill Ziggy for you,"
Charlie said with relish. "When Ziggy first called, I figured it was
just to hang around and make sure this party didn't get out of hand,
but when the Smokies called, I knew things were going to be much
more fun."

"Do you really think a couple of hayseed cops like you can keep
me here?"

Three-hundred muscular pounds of Eldon Tupper placed a
beefy paw on the seated robber-baron's shoulder and smiled down
at him. "Don't see why not," he replied.

Chapter 35

Sunday evening, December 23

"That was a very pleasant tea party," Ziggy said after two of his guests had left in handcuffs, and the third had slunk off into the night. "I must do this again."

"Please don't," Doctor Carnell said. He'd made a fresh pot of tea and was pouring for Ziggy, Sarah, Oliver, and himself.

Oliver shook his head in awe. "You're a one-man vaudeville act," he said to Ziggy. "You could have sold tickets."

Ziggy sipped his tea in silence.

"Talk about making stone soup," Doctor Carnell added. "You were bluffing all along."

"But there was *something* in the skull," Sarah said to Ziggy. "I should have suspected it when you first saw the skull sitting on the kitchen table, and went on about evil living inside it."

"The essence of evil, but not the proof," Ziggy said.

Doctor Carnell nodded. "It was just as we suspected. When Ziggy and I opened it up before the tea party, there was no real proof of any wrongdoing—it was purely circumstantial: the inquiry, a collection of notes on Annette's care, some inconclusive test results, suppositions and suspicions. Will Tierny had put it all on a diskette, and hidden it in the skull, along with the cellophane."

Sarah turned to Ziggy. "Remind me never to play poker with you. Weak as it was, you played your hand it for all it was worth. I watched you looking for a reaction from Harry when you talked about the skull and advances in forensic sciences, but you didn't get any, because he didn't know about the possibility that Annette was murdered."

Oliver nodded. "Like us, Harry realized that Ziggy could only be alive if Doctor Tierny had faked the autopsy. Murdering Tierny was Harry's way of getting revenge and tightening the screws on Ziggy by killing his old friend."

"You've been spending your winters in Florida with him, haven't you?" Oliver said. "But you knew that your name would be in the papers when you won the lawsuit over Myra's will, so you stayed here this winter to protect your friend."

Ziggy sighed, nodding. "Myra Huggard's gift came a high price."

They sat in silence for a while.

"I could see that the skull was making P. Melvin a little nervous," Sarah said after a while.

Oliver nodded. "Especially when he realized that it belonged to Doctor Tierny, and Ziggy talked about 'skull-knowledge.'"

It was Sarah's turn. "Next on the list was what you called my 'insurance policy,' which was just a printout of what was on the diskette that Doctor Tierny hid in the skull back in 2004," Sarah said.

"It wasn't easy to find a computer that could read one of those old diskettes," Doctor Carnell said.

"I'm sure," Sarah said. "But it was a further tightening of the screws on P. Melvin, who had no way of knowing what information might be in the skull."

"'Suspicion always haunts the guilty mind,'" Ziggy said.

"Where did you get that?" Carnell said.

"Shakespeare, quoth the raven."

"I'd hoped you were done with the bird thing," Sarah commented. "Anyway, last but not least, there was the blood sample, which set off both P. Melvin and Harry."

"You don't really have a sample of Annette's blood hidden away somewhere, do you?" Oliver said. "It was just one more of your bluffs, wasn't it?"

Ziggy gave his guests a perplexed look. "Did I say I had a sample of Annette's blood?" He stared at the ceiling, apparently lost in thought. "It's possible there is such a thing, somewhere, though it was so long ago, before——"

"You died and were reborn," Sarah and Oliver said in unison.

Ziggy looked at them benignly. "There are so many blood samples in the world; one of them might be hers, but does it really matter?"

Oliver shook his head. "My God, that was a dangerous game of bluff you were playing. You'd be dead if it hadn't worked."

"And my friends, too."

"And you had nothing to work with except their own guilt," Sarah said.

"A powerful weapon," Ziggy murmured.

Chapter 36

Tuesday evening, December 25

Oliver's house was quiet and still, a hush not unlike the stillness which follows the passage of a hurricane. Or a Christmas morning.

The livingroom still held the faint aroma of a stable, though the combined efforts of Annabelle (the person), Sarah, Cindy, Oliver, and Eldon had transformed the space to its pre-goat state.

Sarah and Oliver sat close together on the livingroom sofa, their feet warmed by the woodstove. Wes lay sprawled across both their laps, snoring faintly. A lot had happened in the two days since the reading of Ziggy Breener's Last Will and Testament, so the fact that they were all tired wasn't just from Christmas day.

"Did you have a good Christmas?" Oliver said.

"Oh, yes. That new dinghy you built is gorgeous; it's perfect for *Owl*." She gave him a long kiss before adding. "I can't believe you were able to build it in the cellar without me knowing."

"It wasn't easy, with you popping in and out of the house all the time—not that I'm complaining about the popping—but sneaky is my middle name. It's a good thing Annabelle was here to help this week, or I never could have finished it in time."

Sarah took a sip of wine. "You know, I was a little jealous of Annabelle being up here with you, while I was in my cabin. You seemed to be spending so much time together." She looked at Oliver. "I stewed over that."

He looked at her, surprised. "She's a good ten years younger than me."

"Thirteen years."

"Oh, right. But she's not my type. Definitely not my type." He kissed her ear. "You're my type."

"Good answer." She took another swallow of her wine. "Anyway, it told me something about myself." She paused. "So, how about you? Did you have a good Christmas?"

"The best ever," Oliver replied. "I got my house back, and nobody I know was murdered." He gave her a long kiss. When they came up for air, Oliver said, "It was nice of you to let Ziggy have your cabin for the winter. Plus, it means I've got a new housemate."

Wes opened one eye and heaved a contented sigh.

"Ziggy has to live somewhere, and there's room for his sister to stay with him for a week or two until he can get around on his own. It's not as though I really need the cabin when you get right down to it. Violet was right about that."

"Smart woman, Violet," Oliver murmured. "Still, I know it was important for you to feel independent there."

"You'll just have to be on your best behavior." She snuggled against him. "And there are advantages to being here, one of which I plan to explore later this evening."

They kissed again, longer this time.

"Your Christmas present for Annabelle-the-goat was a stroke of genius," Oliver said a bit later. "There was something for everybody. I'm just amazed that you found time to build such a luxurious stable and pen for her."

"Sneaky is my middle name, too. Actually, Jeff and Eldon helped a lot. I think the Rices like that goat, though they'd never admit it, and we built the stable so it can be moved out of their back yard to Ziggy's new zoo when he builds a shack next door to the Borofskys."

"Annabelle is a very amiable goat," Oliver mused. "Who knows, maybe the Borofskys will take a liking to her. Anyway, they'll have to be on their best behavior for a while, at least until the police finish questioning Anton Borofsky's goons. It doesn't sound as though they can prove anything, though letting Vince borrow Anton's snowmobile to kill Doctor Tierny and run down Ziggy may be an issue. I hear there was some damage to the machine, which may tie it to Ziggy's injuries. Anyhow, the last thing Borofsky needs is to have the cops thinking he's involved with P. Melvin and Harry. Besides, I expect that Ziggy can string the Borofskys along for quite a while with his Will."

"Speaking of goats," Sarah said. "I saw Harry Penrose on TV this morning. He's claiming that Vince Martell was trying to make him a scapegoat to cover up Martell's little crime spree. It will be interesting to see if the police can prove a connection between the two."

"It could end up just being the word of a former governor against the word of a hit-man. Apparently the police are also reinvestigating the murder of Doctor Hastings, back in 2004, which could be another problem for Harry."

Sarah nodded. "The best thing to come out of all this is that Harry has forgotten about killing Ziggy and has made it his mission to put Edna and P. Melvin in jail for Annette's murder."

"A noble cause, if Harry doesn't end up in jail first."

"Definitely. According to Violet, Harry wasn't the only blackmail artist. Edna had collected an amazing amount of dirt on P. Melvin. Blackmail material, in case she needed insurance. And she won't be shy about sharing it, either."

"Wise of her," Oliver said. "I expect the pair of them will be charged with Annette's death, and at least we helped keep Ziggy from being killed." He paused and added, "It's a good thing that you and Violet were able to fool Edna into trying to finish off Violet. It was the final blow for P. Melvin."

"I just hope he doesn't manage to buy his way out of trouble."

"Sasha was right, by the way; there was a prenup," Oliver said. "According to the papers, P. Melvin's wife gets most his fortune, including damages, if he's caught having an affair."

"I suppose our crafty Edna has proof of their affair."

"Absolutely." Oliver took a sip of wine. "I suspect that losing all that money is almost the worst punishment P. Melvin could get."

"The great manipulator certainly deserves to be manipulated." She paused. "I still worry about Ziggy, though."

"How so?"

"He's lived so long with his self-doubt, guilt, and uncertainty about Annette's death—"

"And now the uncertainty is gone," Oliver said. "He can know for sure that it was Edna's poison, not his negligence that killed Annette."

"Yes, the uncertainty is gone, but not all the guilt. What was it Ziggy said about running like a rabbit instead of fighting like a tiger?"

"Ziggy did the best he could at the time, which was to survive," Oliver said. "He had no way of knowing where his actions might lead, and that Harry would become obsessed with revenge."

Oliver put his arm around Sarah's shoulders and pulled her closer. "Nobody's hands were completely clean on this. P. Melvin may have been using Harry's thirst for revenge and Edna's thirst for power to his advantage, but the Borofskys were helping Harry, too. And there's Vince's crime spree, not to mention that Doctor Tierny was guilty of faking Ziggy's death, and planning to plant false evidence of Annette's murder. Even Annabelle, with her bogus identification of Ziggy's body, was part of Tierny's scam. There was plenty of guilt to go around."

Sarah nodded. "Ziggy is right. Guilt is a powerful weapon for either good or evil." Sarah reached for her glass and took a tiny sip. "Do you suppose Ziggy will change after what happened?"

"Do you mean will he be reborn into yet another Ziggy? Somehow, I think he already has."

"In that case, here's to Christmas and to being reborn," Sarah said, touching her glass to Oliver's. She sipped her wine and rested her head on his shoulder.

"You know," Oliver said, after a few minutes, "P. Melvin was bluffing, too, when he talked about Ziggy being arrested and fingerprinted. I asked Ziggy about that and he didn't remember being fingerprinted. Or so he told me."

A slight frown appeared on Sarah's face.

"Don't forget that it was in P. Melvin's best interest to encourage Penrose to kill off Ziggy, just to be on the safe side. A billionaire can never be too safe, after all—there's too much to lose. Harry believed P. Melvin's so-called fingerprint proof because he wanted to."

Sarah looked at Oliver incredulously. "Are you suggesting that after all this, we *still* don't know for sure if he's the real Ziggy Breener?"

"Of course he's the real Ziggy Breener. I've said it before, and I say it again: He's *our* Ziggy Breener. What else could possibly matter?"

CPSIA information can be obtained
at www.ICGtesting.com
Printed in the USA
BVOW08s1407020118
504219BV00001B/11/P